The Long Way Home

Also by Rob Bauer

Fiction
My Australian Adventure

The World Traveler

The Buffalo Soldier

Darkness in Dixie

Nonfiction
Outside the Lines of Gilded Age Baseball: Alcohol, Fitness, and Cheating in 1880s Baseball

Outside the Lines of Gilded Age Baseball: Gambling, Umpires, and Racism in 1880s Baseball

Outside the Lines of Gilded Age Baseball: The Origins of the 1890 Players League

Outside the Lines of Gilded Age Baseball: The Finances of 1880s Baseball

The Long Way Home

Rob Bauer

This is a work of fiction. Names, characters, places, and incidents either are the product of the author's imagination or are used fictitiously. Any resemblance to actual persons, living or dead, events, or locales is entirely coincidental.

For any inquiries regarding this book, please contact Rob at robbauerbooks@gmail.com.

No part of this book may be reproduced in any form or by any electronic or mechanical means, including information storage and retrieval systems, without written permission from the author, except for the use of brief quotations in a book review.

Copyright © 2020 Robert A. Bauer
All rights reserved.
ISBN-13: 978-1-948478-18-2

For Ally

Thank you for twelve great years together.

Contents

Chapter 1	1
Chapter 2	13
Chapter 3	23
Chapter 4	29
Chapter 5	32
Chapter 6	40
Chapter 7	49
Chapter 8	52
Chapter 9	59
Chapter 10	64
Chapter 11	76
Chapter 12	81
Chapter 13	90
Chapter 14	103
Chapter 15	116
Chapter 16	122
Chapter 17	130
Chapter 18	142
Chapter 19	154
Chapter 20	162
Chapter 21	166
Chapter 22	174
Chapter 23	181
Chapter 24	187

Chapter 25	189
Chapter 26	199
Chapter 27	202
Chapter 28	205
Chapter 29	214
Chapter 30	222
Chapter 31	224
Chapter 32	234
Chapter 33	239
Chapter 34	250
Chapter 35	256
Chapter 36	260
Chapter 37	268
About the Author	274
Acknowledgments	275

I

I take my foot off the gas, the ruh-ruh-ruh-ruh-ruh sound of my truck's lifeless engine fading into the cold morning air. No use flooding it. My coffee steams from the white plastic thermos cup on the dashboard, mixing with the vapors of my breath in the cab of my white '73 Chevy Cheyenne.

I look toward my house but can't see it through the ice on the windshield. "Where is that kid?"

Gingerly, I step down from the cab and bury my hands as deep as they'll go in the wool-lined pockets of my blue denim jacket. I stomp over the crunchy, frosted grass and up three sagging, paint-chipped wooden steps to my front door, my brown work boots leaving deep indents in the frozen turf. I knew Anthony should've mowed it one more time before the late-October frosts began.

Shivering my way into the kitchen, which feels almost as cold as it is outside, the boy is nowhere in sight. "Anthony?" I call loudly. No reply. His brown paper lunch sack sits on the counter where I left it, apparently untouched.

Striding down the hall, I breathe deeply to calm myself before going into his room. I'm already a few minutes late for work; this isn't the time for another shouting match.

I hear the music before I get to the door. Heavy, pounding electric guitar riffs. I forget what kids these days call this music. Metal, or hard rock, or something, but it's garbage. So much grunting and screeching. Who can even follow the lyrics? Taking another deep breath, I turn the handle.

"Anthony!" It comes out as almost a shout, so he can hear me over the music. He's got his back to the door, pretend drumming with two yellow pencils on the edge of his bed. Finally, he notices I'm there.

"Oh, hey Lawrence."

"Time for school, Anthony. You're gonna be late. Again."

"I didn't hear the truck start. And why do you always call me Anthony? I like Tony," he says while finally turning off his cassette player and ending its grating assault on my ears. Why can't Anthony like CCR instead of this noise?

Precious silence restored, I answer, "Because Anthony's your name. Your father calls you Tony, and I won't have anything to do with that man. You didn't hear the truck start because the engine doesn't want to turn over. Not that you could hear it over the music anyway."

"So, how is it my fault for being late if the truck isn't starting?"

"Let's just get going. I need you to scrape the ice while I try to get the engine running. And don't forget your lunch."

"Let me guess. Ham sandwich and an apple. Again."

"Make your own next time, then," I say while Anthony slides past me down the hall. On his way out the door he pulls on a heavy, dark-blue winter coat with a dingy, white collar, covering up his favorite t-shirt, a black one that hangs loosely from his narrow shoulders because it's a size too big. Although I can't see it now, I know the front features a skyscraper with gunsights over it, promoting some band named Def Leppard and their album *Pyromania*. Apparently, they're big among teenagers right now.

I turn down the heat a touch in Anthony's room and prepare to follow. First, however, I can't help but notice the blue- and red-checkered quilt on top of the sheets, and I pause. After a moment, a dull but growing pain tells me I'm biting my lip. Hard. I shake my head and trudge after my fifteen-year-old nephew, grabbing the lunch sack he's forgotten from the counter, despite the reminder I just gave him.

To his credit, however, he's gamely trying to get the windshield clear despite getting no help from the truck's defroster. *He really needs a haircut*, I say to myself as I watch his brown locks bounce off the collar of his coat. Anthony adamantly refuses one, even though the last time I mentioned it, I told him he looked like a girl.

"Thanks, buddy," I say while hoisting myself slowly into the truck's front seat, the cracked brown upholstery sighing under my weight. Wincing, I try to settle in while gripping the key and turning the ignition. Belatedly, I realize I left my coffee cup on the dashboard. It's not steaming anymore. It's not even warm. So, I open the door and toss it out.

"Your back again, Lawrence?"

"I'm fine. It's no big deal." Miraculously, the engine roars to life this time after a couple turns of the ignition.

"When're you gonna get that fixed?" Anthony asks while settling in beside me and buckling up. "One of these days it ain't gonna start, period."

"When I have some money to spare, that's when. Where's your backpack for school?"

"In my locker."

"You didn't have no homework?"

"Nope."

"No BS, Anthony. You really had no homework?"

"Just math. But I'll get that done during first period. It'll be fine."

"Your grade in math last quarter wasn't fine."

"I got a C. What's wrong with that?"

"A C ain't fine. You can do better." I edge the truck out of the driveway, looking over my shoulder for traffic while being careful not to kill the engine as I back up.

"But Mrs. Wilkinson's a bitch. I hate her."

"Watch the mouth, Anthony."

"What? It's not like I've never heard you say that."

"I know. And when you're a man like me, you can curse all you want. But until then, try to keep it polite. Okay?"

He gives a nod that's so slight I'm not sure his head truly moved.

"Besides," I continue, "she's a good teacher, even if she's tough. She was a good teacher way back when I had her for math sophomore year."

"But you suck at math. I've heard you admit it tons of times. And you can't ever help me with math homework, anyway, so why bring it home?"

"Because I was an idiot and didn't pay enough attention until it was too late. I spent my sophomore year chasing girls and working on cars in the rare moments I wasn't thinking about playing baseball. It isn't her fault I got a D. In fact, I probably didn't even deserve a D, the way I used to run my mouth in class all the time."

"You were a loudmouth once?" Anthony asks, his voice rising in surprise on the last word.

"Like I said, I was an idiot back then. I might not be much help at math, but I know how to be a man, and a man doesn't run his mouth and talk back to people who're trying to help him. If I'd had an old man to teach me those things when I was your age, it would have saved me a bunch of grief along the way. That's why I don't want you giving your teachers no trouble, you hear?"

Another nod. We drive in silence for a little while, and soon, we've reached the Port Huron High School parking lot. A sign with an Indian and the words "Big Reds" welcomes us. *Once a Big Red, always a Big Red*, I think to myself, reciting the school motto. I slow the truck and stop so Anthony can get out.

"One more thing. Why'd you rip holes in the knees of those black jeans you're wearing? I bought those new for you just last week."

"Style, Lawrence. Everyone's doing it," Anthony says while giving the door a solid shove to close it. He walks off, hands in the pockets of his ripped new jeans.

Style. Winter's on its way, and the kid's putting holes in his clothes for the sake of style. What's wrong with kids these days? I hope he got my message, though. The last thing I need is to get another phone call from Mrs. Wilkinson telling me my nephew's at risk of failing pre-algebra because he isn't turning in all his work.

Since Anthony gets home from school before my shift ends, he knows how to let himself in and find food if he's hungry. So, after work I decide to stop at Wally's Bar and see who's there. Wally Kauffman's owned his own bar for almost twenty years. Once, it was the best place for a drink in the neighborhood. Now, though, two letters in the electric sign have burned out, so it reads "Wa ly's B r" in the darkening October evening. As I pull in and park, the glowing green letters blur together through the drizzle on my windshield.

Stepping inside, I see a handful of people through the smoky haze surrounding the overhead lights, most of whom I've known for years. Carefully, I sit down next to Brad Duncan on a cracked black leather barstool and wave Wally over.

"What ya drinkin' tonight, Slugger? Usual?"

"Why you still call me that, Wally? It's been twenty-five years."

"I know, but I still tell everyone who asks that Larry Edwards is the best ballplayer I ever played with. I thought you liked it."

"You mean I *was* the best ballplayer you ever played with. I ain't now, that's for sure."

"Back still givin' ya trouble?"

"A little. I'm fine, though."

"You gonna get it looked at like I said?"

"I told you, I'm fine. Just a little stiff. And yeah, I'll have the usual. Shot of whiskey."

"Can you believe the Series?" Brad asks me while clapping me on the shoulder, smoke curling upward from his cigarette. "How'd it ever get to be the Cardinals and Royals, anyway? You could still hit the ball harder than some of those guys, back or not."

"Yeah," I respond, "and the entire Series played on damned Astroturf. Ain't nothin' new, I guess, playing on turf, but still, it bugs me. I'm okay with the Royals winning, I suppose, but I wasn't too partial either way on this one."

"At least it wasn't the Blue Jays."

"Yeah. Canadians. Why'd baseball ever expand to Canada, anyway?"

"Don't worry, the Tigers'll be back there soon, buddy. We both know it."

While Brad says this Wally drops off my drink. I take a sip.

"I thought they finished seventeen games back this year, Brad."

"Nah, only fifteen. And that's with losing eight straight in September. They were in it until that happened."

Like Wally, Brad Duncan is a guy I played ball with in high school. Baseball, football, basketball, you name it, Brad played them all. Tonight, he's got on a white Michigan Wolverines sweatshirt and dark-blue Wolverines baseball cap to go with his blue jeans and sneakers. You don't see as many guys anymore with the bristly brown mustache he still wears, but Brad's had it so long no one even says anything. He has a few strands of gray in the mustache, but nothing too bad. I notice the sweatshirt's wearing thin at the elbows and the Wolverines ball cap has its share of dirt stains.

"Bo's got the Wolverines playin' good ball, though, don't he?" Brad continues.

"I suppose," I say while sipping my drink and contemplating my reflection in the bar's polished, plate-glass mirror.

"Except the Iowa game last week. That kid made the field goal at the end and beat us. Fourth kick of the game, too. It ain't that bad, though, I guess. They were number one in the country, and people say Chuck Long is gonna win the Heisman this year."

"Yeah, it was somethin'."

"If only we had a threat at receiver. Bo's pretty conservative on offense, but ya have to be with the receivers we've got. I guess you can't have Anthony Carter catching passes every year."

"No, probably not."

"You even watch the game, Larry? You don't sound so into it. I thought you were big on college football."

"I work Saturdays now, Brad. Can't watch 'em like I used to."

"Shit, I forgot about that, Larry. I'm sorry, buddy. I shoulda thought of that."

"It's okay. Not your fault my old job disappeared, and I work at the hardware store now. Gotta do somethin', right?" I take another sip of whiskey.

"How long were you lookin' for work, anyway?"

"Three months, give or take. There just ain't no more teamster jobs these days, it seems like."

Wally walks back over to check on us.

"Slow night, huh, Wally?" Brad offers.

"It's only Tuesday. It'll pick up in a day or two," Wally replies while polishing the bar. It's already spotless, just like always, the rich oak deeply worn from countless elbows over twenty years.

"Well, gotta get home. The wife's gonna wanna see me, I suppose," Brad tells us. "Cheers, guys." He drops some money on the bar and strides out.

"How's the boy doin'?" Wally says to me.

"Don't know for sure. Not good, though, I don't think. Math, especially."

"He got Williamson this year?"

"Yeah. I told him to be nice to her."

"We never were, Larry."

"I know, and I've felt bad about it for about twenty years, too."

"Ain't it somethin' Larry?" Wally asks with a sigh. "When we were young, it never seemed like teachers at school were on our side. All that discipline. I just couldn't stand it."

"Wasn't it Williamson who caught you smoking that one time?"

"Yeah, that was her. I hated her for that the rest of my time in school."

"She just had this sixth sense when I tried cheating on my homework, too, Wally. Somehow, she always figured it out. Probably because I got too many answers right and she knew I wasn't that good at math," I say with a sad, weak laugh as I finish my first glass.

"You want another?"

"Yeah, one more."

When Wally returns from filling the glass, he says, "We were just stupid kids, Larry. Back then, no one could have made me believe that teachers did all those things because they wanted us to be good at something. It just never seemed that way at the time."

"Yeah, I wish someone woulda told me that high school would be the last time I'd have an authority figure who actually cared if I did well or not."

"You ever wonder about that, Larry?"

"About what?"

"If things woulda turned out any different if your pops hadn't died in France?"

"Can't say, Wally. I was born in '42, and he shipped out the next year. I never knew him, so I don't think about it much."

"You said Anthony ain't doin' so great, though?"

"He's young and figurin' out who he is, like I was at his age, but I don't get the things he does sometimes. Most of the time, actually." I start on my second drink.

"He and his friends still playing that game with the wizards and dragons and everything else?"

"Yeah. Sometimes they play at my house, sometimes at a friend's house, but they just sit around for hours rolling dice and drinking pop while playing that godawful music. I don't know what's with kids these days. Shouldn't he be under the hood of a car or playin' baseball or somethin'?"

"Maybe the times are changin', Larry. We gotta keep up, somehow."

"Maybe. I ain't so good at change, though. I don't know what to do with him sometimes."

"You're doin' what you can, buddy. His own daddy's doin' time for killing your sister in that car wreck they got into while he was drunk, so Anthony don't got no one else. I'm sure he appreciates what you're tryin' to do for him. He just don't show it all the time."

For the first time that night, I look up and scan the bar in the mirror while Wally speaks. Usually, there's no point; it's the same few regulars every time. That's why I haven't bothered until now.

Then, through the hazy air, I see someone whom I don't recognize. A woman, maybe late twenties or early thirties, sipping a drink at a booth by herself. She's got blonde hair, just a little wavy.

"Who's that in the corner?" I ask Wally in a quiet voice with a slight movement of my shoulder toward the woman.

"Don't know," he replies, also speaking a little lower. "Never seen her before tonight. She just came in, got a drink, made a phone call, and sat down like she's waiting for someone, but she's been here a while now, and no one's joined her yet. Strange, huh? She's just sat there looking out the window the whole time."

"Yeah, weird. You ever seen her before, like, around town?"

"No. You?"

I shake my head.

"You want me to go check on her, Larry? See if she's got a ring?"

I scowl.

"What?"

"She looks fifteen years younger than me. Ten, at least. Let it go."

"It's never too late, Larry."

"For what?"

"Finding a good woman. You deserve one, you know."

"Get real. My time's up. Ain't no woman interested in me."

"How long've we been friends, Larry?"

The Long Way Home

"I dunno. Since intermediate school?" I've never understood why Port Huron has intermediate schools. Why not call them middle schools or junior high schools like everyone else does?

"Have I ever done you wrong?"

"Never."

"Then trust me when I say it ain't too late for you. Now, you want me to go check her out, or not? She's gotta be ready for a second drink by now, anyway, so it won't be suspicious."

"Do what you want. I'm gonna finish my drink and head home soon. I just hope Anthony remembers how to cook himself some macaroni and cheese if he gets hungry."

I turn and pretend I'm studying my drink, so I don't give anything away while Wally goes to check in on his blonde customer. It's been a while since I played this game, but I still remember the rules. After about a minute chatting with her, he heads to the other end of the bar to check in with his patrons there.

Wally's a tall guy, about six-three, and these days he's a big guy, too, maybe two-thirty. Back when we played ball together in high school, he was the first baseman and sometimes a pitcher and was pretty good at both.

I look over at the far wall, and it's still there. The blown-up black-and-white photograph of our 1960 high school team. Wally's right in the middle in the second row because he was the tallest guy we had, and he has the big, goofy smile on his face that he's never completely lost. I used to tease him about it, but he says it helps keep the customers at ease. He has two daughters, but they left town for Detroit after graduating high school, and I haven't seen them in a couple years. I don't think Wally sees much of them, either. Shoot, I don't even know for sure if either is married, but I've never heard Wally talk about any weddings or being a grandfather, so I'm guessing they aren't.

I've nearly finished my second drink when Wally makes it back over to fill me in.

"Nothing to worry about, buddy. She's got a wedding band."

"I wasn't worrying about it, anyway. You learn anything else about her, though? Just curious since I've never seen her before."

"Not much, no. I just asked her if she was from here and told her I'm happy she stopped in tonight."

"What'd she say? About where she's from, that is."

"When I asked if she was from Port Huron she just said, 'kind of,' and left it at that. It didn't seem like she wanted to talk about it, or anything else, for that matter, so I didn't ask her anything more. She sounded a little irritated at something. Maybe more than a little."

I shrug, drain my glass, and then pull out my wallet to pay.

"Don't worry about it, Larry. Have this one on the house."

"Nonsense," I say while extracting some cash.

"Larry, it's okay. You've been a customer ever since I opened this place. I know things have been tight for you lately, so let me be a friend and comp you a couple drinks, all right?"

"No way. I can see you ain't been too busy lately. You need the money as much as I do, and you know I ain't one to not pay my debts. Here." I extend the money to Wally. He steps back.

"Come on, Larry. No one here doubts your honesty. We all know you. Just let me be a friend, okay? It's only two drinks."

"I'm gonna leave the money here, Wally. You can take it, or someone else can. I've never been a freeloader, and I'm not about to start now."

"You're a stubborn man, Larry, refusin' a friend's help like this. Can we compromise at fifty-fifty?"

I turn and stride toward the door. If Wally has anything more to say, he thinks better of it. I don't know what made him do that; he's never tried to offer me charity before.

Back in the cold outside, I see the bar's blinking electric sign reflecting in the raindrops on my Cheyenne's windshield. It's cold, but not freezing. Still, I'll just about be home by the time the truck's heater gets going enough to matter. Figures.

The Long Way Home

I check my watch. 7:30. Damn, I shoulda stopped after the first drink. Anthony has a house key, of course, but I shouldn't have left him alone this long.

II

A few minutes later, I pull into my driveway. All the lights are out in the house. Snatching my keys from the ignition, I slide carefully down from the Cheyenne's cab and then stride quickly to the front door, house key already out and ready. Just as I walk up the sagging front steps and reach for the lock, I see a light come on in Anthony's room. I put my head back, sigh with relief, and then turn the knob and go inside.

While I walk toward his bedroom to check on him, I could swear I hear low voices and a sound like the bedroom window closing. However, when I knock and go in to talk with Anthony, it's just him.

"Working late, Lawrence? I thought you got off work at six tonight."

"I had a tough day and stopped to get a drink. You had dinner?"

"Nah, I wasn't hungry."

"How come the house was so dark when I got home? I thought I told you to always leave some lights on."

"Yeah, you did, but I had a headache, so I decided to lie down for a while and try to sleep it off. That's why the house was dark. I was resting and it just got late before I woke up."

"Okay, just try to remember next time, all right?"

He nods to me, almost too quickly for someone whose head was hurting so much just a little while ago.

"I'm kinda hungry now, though. What we got for dinner tonight?"

"I'm gonna open a can of pork n' beans," I tell him. "You want some of that? Maybe some chicken soup?"

"Either one sounds good. Thanks, Lawrence."

I nod and retreat down the hallway, boots echoing softly on the worn hardwood. My ears still work, it appears. I certainly smelled perfume in Anthony's room, not to mention it was much cooler than the rest of the house, so I don't even need to go outside and check for footprints below his window. We've had the "girl talk" already, of course, but the fact he's sneaking someone in and out of the house isn't a good sign. I wonder if this is the first time he's had a girl over?

It should probably bother me more that he tried to cover it up, but I'm not sure it does. After all, I did the same thing when I was his age. Doesn't make it a good move, though, just because I did it twenty-five years ago. Heaven only knows how lucky I am that I never got some girl pregnant in high school. Still, I don't want Anthony to travel that road if I can help it. Might be time to talk with him again.

But not tonight. I just need to take a load off my back while I think of how to talk to the boy, so I grab the can opener and heat a pot on the stove for two cans of pork n' beans.

That night, I fall asleep to the sound of rain gently dripping from the rooftop.

The following day, Wednesday, I'm stocking shelves at Eddie's Hardware Store. I'm on my right knee straightening up a shelf with boxes of nails when I hear a melodic voice ask from behind me, with just a hint of sarcasm in the tone, "Excuse me, Larry, could you help me for a moment?"

I turn my shoulders and look up, expecting to see someone I knew from back in high school. Instead, it's the blonde woman from the bar last night. Now that I get a closer look at her face, she's got brilliantly blue eyes to go with her wavy blond hair and soft cheeks.

Today, she's wrapped a plaid scarf around her neck because it's chilly once again.

"How did you know who I am?" I start to respond, then, "Oh, yeah, I suppose you read my nametag."

"No, actually, I remember you from last night. You got into a loud conversation with the bartender and then walked out of the bar."

"Yeah, I guess you'd a heard that since you were sitting there. Sorry."

Then the woman lowers her voice a bit. "I also know what game the two of you tried to play. The bartender talking to you, then me, then around to the other customers before coming back to you. I suppose you could have made it more obvious you were checking me out, but you really need to be more creative."

I don't even try to pretend. "It was Wally's idea, if it matters at all to you. I told him it was stupid, but, like you saw when I walked out, we have our disagreements."

She gives me a weak smile, although I'm not sure if it's because she believes me that it was Wally's plan or because she finds my excuse so feeble.

I go on. "Well, you asked for help, so what can I get for you? If I didn't blow whatever confidence you might have in me last night, I'll sell you whatever piece of hardware you're looking for." Then, I notice. Last night's wedding ring isn't there today.

"I've got a dead car battery. You sell those?"

"Not here, no. You need an auto parts store for that."

"Great. Where's the closest one?"

"A couple blocks down." Just then, thunder sounds outside. A quick glance out the store windows shows fat raindrops starting to splatter on the pavement.

"Just my luck," the woman says, running a hand through her hair. "Outside in the rain again, just like last night."

I see the woman has no umbrella, and a thought hits me. "Here, tell you what. If I didn't offend you too much last night, I'll drive

The Long Way Home

you over there. I'm due to go on a break in about ten minutes, anyway, so if you don't mind waiting just a bit, I can take you, and you'll get to keep dry."

She rolls her eyes and gives a deep sigh. "Great. I get to spend more time with the local bar gang. Yeah, what the hell, I'll wait. Better than getting soaked."

After getting permission from Eddie, my manager and the store owner, to take a couple extra minutes on break, the woman and I stand at the door, ready to make a break for my truck through the downpour. "Just wait a minute and I'll pull up and get you," I tell her before striding away.

Moments later, we're both in the cab of my truck, windshield wipers slashing back and forth. I set the heater at a medium setting, so the windows don't fog up, and then, pointless though it may be, I decide to attempt polite conversation. "You weren't at Wally's by choice last night, were you? Did your battery die before that?"

"Yeah. I went to the bar to call my boyfriend and tell him what happened. It was the closest building I knew would have a phone."

"He sure did take his time coming to get you. I guess that explains why you were pretty short with Wally."

"You got it. Rickey wasn't even home when I called. Didn't make it to get me until nearly closing time."

"That's rough of him. If I'd a known, I woulda offered to help last night, but I have a feeling you woulda turned me down."

"Probably," she says curtly as we turn into the parking lot for Ted's Auto Parts.

"And then he put you in charge of getting a new battery today?"

"He had to get up early to work his construction job, so, yeah, I have to do it."

"Ever bought a car battery before?"

"Nope."

"Want me to go in with you, then? I know the owner, Ted. We went to school together. I'll make sure you get the right battery and then drive you back to your car and help you install it."

"Don't you have to get back to work?"

"Nah, Eddie gets it. He's an old-time guy. Eddie'd rather we go out of our way to help a customer. He feels like it generates trust with the community."

"I'd like that, I guess," the woman says while stepping down from her seat. "I'm Anna, by the way."

"Well, Anna, let's go find what you need."

After shopping for a few minutes, we're back in the Cheyenne and on our way to Anna's car. It isn't all that far; Port Huron only has about thirty-three thousand residents. At least the storm has passed by, and the rain is a mere drizzle at this point.

When I pull up, I see someone standing at the car. He's a large man both in height and size, maybe even a bodybuilder from the width of his frame, with a short beard. He wears a hunting parka and blue jeans. A Stihl Chainsaws hat rounds out his appearance, almost concealing his bushy eyebrows but not the long, dark hair spilling out from the back. He's got the hood of the car up and looks like he's about to hoist a new battery into place when he sees Anna and me stop a few feet away.

"That's Rickey, my boyfriend," Anna mutters, as if I had any doubts on that question. "His new worksite must not be too far from here."

Anna jumps down to speak to Rickey. I follow, easing out of the cab slowly and wincing just a bit.

"Hi, honey," he says to her, leaning in for a kiss. "I'd give you a hug, too, but I'm a little dirty from fixing this. Who's that?" He nods in my direction.

"That's Larry," Anna chirps on my behalf. "He works at the hardware store, and he's just giving me a ride here to put a new battery in the car."

"A new battery? What're you talking about? I've got one right here, see?"

"But, last night on the phone you told me to take care of it this morning."

"No, I didn't. I said *I'd* take care of it in the morning."

"You did not. You told me to do it, Rickey."

"You're making that up."

"I heard you," Anna says in a defensive tone, her expression changing from a winning smile very quickly as she frowns, clutches her purse to her chest with one hand, and digs the other into her pocket.

Rickey's face, which had tensed in the brief argument, softens, and he says, "Well, we've got a battery now. No need to argue about it, I guess. You can take off, Terry, we've got this under control."

"Sure," I say, ignoring his failure to remember my name after thirty seconds. "You know how to install one, right?"

"What does it look like, old man?" Rickey hoists the battery he brought for me to see. I notice he handles the battery's weight easily using just one arm. The idea that he's a weightlifter looks more probable by the minute.

"Yeah, like you said, under control. Okay, I'm headed back to work." Old man. That's a new one. Well, what can I say? He's about half right.

Rickey's already turned his back on me to put the new battery he brought into place.

"Wait," Anna calls out when I turn around. "What about the battery I just bought?"

"I'll take it," I respond. "Don't worry, I'll have Ted tear up your check when I return it. His store is on the way back to work, anyway."

"You trust this guy already?" Rickey shouts from under the hood.

"Well, you know where to find me if I don't keep my word," I say while hoisting myself into the Cheyenne's cab. It takes a couple turns of the ignition for the engine to start, but it finally does, and I go on my way.

"What're you doin', Lawrence?" Anthony asks me that same evening as his wooden chair scrapes across the gray-and-white-checkered linoleum floor of the kitchen. He sits down, TV dinner in hand.

"Checking the 'Help Wanted' section of the newspaper."

"Why? You've got a job."

"For now. Business hasn't been too good at Eddie's lately. If he needs to let someone go, it'll probably be me since I'm the newest employee Eddie has."

"How come business is slow at Eddie's? You always say what an honest guy he is and how much he tries to do for his customers."

"Yeah, that's all true. Eddie's a great guy. But, Anthony, did you see that new hardware store chain start construction across town? That's gonna be competition for Eddie when the store's finished, and it'll probably mean he gets fewer customers. It's nearly finished right now."

"That doesn't seem right."

"Right or wrong, that's how things are sometimes. You gotta keep your eyes open and anticipate what might happen in the future. Try to be one step ahead if you can."

"I'll keep that in mind for the future."

"How about the present, Anthony? It's never too early to start, you know."

"From some of the stories you've told me, it doesn't sound like you were too good at that back in your day." He says this matter-of-factly, without meanness or spite. I wouldn't deny it, anyway, because I know it's true.

"Well, that's part of bein' a parent, I guess. Part of your job is to try to save your kids from doing the dumb stuff you did. Problem is, the world's inventin' new ways to do dumb things all the time, and it's hard for parents to keep pace."

Anthony laughs. He doesn't do it often, so I relish it when he does.

"Let me tell you one more story, Anthony. You know that small river down the way where kids like to go and swim in the summer?"

"Yeah, of course. I go there sometimes."

"They still have that rope swing over the deep eddy?"

"No, I've never seen it."

"That's because about two years after I graduated high school, a kid got killed there. You see, they had this rope swing, and as long as you let go of the rope in the right place and landed at the right spot in the deep pool, you were fine. But if you let go of the rope late and went to the right too far, you'd hit a big rock in the water. Anyway, from what I heard, this kid was new and had never tried the swing before. He let go too late, hit his head on the rock, and died on the spot."

"Damn," Anthony says, shaking his head. "That's sad. The kids at school sometimes tell rumors about someone who died there, but you know rumors. You can never tell if they're really true. How many times did you swing there?"

"Hundreds," I say, shaking my head, too. "At first, I did it in the name of proving my manhood. It was just something you did back then. It was fun in a way, though, because of the excitement, the risk, and the danger. But thinking back now, I'm wondering why I insisted on taking that chance so often. A couple times I came within inches of that rock myself, you know."

"On purpose?"

"Of course. That was part of the game. Proving you weren't scared. Your grandmother would've had a heart attack if she'd known."

"You think she ever found out before she died, Lawrence?"

"I don't know. I hope not. She acted kinda like I'm acting now for you. Your grandma tried to keep me out of trouble, but I had a way of finding it anyway. It's part of what parents do. Try to shield their kids from trouble whenever they can."

"You think they'll ever let my dad out of prison?"

"You know I don't like to talk about that, Anthony. After your father killed my only sister in that car crash, I swore I'd never forgive him. I still haven't. I know he's your dad and all, but I just can't do that yet."

"You two never got along that great, I know."

"Again, I know I'm talkin' about your father, Anthony, but I never trusted him. I tried to talk Samantha out of marryin' him, but it didn't work."

Anthony doesn't respond. Instead, he looks down and prods his turkey with his fork.

"Maybe I shouldn't have said that," I say, not knowing if it's a good idea to continue the conversation. "It's just that after my own mother died, Samantha was the only family I had left. Now, I don't have any family at all. Well, other than you."

"How many beers did he drink that night, again?"

"I don't remember. Way too many."

There's a long pause, as if we've mutually agreed to let this conversation topic end.

Then, Anthony asks, with a little pep back in his voice, "Can I ask a favor, Lawrence?"

"What do you have in mind?"

"You like football, right? Will you take me to the game at school on Friday night?"

"You want to watch a football game?" I pause for a moment, chewing my lip just a bit. I didn't expect this, for sure. Anthony doesn't care much for sports. Finally, I ask carefully, "You gonna meet someone there?"

"Yeah, her name's Theresa Wagner. She likes football and asked if I'd watch the game with her."

"Is she the same girl who jumped out of your window when I got home last night?"

"You figured that out after all, I guess."

"Sure did. Remember, everything you're doing now, I did it myself once. Just be careful, nephew."

"She's a good girl, Lawrence. We just started dating the other day."

"Then why sneak her in and out of the house?"

"She was scared because I didn't tell you she was coming over."

"Were you nervous to tell me?"

"A little, I guess."

"Don't be. You're the right age, and dating's a normal thing. But be careful who you spend time with. Before too much longer you'll have your driver's license, and then you've really gotta watch out and make good choices."

"I told you she's a nice girl. She likes the same music I do."

"Still, be careful. That's part of what I meant by trying to stay one step ahead."

"Careful about what?"

"Everything. Sometimes people aren't who they seem. Just remember that."

III

Friday night comes around, and I'm at my first high school football game in several years. It's a crisp evening, but at least the rain is over with for now. Still, we've had enough in recent days that the field's in lousy shape, and the game turns into a mud slog before long. Port Huron High, Anthony's school, clad in red, white, and black, plays rival Port Huron Northern with their gold and blue uniforms.

I sit next to Brad Duncan, who continues going to Port Huron games religiously a quarter-century after we graduated, and Sammy Williams, another guy we played ball with in school. The unusual thing about Sammy is that he's black, and we didn't have too many black kids in school growing up, but Sammy had such a combination of athletic skill and a sense of humor that it was impossible for me not to like him. Brad and I both stuck up for him a time or two back in school when people tried to pick fights with him because of his color, and I still enjoy seeing him today.

I'm watching Anthony and a girl who I presume is Theresa more than I am the game. She's got dark hair, almost black, and way too much dark eye shadow around her eyes, but outside of that, she looks like any other teenager cheering at a football game in her jean jacket and black jeans. I'd rather concentrate on the game on the field, but Brad and Sammy keep me filled in on what's happening.

"Boy, that running back Ronnie Bradley we've got can sure play," Sammy's saying as the second quarter winds along. Sammy would know; he was our team's running back his senior year in addition to playing center field on our baseball team. "He's as big as most of the linemen, but he's also the fastest guy out there."

"Yeah, his brother Rickey was a player, too," Brad replies. My attention perks up at the name. "About a decade ago, I think, he was one of the best linemen in the conference."

"I remember that dude," Sammy says. "Whatever happened to him? He had a body like a tree trunk."

"He went to Western Michigan, or maybe it was Eastern, but washed out before he ever played, I think," Brad tells Sammy. "I don't recall if it was because of injury or attitude."

"I think I might bet on attitude," I put in.

"What makes ya say that?" Sammy questions.

I tell them about my encounter with Rickey, Anna, and the car battery on Wednesday morning.

"You sure it was the same dude?" Sammy asks.

"Seems likely. He looked late-twenties, he was huge, and Anna called him Rickey. How many people who fit that description can there be in Port Huron?"

"You're on a first-name basis now with that woman at the bar?" Brad asks, jabbing my shoulder with an elbow.

"Come on. I was just doin' my job. You know how Eddie feels about making sure we value customers. Even though she turned out to not even be a customer."

"Eddie's a good man," Sammy puts in. "I still travel crosstown to buy from him instead of the place by my house. It costs me extra in gas, I suppose, but it's worth it just to check in with him and see how he's doin'."

"How'd you get free from work to be here?" I ask Sammy. "You're, what, assistant manager at the restaurant now? Shouldn't you be working?"

"Yeah, I'm a manager, but the owner likes to run things on Fridays. He says that's when things are most likely to go wrong, people blowin' off steam after a week at work and all, so he likes to be there himself to put out the fires when they spring up. Fine by me."

"I'm gonna get some popcorn, I'll be back in a few minutes," I tell the guys before striding down the bleachers to the concession stand. Anthony and Theresa seemed engrossed enough in the game that I figure I can take my eyes off them for a few minutes, and this way I'll also beat the halftime rush.

I'm waiting in line to get my popcorn when once again I'm surprised by an upbeat voice behind me. "Thanks for helping me the other day."

Turning around, I see Anna in the spotty light filtering to the edge of the stands from the stadium lights above. She's by herself, no Rickey in sight this time. Tonight, she's pulled her hair back, and she's wearing a heavy red sweatshirt over blue jeans.

"Miss Anna, good to see you," I say clumsily, not knowing quite what else to do. I take off my Tigers ballcap and run a hand through my hair before replacing the cap. The hair is a little thinner than it used to be, but I've still got most of it.

"Actually, it's Miss Nicholson, but you can just call me Anna."

"Did everything go okay after I left Wednesday morning?"

"Sort of. Rickey gets a little mad when he thinks he said one thing but really said another, but it's okay. He shouts a little sometimes, but he's usually sorry afterward. Too much beer does that to him. Things are okay again now, though."

"I meant did everything go okay with the battery, not with the little argument you had, but I guess that's good to hear, too."

"Oh, yeah," Anna replies, blushing just a touch. "Since you saw us argue, I figured you were referring to that. Maybe that was more than you wanted to know. The battery's fine. My Honda runs again. That was very sweet of you to help me out, driving me all around. I probably should have been nicer about it at the time, but I was having a bad morning."

"Nothing to worry about. You weren't the toughest customer I had to assist that day. This one guy kept complaining his chainsaw wouldn't start, said we'd sold him a piece of junk, but he never even put gas in the thing."

She laughs while I step up to the window and request a small bag of popcorn. Anna buys a large bag and adds two Cokes, and then she hands one Coke to me. "For your help. And to make up for my attitude."

"I can't take that. I really didn't do anything to earn it, you know."

"Oh, please," she says while smiling brightly and nudging my shoulder with the popcorn bag. "Not another repeat of the night at the bar. It's just a Coke. We may never see each other again, and I don't want to end this week feeling like I was a bitch to a stranger who helped me out."

I don't know why, but I reach out and take the drink. Maybe it's because her smile is brighter than anything I've seen in months. It's certainly not because I love drinking pop. Whatever the reason, I take a sip.

"There, you go. You've had a drink, so it's yours now," she says with a small giggle and another smile. "See ya around, Larry. And thanks again for being a gentleman."

With that, she walks off, leaving me standing in the muddled twilight on the edge of the range of the lights at the high school football stadium. Sighing, I shake my head and walk back to my seat, wondering what just happened and why. I can't remember the last time someone called me a gentleman, if anyone ever has. Growing up, I always associated that word with older people. At least Anna didn't call me "old man" like her boyfriend did the other day.

I spend the second half of the game watching the action some, reminiscing with Brad and Sammy about the old days, and keeping an eye on Anthony. As far as I can tell, he has a good time, and he and Theresa keep their hands to themselves. It's a good evening and a nice change of pace from my routine Friday night of unwinding with a beer on the couch watching whatever's on television. I'd even consider going again next week until I remember that teams play their rivals in their final game of the season, so this is it for high school football in 1985. I catch one glimpse of Anna, almost by accident. She and Rickey stand and cheer when Ronnie Bradley scores his third touchdown of the game. It's easy to spot Rickey because he's the largest guy in the crowd. After clapping for several moments, they kiss and hug before sitting down.

Back at home that same evening, I need to get a little sleep, so I can work tomorrow. That means getting Anthony to turn the music down again. I knock and wait for a moment. Nothing. So, I knock again. Still nothing. Frowning to myself, I decide to just go in. He's lying on the bed with his eyes closed, drumming away on his stomach with his pencils. Somehow, he notices I'm there and looks up.

"Anthony, I gotta get my rest for work tomorrow. Let's turn the music down, okay?"

"Sorry, Lawrence. I got caught up a little, I guess."

"You enjoy the game tonight?"

"I suppose. Football's not really my thing, but it was okay."

"You ever think about trying to play in the Big Red Band or whatever they call it? You like music, and you're always drumming to yourself whenever I come in. Maybe you should try playing in the school band. You might like it."

"I don't think so, Uncle. They don't play my style of music."

"Mine neither, but you might make a few new friends that way."

"There's nothing wrong with my friends. Besides, who wants to hang around with band geeks, anyway?"

Even I give a wry smile at that one. "You taking good care of your mother's quilt?"

"Yeah, I always fold it away when I'm eating in here, so I won't get food on it."

"That's good. It was your mom's wedding present from your grandmother, you know. After she died in the car crash, I thought you should have it."

"Grandma sure was good at sewing."

"She was, for sure. It's a good thing she wasn't afraid to hang around with the sewing geeks, isn't it?" I say to Anthony while raising one eyebrow and grinning. "Goodnight, buddy." I close the door and walk out without waiting to see how long he needs to get it.

IV

The next evening, I pull into Wally's Bar, driving over the curb with one tire and skidding to a stop. Barging through the door, I march up to the bar and slap my palm on the polished oak. "Whiskey. Now."

Wally nods and hustles over from where he was talking with a few other customers. "Tough day, buddy?"

"Don't wanna talk about it. Just gimme a drink, and when this one's done, keep 'em comin'."

"Whoa, Slugger, what happened? This ain't your style. You always stop at two drinks."

"Not tonight. Fill it up," I growl.

Wally brings over my drink, but before sliding it to me asks, "It's work, ain't it?"

"Not anymore. Don't have no work," I say while taking the glass from him and beginning my first drink.

"Eddie had to let you go?"

"He said there weren't enough business to keep me on right now. Said things usually slow down in the winter because people'r doin' less outside work. Sounds like a bunch a bullshit to me." I say all this between my next couple gulps.

Wally glances over my shoulder, toward the parking lot. I don't care if I left any cans of Bud open on the dash or not. I look at my glass. Already half gone. "Get another round ready, Wally."

"You sure, Larry? You're drinking this first one a little quick. Tell you the truth, you don't look so good. Maybe I'll call you a cab?" He reaches toward the rotary phone behind him.

"Hell, no. I said gimme another drink. I'm fine."

"You ain't fine, Larry. Now, just slow down. Let's get ourselves together for a minute, okay?"

"Don't you cross me too, Wally," I snarl. It's possible other customers are looking our way, but I don't care.

Wally leans in close and speaks softly. "Larry, you know I'm on your side, and I'd never do you wrong. Your sister and me were good friends, too, and after what happened to her, I can't let you do this."

"You leave Samantha outta this!" I roar in his face. "Now, more whiskey!"

"I can't do it, Larry. Come on, lemme call a cab for you. I'll come by and check on you tomorrow, okay?"

"That's it," I bellow, snatching my keys from the pocket of my denim jacket and storming for the door. The faces and colors in Wally's Bar blur even as I bump a chair on the way. I curse when it bruises my hipbone.

While I gather myself, from the corner of my eye I see Wally wriggling around the end of the bar to intercept me. "Larry, stop, buddy. Just slow down!" As I reach the door, he puts his hand softly on my shoulder. "Slow down, Larry. Let's talk it over."

Although something in the back of my mind tries to tell me it's a bad idea, I ball my fist and slug Wally in the gut. He doubles over in the doorway. I push past him and leap into my truck, shouting in pain when that wrenches my back. I stomp on the gas, throw my view over my shoulder, curse when my back protests again, and squeal out of the parking lot and into the street. This time two tires go over the curb with a jolt.

Again, this jolts my back, and I curse while reaching my right hand around to massage it. Next, I reach for the can of Bud I was drinking before getting to Wally's, to see if there's anything left.

This requires taking my eyes from the road for just a moment, long enough that I miss the four-way stop sign at the next intersection. My foot still on the gas, I plow through. Right into a gray truck that's accelerating into the intersection after stopping. With the screech of metal on metal, we collide. I'm thrown against the driver's door, my head hits the cab frame, and as I hear glass shattering, the last thing I feel is the fresh blood on my left cheek as I lose consciousness.

V

"Larry? Larry, can you hear me, buddy?"

I hear the words, and the speaker seems like he might be familiar, but the sound seems far away, like someone's speaking to me through a fog so thick I can't tell where he is. I can't quite open my eyes, either, but I think I see alternating lighter and darker blurs above me. When I try shifting my body, my left shoulder screams at me to hold still, so I do. It's possible I give a weak cry at the same time, but I'm too groggy to tell if it's my voice or someone else's.

"Larry, we're gonna get you all patched up, buddy. You'll be okay," the voice shouts again before other voices start to babble above me. Without the single voice to concentrate on, I lose focus and drop into blackness again.

When I come to, I'm in a hospital bed. My left shoulder has a cast around it, and I see an IV tube inserted in my left forearm. Slowly, ever so slowly, my vision comes back into focus. After repeated blinking, the sign on the wall with my room number only appears one-and-a-half times instead of twice whenever I look at it. I sink back into the pillows.

"Welcome back, Slugger," a voice says from bedside. This time I recognize it.

"Wally," I mumble, turning slowly to my right to look at the voice. "What time is it?"

He glances at his wrist. "About four in the morning, buddy."

"What happened? How'd I get here?"

"Should I start with before or after you punched me last night?"

"I punched you?"

"Yeah, you hit me like I was a belt-high fastball. You can still pack a wallop when you need to."

"Why did I punch you, Wally? You're my friend."

"Do you remember coming in for a drink last night?"

"Sort of. I got mad because I lost my job, so I had a few beers. The rest after that isn't too clear to me. I'm gonna guess I said some things I shouldn't have, didn't I?"

"Yeah, a few. Okay, maybe more than a few."

"I don't remember most of them."

"It's okay, Larry. The doc said you might have a concussion from the collision, and one thing that concussions do is make it hard to remember recent things."

"I was in a car wreck?"

"Right after you left my bar. That's why your shoulder's all bandaged up right now. The doc told me you didn't break anything, but you've bruised it really bad, so you've got to have a cast on there for a little while. Your face is scraped up, too, and you bled some, so they put an IV in you to keep your fluid levels stable."

"I remember some of that, now that you say it. After Eddie told me he had to let me go, I just got so mad. Not at Eddie, just at life in general. I'd even been looking for other jobs just in case this happened, but I hadn't found one yet. So, I went out and bought a twelve-pack of Bud and started drinking. Somehow, I knew it was a bad idea and I shouldn't do it, but the anger and frustration just took over, and before I knew it, the Bud was gone. That's when I started for your bar, and I don't remember much of what happened after that."

"Yeah, about the Bud, Larry. The police saw the beer when the ambulance showed up to take you here. They're probably gonna take away your driver's license for a while."

"I deserve that for being stupid, I suppose."

Then, a thought hits me, and the tears well in my eyes. Seconds later, I'm sobbing, and I raise my right hand to cover my eyes and rub my forehead.

"What's wrong, buddy? You'll get your license back before too long. It's your first offense for drinking and driving, isn't it? People'll understand."

"It ain't that. What happened to the other driver? The person I hit?"

"Minor injuries. The guy came along in the ambulance, but it turns out he only has bruised ribs and a few little cuts where the glass scraped him. He said as long as you pay his hospital bills and fix up the damage to his truck, he'll consider the matter closed."

Although I hear Wally, I keep crying.

"What're you still crying for, Larry? That's good news, ain't it?"

"Yeah, it is."

"Then what's the matter?"

"How can I ever look at Anthony again? When he came to live with me, I promised I'd take good care of him, and I ain't done it."

"Anthony'll be fine. He was here for a couple hours, and then the police took him over to a friend's house for the night. Timmy was the friend's name, I think. The parents said he could stay there until you're back home."

"I don't mean that. He came to live with me because his own father was a drunk and killed my sister in that crash. Now, I'm no better'n his dad is. How can Anthony ever respect me after this? I failed him because I was stupid and weak."

"Don't worry about that now, Larry. Let's just get you better first, okay? Then we'll talk about the other things. You feelin' like you need some rest? It is four in the morning, after all."

"I suppose."

"Are you in pain? You want me to ask the nurse to check on you?"

"It ain't that bad. Just let me rest, I guess."

"I'm gonna go home and sleep a bit, Larry. I'll come by to see how you're doin' this afternoon, okay?"

"Okay. Oh, and Wally, if I really did hit you, I'm sorry. I shouldn't have done that, either."

"It's okay, buddy. I got plenty of extra padding these days, anyway," Wally says with a laugh as he slaps his stomach, causing the fat to roll.

Then, he draws the doorway curtain aside and departs. My vision's just good enough to see that the curtain has a subdued, light-green floral pattern on it. It's about the only thing with any life in the hospital room. The walls are white, the sheets and pillows are white, everything's white. Well, okay, the floors have a tan-and-gray diamond pattern, but almost everything else is white.

While I drift back to sleep, the only thing I can think about is Anthony. I only had one purpose in life, and that was taking good care of him. Turns out, I couldn't even do that one thing right. As I drift back into sleep, I feel tears wet my cheeks once again.

Later that day, Sunday, the doctor monitoring me says I need to wait another day or two before he'll discharge me because he's worried about the lingering effects of a concussion. I try to tell him I'm fine. Staying any time in a hospital costs money, and I don't have much of it, so I need to go home. However, since I totaled my truck, I can't leave unless someone will drive me, and Wally says I should listen to the doctor and stay one more night, so I'm stuck one more night.

I'm almost ready to sleep again, having turned off the television after watching more sit-coms and game shows today than I usually do in a whole year, when I hear light, booted footsteps outside the curtain to my room. The footsteps pause for a minute, as if their owner is debating whether to come in, but then the curtain slowly peels back.

In walks a face I never expected to see. The woman's dark brown hair reaches halfway down her back, and her gentle smile reveals the soft lines on her face. She wears a heavy white turtleneck sweater along with blue jeans and the brown leather boots I had already noticed.

I try to speak, but she beats me to it. "Hello, Larry. It's been a long time."

I nod but can't find the words to reply. Then, she continues. "You look like you've had better days."

"Yeah, I—"

"You don't need to tell me all the details. Wally called this afternoon and described what happened last night. He said I probably wouldn't care but thought I should know, anyway."

"Yet, here you are."

"Here I am," Shawna English says to me while taking a seat near the bed.

"Why'd you come?"

"Because I do care. I know things didn't end that well between us, but that was mostly my fault. I thought I owed it to you to at least see if you were okay."

"But why did Wally call you?"

"You forget we were good friends in school and grew up almost next door to each other. We've kept in touch a little."

"I'm hoping they'll discharge me tomorrow. I'll be back on my feet quick enough."

"With a cast on your shoulder?"

"It ain't broken. Just a bad bruise."

Shawna nods, then moves to the side of the bed and pats my good arm. "I'm sorry this happened to you. Wally told me about the job, too, and about how you take care of your nephew now. You've been trying hard to do the right thing, and I'm proud of you for that."

"I'm nothin' to be proud of. This is just the most recent time I've failed to save me from myself."

"Don't be too hard on yourself, Larry. Everyone makes mistakes."

"This was a pretty damned bad mistake, Shawna."

"We all make those. Sometimes, though, what makes it bad is the timing, more than the action."

I think on this for a moment before asking the biggest question on my mind. "Does your husband know you're here?"

"Of course. He's the one who spoke to Wally on the phone. After I got off work at the beauty parlor, he told me. I drove over from Lansing as soon as I could eat some dinner."

"I thought he hated me."

"Hate is a strong word for it, Larry. He was suspicious of you when I first met him. Thought you might try to get me back, even though I knew he didn't have anything to worry about. You're way too honorable for that. Besides, we both know our breakup was because of me, and you've never been one to pine over the past."

"I might have said a thing or two the night you walked out that I shouldn't have. I seem to remember telling you to get your head out of the clouds and live a real life. Or something like that. I don't think I was all that polite about it, either."

"No, Larry, you said exactly what I needed to hear. Like you always did. I just wasn't mature enough to realize it at the time. When I think back to who I was back then, now I can laugh. Imagine being thirty-four years old, barely employed, and still expecting to live this rich, glamorous life someday. Pretty crazy for a woman who barely graduated high school, huh? I was so hooked on celebrity lifestyle magazines, not to mention booze and cigarettes, I'm surprised you stayed with me as long as you did."

"I thought you had potential if I could only get through to you."

Shawna laughs and smiles. "You were right. It just took me a bit longer to figure that out than you could afford to wait."

I sigh and close my eyes for a moment, feeling the fatigue gnawing at me. Shawna's voice brings me back. "I finally did give up smoking. Drinking, too."

"I'm proud of you for that. If only I could say the same, I wouldn't be here now."

"That's part of my point, Larry. I drank longer and harder than you ever did, by far, but somehow, I got away with it. You've never been a heavy drinker. Just one night of bad luck, though, and you're here. I can think of a hundred scenarios where our places would be switched right now, but sometimes life does crazy things that don't make sense."

I give a wan smile. "I don't know if I believe you, but thanks for saying that."

"I believe it. Sometimes, even things that seem like a mistake at the time can turn out for the best in the long run, you know? You think life's awful right now, but later, you look back and see it was good for you."

"Since when did you get to be so deep? You're sounding an awful lot like the grown woman I always thought you could be." I smile as I say it, and Shawna laughs.

"Well, I've had a little help."

"Your husband?"

Shawna hesitates just a moment. "My therapist. Yeah, I see one twice a week. After a few sessions, we concluded I suffered from occasional bouts of depression, so I use some medication to manage it."

"Huh."

"It's not something you would ever do, I know, but I think it's helping me. I also take some stuff to help me calm down and sleep at night."

"No more card games at two in the morning, then?" I ask with a cautious smile, remembering how many nights I'd wake up to find lights on in my house and Shawna, eyes bloodshot and hands shaking, playing cards at the kitchen table, several cans of beer nearby. I just got so frustrated seeing her waste her life like that. It's one reason I finally decided our relationship needed to end.

"Like I said, I finally left that life behind. If it takes a few pills and some therapy to do it, I'm okay with that."

I'm about to reply, but before I can, a yawn escapes me.

"You tired, Larry?"

"A little, yeah."

"I think I'll go, then. It's been good to see you."

"I agree."

"Good night. I'll leave my phone number at your bedside if you ever want to call me."

"You sure your husband won't care?"

"Yeah, I'm sure. He always says I should try to make some new friends since we moved to Lansing, but maybe I'll be just as happy if I can regain an old one."

"One last thing, Shawna. When did your hair get so dark? I seem to remember it being light brown. Don't tell me that's the concussion messing with me."

"I work at a beauty parlor, remember?" she says with a grin while standing to leave. After Shawna grabs the straps to her purse, she leans over the bed and kisses me softly on the forehead. Without saying anything else, she walks out.

VI

Although speaking with Shawna on Sunday night was a very pleasant surprise, by Monday afternoon when the doctors release me, the reality of what I've done sinks in once again. I had one thing to worry about in life. Taking care of Anthony in place of his parents. Just one thing. And I failed to set the right example for him. Timmy's parents dropped him off at home earlier in the afternoon, so now, when Wally drops me off at my front door, I've got to face him.

While I trudge up the creaking steps, for the first time in my life I'm scared to talk to the boy. There've been lots of times when I didn't know the best words to say to Anthony, but I've never been scared to say something. Until now.

When I pause outside the door in the fading light of the late afternoon to try to think of how to approach him, I notice just how badly the white paint on the front of the house has started peeling. One more thing to worry about. I turn the worn, tarnished brass doorknob and step inside.

I expect Anthony to be in his bedroom, drumming away, but instead, he's sitting at the kitchen table, half-eaten apple in hand. He's wearing his second-favorite t-shirt—it features an angel with wings, except the angel has the face of a grown man and a cigarette in his right hand. I think he told me it was from Van Halen's album *1984*. He's had the shirt since last year, so I guess that makes sense.

"Hi there, buddy," I tell him after a few quiet, awkward moments of looking at each other.

"Hey, Lawrence," comes the dull, monotone reply. Then, while I stumble for what to tell Anthony next, he continues, equally monotone, "How's the shoulder?"

"Sore. But it's gonna be okay."

"How about your head?"

"About the same."

"Wally told me you might have a concussion, and you might have trouble remembering things for a while."

"Nah, it ain't that bad. My head'll be okay."

"Just like you were okay on Saturday night when you left Wally's bar?"

Normally, I'd get upset over a comment like that, but this time, I just bite my lip and take a deep breath. "About that night, Anthony—"

"What about it? You got drunk. Just like Dad did the night he crashed his car and killed Mom." The tension in Anthony's voice rises.

"I'm really sorry about that. It's just that—"

"Just that what? You lost your job, and then decided to go and make things worse?"

"I'll find another in no time. There's always work if you're willing to work hard, Anthony."

"That's not what I mean. I know we argue sometimes and all, but I trusted you not to do that to me." Anyone could detect the ragged edge in Anthony's voice. Even me.

"I made a mistake. I know it—"

"Now I can't trust anyone! Not you, not Theresa, not my dad, not anyone! I guess I can only trust myself."

"What happened with Theresa?"

"Her parents said she had to break up with me because my guardian is a drunk and a bad influence." For the first time I can remember in the year since he came to live with me, I hear Anthony start to choke up. "Yeah, that's right, everyone at school knows already!"

Standing motionless, I stare down at the kitchen table, unsure how to answer. While I fumble for something to say, he goes on. "Some of the kids tried teasing me, too."

"What'd you do? Did you fight again?"

"Not this time. I wanted to, but the bell rang before anything bad happened."

"I'm glad you didn't fight, Anthony. That was a good move."

"Whatever. They teased me about how it felt to walk to school since you were gonna lose your license. Is that true?"

"My driver's license is suspended for six months, yes. But, why would you have to walk? Can't you ride your bike for a while, like you did in intermediate school?"

"That's what I did today, but somebody slashed the tires, and they're flat now. I had to wheel my bike home."

"One of the kids teasing you did that?"

"I think so. They know what Dad did, and now you, and they teased me. They said no one in my family was fit to drive, not even a bike."

Again, the words elude me, and my eyes drop. I see the wet spots around Anthony's eyes, although he's trying not to cry. I want to apologize once more but just can't think of how to say it right. So, pathetically I try to change the subject.

"How'd the weekend go at Timmy's house?"

"Fine."

I've learned no more ambiguous word exists in the English language than when a teenager replies to a question with the word, "fine," so I try again.

"You guys play your dragon game?"

"It's Dungeons & Dragons, and yeah, we played some. What do you care? I thought you hated that game."

"That's a bit of a strong word for it, Anthony."

"No, it isn't. You're always telling me to get outside, and play ball, or ride my bike—which I can't do now, anyway—instead of playing D & D with my friends. Every time! You think I need to be like you were, or else I'm not normal. I don't want to be like you. Look at you! You lost your job and your driver's license, both in the same day! Who'd want to be like that?"

My cheeks flush. I can't see them, but I know they're getting red because I can feel the blood rushing to my face. Anthony's never said anything like this to me before. I raise my unbandaged right fist to pound the table and shout at him.

But I don't. I stop. I can feel how quickly my heartrate has gone from normal to racing, and how I'm taking gulping breaths. Slowly, I turn my head and look at Anthony. His eyes are wide, and his arms are up to cover his face. He thinks I mean to hit him. In this moment, I feel smaller and less of a man than I've ever been. The last time I remember feeling this ashamed of myself was when I was fourteen years old and my mother caught me smoking. She didn't say anything. She didn't have to. The disappointment in her face scolded me more than words ever could, and I haven't touched a cigarette since.

Now, with that memory flashing through my mind, I look at Anthony, and the fear I just saw in his face gives me the same sinking feeling I felt nearly thirty years ago. Slowly, my arm drops to my side, the color leaves my face, and I realize I've failed him again.

"I'm sorry, Anthony, I didn't mean that," I tell him as I turn and walk to the door. "I think I need to go for a couple hours."

He's already pushed his chair out and started toward his bedroom at a half-run. I don't blame him for wanting to get away from me. "I'll cook some dinner when I get back," I call out uselessly down the hallway before opening my front door and walking into the still air of the darkening evening.

It's been another rainy day, and a light mist still falls, with gray clouds veiling the starry sky above. The weather is the damp cool of early November rather than the frosty chill of late November, so my denim jacket should be enough.

I have no idea where I'm going, so while night falls around me and the mist dampens my hair, I just wander along the pitted gray sidewalk with the stunted dandelions growing in the cracks, letting my feet take me wherever they want to go.

Slowly, I shuffle along with my head down. A handful of vehicles drive by, their tires making the familiar sloshing sound as water kicks up behind them. The drizzle continues, but it's not enough to get my jacket wet; there's just a light coating of moisture on it while I walk.

I hadn't planned to go there, but eventually I get to Port Huron High School. Not knowing what else to do, I walk to the baseball field and lean against the metal pole by the third base dugout. I scan the diamond, just like I did twenty-five years ago when I played here for the last time.

For several years, I'd continued coming to some of the games after I graduated, but eventually work just seemed to take up too much time. Then the coaching staff changed, and the younger brothers of guys I played with graduated one by one, and I didn't have much reason to watch the Big Reds play baseball anymore. The handshakes and high-fives from parents who'd seen me play got rarer and rarer, and one day, I realized I was just another twentysomething has-been with no connection to the people out there on the diamond. Someone who should've moved on a few years back but still hadn't.

At the time, I told myself I kept going back because I loved the game, and it wasn't complete self-deception, but now I realize my main reason was that playing baseball was the last time in my life that people outside my family and a few friends cared about me. It was the last time anyone cheered for what I did or encouraged me to do better. The highlights of my life were over by the time I turned nineteen, but I hadn't realized it until nearly a decade later. So, I kept watching a few high school baseball games a year, hoping that would somehow rekindle the inner spark that'd burned in my teens.

Unbidden, various other memories come back to me. The time I got in a fight my junior year when some angry seniors looking for trouble called Sammy a nigger and we had it out with them. Sammy and I were getting the worst of it when some teachers arrived and broke things up. But I'd never felt prouder than when Sammy's father called me on the phone to thank me for sticking up for Sammy and then took me out for a hamburger and milkshake after our next ballgame. Spending that dinner with Sammy's mother and father and hearing their stories about all the prejudice they faced each day growing up in Mississippi was when I fully understood why a person's actions are more important than their skin color.

Then I remember my first, and only, high school dance. It was also my junior year. I had no idea how to dance and probably moved as awkwardly as I felt in the silly clothes high school kids wear to dances, but the kisses I got at the end made me feel as alive as I'd ever felt before.

I even recall the time my English teacher complimented me on my poetry. At the time, I thought poetry was silly and feminine, and, to tell the truth, I still do. But my teacher was also the wrestling coach, and he was a tough guy, so I figured I must've done okay. It was one of the few compliments I ever got on my schoolwork, and I was a mediocre student who didn't deserve many compliments, but for a couple days, I felt great about myself.

Compared to these memories, however, nothing I've done since high school has ever been quite the same. After graduation, I got a job working construction, and over time I saved enough to buy my house and the Cheyenne. I've socked away a little extra, too, although I think most of that is going to end up paying for my hospital stay and another truck. At the time, I felt good because I figured I was doing what an adult is supposed to do. Get a job to support myself and pay the bills. Put some money aside, just in case. Buy a house and a vehicle. Find a wife and start a family.

Except, I never did the last part. I've dated plenty of women since high school and liked a couple of them enough that I thought about proposing, but I never pulled the trigger, and eventually, they walked away. Time passed, I hit my thirties, and I still figured I had time to meet the ideal woman. One day, though, I realized I was nearing the end of my thirties, that woman still hadn't materialized, and the single women who used to talk to me now just glanced the other way when I came around. Just another of my failures.

Eventually, I stopped going to parties and gatherings with some of my old friends. They meant well by inviting me, I'm sure, but it felt weird going to a birthday party for their kids and being the only one there without a child to join in the fun. No one ever said it to me in so many words, but just the looks in their eyes seemed to question me about why I was there alone. At least, I felt like that was true. Same thing with parties for New Year's Eve and other special occasions. While everyone else toasted their spouse, there I was, on my own. It was uncomfortable, so I went less and less often. Which meant the slow loss of some friends I should never have lost. Failure.

As I stand looking out at the place where I had some of the greatest times of my life, the list of failures lengthens. My refrigerator has no photos of my kids doing all the crazy things young people do. I've never bought my wife a present for no other reason than to just tell her I love her. There's never been a movie night where I made popcorn and sat with my kids, or a pizza party and sleepover for someone's birthday. I've never played catch with my son, or read a storybook with my daughter, or gone to meet my kids' teachers at school. Likewise, I never gave my mother the thrill of holding my grandchild while she was alive. She died knowing her only son had let her down. More failures. So many failures.

Perhaps that's why I haven't done well with Anthony. I didn't have much practice with kids of my own before he came to live with me.

Now, I'm not even a success at the things I used to be good at. A real man has a solid job to support his family. I don't anymore. I still own my home, but it's starting to fall apart, and my truck's wrecked. All the money I squirreled away for a rainy day, well, that rainy day is here now, and I have nothing to replace the money with once I spend it. Failure, failure, and more failure.

What made me think I could take care of Anthony, anyway? I volunteered after his father killed my sister, of course, because that's what a real man does—takes care of his family. I thought I was up to the challenge, but looking back now, I was wrong. Another poor judgment in a long line of poor judgments.

I have no idea how long I've been here staring at an empty baseball diamond. There's just no avoiding the fact that my life's been a long, slow letdown for the past twenty-five years, and I've never felt as good about myself or what the future holds as I did on those days when I played ball here. Even though I wasn't thinking of it consciously most of the time, I've spent the last two decades trying to get that feeling back. The feeling that I matter to someone. The feeling that what I'm doing means something. The feeling of enjoying life.

It's hard to escape the irony. Most of my teenage years, all I wanted was to be an adult and have people respect me. Be a real man. Now that I'm an adult, I spend so much time thinking back on how much more *alive* I was at age seventeen.

Glancing down, my watch tells me it's past eight. I also notice the rain's picked up a bit when a drop cascades down my forehead. I look up, but all I see is blackness overhead while larger raindrops hit my face. Since I've found no answers anywhere, I retrace my steps for home.

The rain falls even harder while I walk, and by the time I'm back on my sagging porch, I'm drenched thoroughly. When I enter the kitchen, everything looks just like I left it hours ago. I go to the cupboard, pull out a can of chicken noodle soup, and start heating it in a pot on the oven. I set a second can on the counter for Anthony and consider just pouring it in with mine but then decide I should go check on him.

Standing outside his room, I expect to hear the music like usual, but I don't, so I knock and then turn the door handle. He's there, sitting cross-legged on the bed, thumbing through a booklet.

"You have any dinner?"

"Not hungry," he mutters without looking up.

"I'm making some soup if you want it."

"Not hungry."

"You sure?"

Anthony nods, barely perceptively. "I'll get something if I need it." He still hasn't even looked at me.

"You watching the time?"

"Yep."

I nod, even though he still hasn't looked up and can't see it. Normally, I'd remind him of his bedtime. It's not a hard-and-fast rule—he's fifteen, after all, and he needs to learn independence—but more of a guideline. Tonight, though, I don't say it. Nor do I ask if he's done his homework. I should ask, especially since I know he hasn't always done his math recently, but tonight, I don't. Better to give Anthony some space and avoid another mistake, another failure, on a day when I've already made so many.

VII

The next morning, Tuesday, I'm up to see Anthony off to school. I'm used to getting up around 6:30, anyway, so I decide to get his breakfast ready to help him out. Besides that, I need to find work, so I'm anxious to get the newspaper and chase down whatever leads I can find there. My coffee mug is on the table, steaming, and I'm about to take my first sip when Anthony walks in, fully dressed, with his blue winter coat, backpack on his shoulder. At least he didn't leave it in his locker this time.

"I got your Cheerios out. They're right there on the table," I tell him.

"I'm not that hungry. I'll just eat a couple Pop Tarts on my way."

"Is that gonna hold you until lunchtime?"

"I don't have time to eat a bowl of cereal. Now that I have to walk to school, it takes longer, so I'll just eat the Pop Tarts while I walk." I hear the tear of plastic packaging as Anthony drops two into the toaster. "It's still about a month before Timmy gets his license, so I'll probably just skip having cereal for breakfast until that happens."

"At least take a banana, okay? We've got a couple left, but they might go bad if we don't eat them soon."

"You eat one, then. I didn't ask for bananas, did I?"

Briefly, the blood rushes to my cheeks again, just like last night, and I feel my pulse speed up. This time, however, I fight it down and hold my tongue. Instead of getting upset, I pause a moment, breathe, and ask, "You coming straight home after school?"

"I think I'll go over to Justin's house to play some Atari. We got really far last time, and I think we can beat it this time."

"That's different than the dragons game, right?"

"Yes, Lawrence. I've told you about it a hundred times. Atari is a video game system. You play it on the television. I asked you for one for my birthday, but you got me a baseball glove instead, remember?"

Biting my lip, I think back. Anthony's birthday is in May, and I thought getting him a new baseball glove was the perfect gift for that time of year, with the summer coming on and all. I also seem to remember that a baseball glove was quite a bit cheaper than an Atari when I went to the toy store and looked at one. Not to mention, what fifteen-year-old kid would want to spend his summer break in front of the television? That isn't what teenage boys are supposed to do. It's bad enough he spends all evening tossing dice to kill imaginary monsters when his friends come over. Once, he bragged to me about killing a dozen orcs in one battle. I don't even know what an orc is. Ridiculous. Wasting the day in front of the television just makes it twice as bad.

It's possible I should have explained all this to Anthony back in May when he opened his present and saw the baseball glove. I was sure he'd like it, but, instead, all I saw was disappointment in his eyes. I dragged him outside for a game of catch anyway, hoping he'd get into it, but that only lasted about ten minutes before he announced he was bored. We've only played catch a couple times since then.

Before I can reply, the sound of the toaster finishing the Pop Tarts spares me the need. Anthony wraps them in a paper towel and starts for the door. "See you this evening, Lawrence."

He's gone, and I'm alone in the kitchen. I just close my eyes for a moment, waiting for the anger to subside. Anthony hadn't even asked to go to Justin's house; he just stated that's where he was going. That's never happened before. I raise my arm to make a fist and pound the table in frustration, but then a thought hits me. Why should he ask for my permission? With all the mistakes I've made, I can't claim good judgment.

Besides that, he's fifteen. Maybe it's time Anthony takes full responsibility for what he does. I've failed him often enough; he can't do worse than I'm doing.

VIII

On Thursday, December 19, I walk to the kitchen when the phone rings. I lift the bright red receiver from its cradle where it's mounted to the wall. "Hello?"

"Is this Mr. Edwards?"

"Speaking."

"I'm Mr. Soward, the principal at Port Huron High School. I'm sorry to bring this to your attention, but we've had a bit of trouble with Anthony today."

I just stare at the light blue paint on the kitchen walls for a moment, gently bumping my forehead into the door frame. What has he done now?

"Mr. Edwards?"

"What kind of a problem?" I sigh into the phone.

"Anthony was in quite a fight during lunch today. We need you to come and pick him up from school."

"What happened?"

"He claims that some older students taunted him, that they'd been doing so for weeks, and he'd finally had enough."

"Do you believe him, Mr. Soward?"

"He may well be telling the truth, Mr. Edwards. The two boys he fought with have been in trouble a few times before. However, our school has a no-fighting policy, as I'm sure you're aware."

I am aware. Anthony was in one fight previously, back in September, and I'd cautioned him to try not to do it again. So, I say, "I know this is the second time he's fought this year."

"That's correct. According to school policy, the second time a student fights, he or she faces a three-day suspension from school."

"I see." I'm not sure if I should be mad at Anthony for losing control, proud of him for sticking up for himself, or both.

"However, Mr. Edwards, here's what I'd like to propose. Tomorrow is the Friday before Christmas Break. Why don't you hold Anthony home from school tomorrow, have a talk with him, and then we'll see him again on the first Thursday in January when school resumes. I'm skirting school policy a bit here, but I think he probably was responding to excessive provocation, and I'm hoping that the layoff over break will be enough to get everyone to calm down."

"That's probably a good plan. I appreciate your thoughtfulness, Mr. Soward."

"The Friday before Christmas Break is not, shall we say, known as a day of intense concentration by students or teachers, so it seems a course that will result in a minimum disruption of learning for Anthony."

"I think you're right about that. I don't remember too much about high school at this point, but the day before a holiday is tough for everyone."

"I need to mention two more things, however, Mr. Edwards. First, I spoke to each of Anthony's teachers during lunch break, and he does have two exams scheduled tomorrow. He'll have to take those after school in January."

"That sounds fair enough. More than fair, actually."

"That was my thought, as well. Here's the other thing I believe you should know. Anthony's teachers report that his grades have slipped of late and that he spends a great deal of time drawing sketches of fantastic monsters in his notebook. Dragons, elves, and other things I don't claim to be able to recognize."

"It sounds like that damn game, I mean, silly game, that he plays with his friends after school. Please excuse my language, Mr. Soward."

"Whatever the cause, he's not turning in much homework, and that's resulting in poor performances on his exams. Anthony's teachers asked me to mention this in the hope that you'll engage him in a little heart-to-heart talk before school resumes in January. They also told me they'd provide me with a list of some of the assignments he's missed in the hopes he can catch up a bit over the next two weeks while school's out."

"That's very kind of them. I'll try to give Anthony some encouragement."

"Please do, Mr. Edwards. Anthony's teachers tell me he has plenty of intelligence when he applies himself. With a bit more self-discipline, they believe he can get back on track and finish his sophomore year in good standing."

With nothing more to say, I hang up after the usual closing courtesies. I should probably go right away and get Anthony, but what can I say to him? I've lost most of my credibility in his eyes. He's simply doing the same stupid, immature things I did at his age, and he has no reason to respect me or listen to me as a parent. Hell, I don't even have a vehicle to pick him up with anymore. But, there's no dodging the issue, so I grab my heavy black parka and step into the subfreezing chill of the December afternoon. The iron-gray skies threaten the first big snowfall of the winter.

I'm determined to get to the school before it lets out—I don't want to add more shame for Anthony by him having to walk home with me when all his classmates are around. Reaching the main office with about twenty minutes to spare, I enter and find Anthony seated in a red plastic chair. He looks up for a moment when he sees me come in and then puts his head back down like a dog who knows it has done wrong and is about to get a scolding. When he looks up, though, I can see his right eye socket is very swollen—looks like he took a hard shot to the face. I notice some bloodstains on his white t-shirt, too. Given the small wad of gauze in one of his nostrils, I assume it's his blood.

After I sign Anthony out with the school secretary, we start the walk home. For a while, neither of us has anything to say. We just plod along, watching the vapor from our breath billow out in front of us. On the way home, we pass red maples, beeches, and birch trees planted along the street. A few desiccated leaves still cling to some of the maples, making a forlorn sighing sound as we pass. It seems about right, given the mood of the day.

Finally, I decide I'd better say something. "You gonna tell me what happened today?"

Anthony takes several more steps before responding. "What's there to say? Some assholes were teasing me again about you and the rest of my family. They asked me if I was a drunk, too. I'd had enough, so I punched one of them."

"Did you at least give 'em a good shot?"

Anthony raises an eyebrow and cocks his head to the side while he looks at me. "Yeah, pretty good. Except there were two of them fighting just me, so it didn't go too well. Does my right eye look as bad as it feels?"

"Yeah. You're gonna have trouble seeing straight for a while, I think. Two against one, huh? Cowards."

"I'm in big trouble, right? You told me not to fight again after the last one, back in September, but I guess I just couldn't take it."

I just continue walking, thinking things over. Finally, I say, "Well, did Mr. Soward tell you what he decided about your punishment?"

"There's nothing to decide, is there? The second time you fight, you get a three-day suspension from school. Everyone knows that."

"When I talked with him on the phone, he said to keep you home tomorrow, but you could go back to school when classes start in January. You'll have to make up some exams when you do."

Anthony thinks things over for a while and then replies, "So, then, that's what, a one-day suspension?"

"I think so. You know he's doing you a favor, right?"

"I guess so."

"He is. He told me you were probably right that those other boys egged you on, so he was going to bend the school's policy a little."

Anthony sighs while sidestepping a part of the sidewalk that's crumbled into little bits of cement. "And how much trouble am I in with you?"

I do some footwork of my own, stepping over a section where a tree root has elevated the pavement several inches. "I'm not sure."

"But, in September you told me if I fought again, I'd be grounded for two weekends."

"I know I said that."

"You mean, you've changed your mind and I'm not grounded?" The boy has a hopeful look in his good eye.

"I'm not sure. You know fighting ain't gonna solve things, right? Especially when there's two of them and one of you?"

"Yeah, I guess I shoulda considered the odds a little more. I just got so angry. I'm tired of people givin' me shit all the time. It ain't right."

"No, it ain't right, but it still happens. There's nothin' you can do about it, either, because you can't control other people. Only yourself."

"It's hard, though, Lawrence, when there's people all around, expectin' you to stick up for yourself. Still, I guess it was pretty stupid to hit someone bigger than me when his friend was standin' right there."

I just nod. I've reached my decision, so I stop and turn to face the boy. "Anthony, you know I ain't a good role model. I've made a bunch of mistakes, and I barely know how to act like a parent. The only reason you're staying with me is that I'm the closest blood you've got while your dad's in prison. Even though I try to do right, I fail more times than not. Maybe it's better if I don't try to act like a father and just let you work things out for yourself."

Anthony stops walking, takes a step backward, and goes stiff. He's looking at me as if I'd just asked to play his dragons game. "So, I'm not grounded, then? I'm not getting more punishment for fighting?"

"Here's what I'm sayin', Anthony. When you came to stay with me, I wanted to show you how a man acts, how a man behaves, and how to be a grownup, because you don't have a father to do that for you right now. But, when I went walking that night in November, I realized I ain't suited to do any of that. Almost everything I've done since I graduated high school I've failed at. I'm not a good example to follow, and you shouldn't want to be like me."

"But what does that have to do with me fighting today?"

"It means you got to work out for yourself who you want to be and how to get there."

"I'm getting kicked out of the house?" Anthony's shoulders sag, falling in on themselves while his eyes go wide.

"No. Who said anything about that?"

"Didn't you just say I have to work things out for myself?"

"Yeah, but I'm not kicking you out just because you got in a fight. You can't go stay with your dad's brother. He lives in Wisconsin, and, well, shit, I don't even know what he does for a living. Not much, last I heard. I just mean you got to be responsible for your own decisions since I'm not a good example."

"So, I decide my own punishments when I screw up? I'm still not sure I get it."

"I haven't worked out all the details, but somethin' like that. You got to understand, though, that I ain't talkin' about no free ride and just doin' whatever you want. In life, if you screw up, there's consequences. Just look at what happened to me when I lost my license. So, if you're callin' all your own shots, you also gotta take the consequences on your own shoulders."

It's hard for me to read the expression on Anthony's face at this moment. Surprise, for sure, but also shock and uncertainty. I guess I'm a bit surprised myself. Before this moment, I had no idea if I'd actually go through with it and say all of that to him. It's done now, though, and there's no taking it back. Come January and the new school year, we'll see if I've helped him or just found a new way to fail as a parent.

IX

One afternoon in early February, I'm sitting at my kitchen table, looking through the want ads. I'm getting desperate because my savings have all but disappeared, but Port Huron isn't that big a place, and I haven't found anything steady since November. Just a couple of part-time things that lasted about a week. I can't even drive a snowplow for the City because I've lost my driver's license. Sighing, I fold up the paper and hope tomorrow will bring better luck.

Just as I do, I hear the rumble of a large truck engine outside. I go to the window to see who's there, and it's Brad Duncan climbing down from a new Ford truck. He's got it jacked up, with huge tires, and the truck's painted red. Not bright, cherry red, a duller red. Still, I'm half-surprised he didn't have yellow flames detailed on the sides.

Brad stomps up the gravel walkway in his work boots, and I let him inside. He's got on a midnight blue sweatshirt with the Tigers logo on it, surrounded by the slogan "Tigers Roar in '84!"

"Brad, come on in. Can I get ya a beer?"

"You still drinkin' after your accident?"

"Just a couple per week. Gotta keep somethin' on hand for when a friend stops by, don't ya? Besides, it ain't like I can get behind the wheel again for a while yet."

"All the same, I'll pass. Gotta go back to work in a little while here."

"So, why'd you stop by, then? You wantin' to show off your new truck? Is that an '85 model?"

"Sure is. F-250 with a V8. Brand new, built in Dearborn. Just bought it off the lot this weekend. I want to take you for a ride."

"That's a great offer, but I've ridden in a Ford before."

"I know you have, but I want to drive you down to Public Works, Larry."

"The City?"

"Yeah. I just found out they've got a job opening, and I want you to be first in line to apply."

"What kind of work?"

"Well, Larry, it ain't glorious, but it'll bring in some cash until you find somethin' better. One of the guys at my worksite says his brother worked sanitation, but the brother just decided to move to Ypsilanti to be with his girlfriend."

"Sanitation? You mean I'd be a garbage man?"

"Yeah, that about says it. Assuming your back can take it?"

"My back's doin' a lot better, Brad. Since I haven't been workin' much, it's had time to heal up a bit. But, sanitation?"

"I keep offerin' you a job on one of my construction crews, but you won't take it."

"Because it ain't right to ask a friend for charity like that."

"I'm offerin' it freely, so I don't see it as charity, but you still won't take it. Well, how about this. We'll get you this job—"

"How do you know they'll hire me?"

"I know a guy—one of those desk jockeys who pushes papers in city government. Worked with him a few times gettin' permits for some projects. He's an okay guy, even if all he does is sit around all day. It'll put some money in your pocket. Then, when April comes around and the weather gets better, if you don't like sanitation, I'll offer to hire you on one of my construction teams again. Hopefully, by then, business will pick up, and I'll need another employee. Then, you won't need to feel like it's charity because it won't be."

"I guess that's a good plan for now. Lemme get my coat."

It isn't far down to the offices of the city government, but we have time for a little conversation because we keep hitting the stoplights red. "This is a nice ride," I tell Brad. "Since when did you start listenin' to country music, though? I thought you liked the Stones."

"Ah, that ain't my station, Larry. Yesterday the wife said she wanted a ride, and she picked it."

"What would someone in Michigan care about cowboys for? It's not like she's from Texas or Wyoming or whatever. Sandy went to high school with us."

"I know. I can't explain the attraction, either. But she likes it. I guess I can tolerate bad music in small amounts. As long as my wife likes being a cowgirl at home, too. Or a reverse cowgirl," Brad finishes with a snicker.

I join for the sake of laughing, but without much enthusiasm. It's hard to tell if Brad notices because he's still guffawing at his own cleverness. After a few moments, however, he calms down and asks, "How's Anthony doin'? He hangin' in there?"

"Not the best. He hasn't gotten into no more fights, and that's a good thing, I think. But he just don't take his schoolin' very serious, and I can't convince him that he should. He spends so much time playin' that magic game with his friends."

"I guess if he's rollin' dice and bein' a wizard or whatever, at least he's not out stealin' or gettin' in trouble some other way."

"Maybe, but it don't seem right, Brad. Just the other day, for instance, I asked him how he was doin', and he said he was doin' good because he had fireballs now. I thought he was talkin' about some new candy, until he told me he played a magician who could cast fireballs and that he used them to waste three trolls at once the other day. Who gets that excited over a game you play with paper and dice?"

"I don't know what to tell you, Larry. It seems weird to me, too. We didn't have nothin' like that back when we were kids. All we did was look at car engines and play ball."

"How do you do it, then, Brad?"

"Whaddya mean?"

"You've got two daughters. They're both nice girls who stay out of trouble and do great at school. What's your secret?"

By now, we've reached our destination, and Brad stops the truck, but we don't get out right away because I want to know what I'm doing wrong.

"There's no secret, Larry. Sandy and I ain't done nothing special except just feed 'em, give 'em hugs every night, and take 'em to the library when they tell us they need some more books to read."

"That's it?"

"Pretty much. I don't think there's a magic formula. We watch movies together once or twice a week at home, and we always eat our meals together at dinner, but there's lots of people who do those things."

"You got one of those, whaddya call them, VCR things now?"

"Yeah. You just go to the video store, find a movie that looks good, and take it home and watch it on the television. It's not quite the same view as the theaters, but it's cheaper, and you can watch whenever you want to."

"That doesn't sound so complicated, Brad. The part about takin' care of your girls, that is. So, how come I'm so awful at raisin' kids? How come none of that works very well with Anthony? Maybe it's different with boys. What do you think?"

"Well, you know I'm not one for deep thinking, Larry. Sandy's the one who reads those advice books on how to raise girls."

"There's books that tell you what to do?"

"Books and magazines, yeah. Plenty of 'em. But, here's the thing. I don't think it's the books that are the key. Some kids just have different personalities than others. Sandy and I just got lucky that we got two girls who don't cause trouble and are easy for us to raise. Our girls've always been that way, and I don't think it's because of me. I mean, look at me, Larry. There ain't too much difference between us. We did the same things growing up, we were both C students in school, we both love sports, and neither of us ever went to college."

"But you're a construction manager, and I'm, maybe, a garbage collector."

"Only because my dad owns the construction company. If it wasn't for that, who knows what I'd be doin' right now? Not drivin' a new truck, probably, or thinkin' about sending my girls to college. Some people just grab a lucky break. My break was bein' the son of the owner of the company. You didn't have no father to help give you any breaks, and Anthony doesn't have his real father, either."

"But that ain't no excuse. I can't have what doesn't exist, so what's the use of thinkin' about it?"

"I just copy what I remember my father doin' for me, and it seems to work. You don't have that example to call on when you need it. You've learned to do lots of things for yourself over the years, but raisin' kids is different than buildin' a house."

"How come we're talkin' about me all of a sudden? What's all that have to do with Anthony?"

"Anthony's just a different type of kid, I think. To tell you the truth, if my daughters wanted to play games where they had fantasies about killing monsters with fireballs or whatever, I'm not sure what I'd do, either. But that ain't under our control. Maybe it's just one more way that I got lucky and you didn't."

"I gotta make my own luck, then."

"Everyone knows you're tryin', Larry, believe me. All your friends know you got put in a tough spot when Anthony came to live with you. Not because he's a bad kid, but just because everything happened so fast with his mom getting' killed and you not havin' a chance to prepare ahead of time. We all know you're doin' the best you can."

"I don't know, Brad. It sounds to me like you're just makin' excuses for me."

"Well, like I said, I ain't one for deep thoughts. That's just how it seems to me. Let's go get you a job, okay, buddy?"

X

True to his word, Brad got me the job, and now I collect people's trash. The job's about as simple as can be. I drive a big truck around to whatever neighborhood is scheduled for trash collection that day, I toss the trash in a compactor in my truck, and then I take the whole stinky mess to a collection site. It goes to the landfill from there. It's simple, and dull, and I wear nose plugs to deal with the rank smells, but it does bring in a bit of money until I can find something better. My partner Nick must do all the driving, of course, because I don't have my driver's license restored yet, but he doesn't mind.

Today is a Thursday, and I've been on the job for a little over two weeks, so I'm getting to know the routes. Thursday's our day to get the trash from an apartment complex near St. Clair County Community College. This complex looks run-down compared to most in town. Some of the gutters hang askew on the roofs of the buildings. I also note some cracked windows and wet rot on the siding in some areas, not to mention plenty of broken glass bottles and beer cans in the alley where Nick and I work tossing garbage sacks into our truck. That's what I get for having a job where I pick up after college kids, I guess. The buildings themselves are gray, just like today's sky, except where someone's graffitied them in black spray paint.

It's early afternoon when we ease to a stop at the end of the alley, and I climb down to get the last few bags of trash in the garbage cans there. When I do, however, I notice a woman sitting on the curb, her back to me, just staring off across the street. Curiously for a day this cold, she only has on a lightweight yellow sweatshirt rather than a coat. If she's noticed me, her posture doesn't show it. I decide I'd better say something because the alleyway is narrow for a large garbage truck, and her legs are in the street where we'll need to drive in just a moment.

"Excuse me, miss?"

No reaction. I'll try one more time.

"Excuse me, miss?" I try louder, but still nothing. So, I take off my gloves and touch her left shoulder as gently as I can to get her attention.

When I touch her, however, she yelps and spins to face me rapidly, almost falling over in surprise as her right hand goes to the spot I touched on her shoulder. In the process, the woman's sunglasses fall from her face and clatter to the pavement.

It's Anna, or, at least, I think it's her. The reason I have trouble recognizing her is that the left side of her face is a combination of bright red, hideous purple, and ugly black, swollen and ghastly.

"Anna, is that you?"

For a moment, she looks right past me, her eyes unfocused and darting wildly back and forth. Finally, they focus, and the light of recognition comes on. "Larry? Larry from the hardware store?"

"Yeah, it's me. What on earth happened to you, Anna?"

"Oh, yeah, my face," she says, trying to sound apologetic while her mind comes back to the present. "I fell down the stairs this morning. Just tripped because I wasn't paying attention, and I landed on my face and shoulder. I just sat down here for a while to get my bearings. Serves me right, I guess, for being late for class and rushing."

"Are you sure you're okay? Those injuries look really bad."

"They probably look worse than they feel because it just happened. I was about to go to school for my classes today, like I just said, but I think I might try and go tomorrow instead."

The Long Way Home

By now, Nick's come over to see what's holding me up, but when he sees Anna's face, he takes a step backward. "My goodness, what's the matter, lady? Were you in an accident or something?"

"It's okay, Nick, this is Anna. We've met before, sort of. She says she fell down the stairs in the apartment building."

Even though I repeat Anna's story to Nick, I don't believe it for a moment. Although it has been several years, my friends and I were in enough fights as teenagers for me to know the difference between how a person's face looks the day of a beating and how it looks the day after. Given the heavy swelling and the mottled purple-and-black bruises coloring her face, I'm betting this happened yesterday, not this morning on Anna's way to school.

Now isn't the time to ask about that, however. She needs to see a doctor, or at least put some ice on the bruises to get the swelling down.

I say to her, "Anna, I think it'd be a good idea to put some ice on your face. Maybe your shoulder, too. Those bruises can get worse if you don't take care of them, and they'll hurt more if they do. Since you live here, let's go up to your apartment and get you taken care of."

She sits silently for a moment looking down, then says to the pavement, "I left my keys inside. That's why I was sitting down here on the curb. I'll have to wait for Rickey when he gets off work today."

"How long will that be?" Nick asks her.

"At dinner time," Anna says, her eyes getting wet.

"That won't do," I say to both Anna and Nick. "You need help before then, and you can't just sit outside for hours waiting. Especially in February when it's cold and you've only got a sweatshirt. Can we take you to your parents' house, or maybe a friend's place?"

"My friends are all at work, and I don't know their work phone numbers, or else I would've called them already. My parents don't live in Port Huron. I'll just have to wait here. I'll be okay."

Even Anthony's lies when he pretends to do his homework aren't this unconvincing. Anna looks very far from being okay. Plus, if she were on her way to school when the accident happened, shouldn't her books or a notebook be somewhere nearby? No books are anywhere in sight. I'm thinking she could let us help her upstairs but doesn't want us to see whatever happened in her apartment last night. That's probably also why she hasn't tried getting hold of her boyfriend today, since he should also have a set of keys.

There's also the fact she had on sunglasses when I touched her shoulder. I haven't seen the sun yet today. I'm guessing it's because she doesn't want anyone to see her whole face.

"I've got an idea," Nick puts in. "Larry, your place isn't far out of the way. I'll drop you two off there, you help Anna at least get a warmer coat or something, and I'll pick you up again when I finish our route. We don't have that much left to go. I think I can handle it myself."

I look to Anna for her response. Although her eyes shine and she's nearly in tears, she nods an okay.

"How's that feel?" I say while gently touching an icepack made with a zip-lock freezer bag to Anna's cheek.

She grimaces but doesn't pull the bag away. "Okay, I guess." She takes it and holds it in place with her right arm, although her arm trembles a bit.

Anna's lying down on my worn, dark-brown couch, glass of water at her good elbow and a pillow propped beneath her head. Her normally wavy blond hair is just a mess, sprawled about her face and not made up at all. *Another sign*, I think to myself, *that whatever went wrong happened yesterday. It doesn't seem likely that a woman as attractive as Anna would ever go to school with her hair looking like a mop. Not that women have to pretty themselves up for all occasions, but it looks like she hasn't touched her hair in a week.*

As inexperienced as I am at being a parent to Anthony, I'm even less experienced at comforting young women who've experienced physical trauma and have ended up prostrated on my couch because of it. I've nursed some girlfriends through bad hangovers but haven't ever encountered a situation quite like this.

I don't know what to say at all, but find myself mouthing the words, "You want a Coke or something? Maybe some food?" because it seems like I should attempt something comforting.

"No. Thank you, though," Anna replies. She closes her eyes after adjusting the icepack, although the left one blinks open again because of all the bruising and swelling.

"You want to talk about what happened this morning?" I question while sitting down in my lone armchair, the faded blue one with the cushion upside down to hide the large tear that I had to duct tape last year.

"Your partner sure was nice to do the rest of your route for you," Anna replies.

"Yeah, Nick's kinda a strange guy. But strange in a good way. His family is super religious, so he never cusses, and he hardly even gets mad when people at work tease him about it. One time," I chuckle at the recollection, "a guy slipped a *Playboy* magazine into his locker at work, and you should have seen how red his face got when he saw it."

Anna gives a weak smile that fades quickly.

"I'm sorry, maybe that's only funny for guys," I tell her. "I shoulda known better."

"It's okay. I would have laughed, except it hurts pretty bad when I do."

"You need another icepack?"

"Let's keep it at one for now."

"Anyway, Nick's a real nice guy. Pretty smart, too. I have no idea why he works sanitation for Port Huron. He seems like he'd be a good accountant or something like that."

"How come you don't work at the hardware store anymore? It seems a better fit for you than picking up garbage."

"I got laid off at the hardware store. Eddie doesn't need as many employees in the winter because people don't do as many projects that need hardware. Plus, that new store that just opened near downtown is stealin' some of Eddie's business, I think. I doubt he'll ever ask me to come back."

"Sell any more useless chainsaws before Eddie let you go?" Anna doesn't laugh out loud, but I see a glint in her right eye telling me she remembers the joke I told the day we met at the store. I laugh a bit.

"Nah, no one else returned their chainsaw without putting gas in it first. But I've got a question. Why'd you say selling hardware is a better fit for me?"

"Because you seem like a real courteous guy who can relate well to people. And compassionate. I still can't believe I'm lying on your couch, out of all the places in the world I could be right now, but somehow I just feel like I can trust you, and you're sincere."

I know full well I'm none of those things she just said, other than sincere, possibly, so I reply, "*I* can relate well to people?"

"I know it's weird for me to say it, but I think so. We've only spent a little time together before today, all of it by accident, but you seem like a decent and honest man. When I'm around most guys I know, I'm usually scared they're trying to take advantage of me somehow, but with you I don't have that feeling. Strange, isn't it, when the people you've known for years make you nervous, but you feel comfortable with a man you barely know?"

"You're being a little generous, I'd say. I appreciate your sincerity, but those aren't words I hear too often."

"Your wife never says those things to you?"

"I'm not married. Never was."

"Never?"

"Nope. You still believe I can relate to people after hearing that?"

"I just thought that the pizza boxes by the door in the kitchen must be there because your kids forgot to take them out. You don't seem the type who would leave pizza boxes sitting around."

"I'm the guardian for my nephew. He lives with me because his mom's dead and his father's in prison."

"That's so sad. About his mom, I mean. But that's great that you take care of him."

"What's also sad is that I ain't no good at it. If Anthony had anyone worth their salt on his dad's side of the family, I'd step aside, but there ain't."

I'm not sure why I just told her those things. I guess I figure that an injured woman lying on my couch isn't much of a threat to judge me for my inadequacies. Plus, she showed a lot of trust in me by agreeing to come to my house, so I'm showing a little back to her.

While I muse on that, Anna speaks again. "I can't believe that. You're better at it than you think, I bet. I mean, you just seem like the solid, dependable, caring type that a woman would be lucky to have." Anna stops short. Suddenly, I realize that now I'm the one staring off into nothing.

"I'm sorry I said that," she tells me quickly. I can't tell if she's blushing because of all the damage to her face, but it's possible. "Not my place. I guess I'm just so lucky that you happened by and volunteered to help me out today that I just meant to give you a compliment to say thank you. That's all I meant to say. You got a distant look on your face when I said it, though. Did I make you upset?"

"It's all right. It's just that I've heard all that about a thousand times from people I know. But, since it's the first time I've heard it from you, I'll take it as a compliment." I try to give her a reassuring smile to take the sudden awkwardness away. Anna tries to return it but again winces in pain.

"What are you studying at the college?" I ask, hoping to move the conversation back to more comfortable ground.

"Child psychology. I'm hoping to be a schoolteacher someday, or run a daycare, or something like that. This is my first year in college, and I haven't been in school since I graduated high school ten years ago, so I'm really not sure what I'll do eventually. Have you ever been to college?"

"No. I was never too good at school. I don't think anyone would let me in even if I wanted to go at this point."

"What did you want to be when you were younger?"

"What do you mean, Anna?"

"When you were getting out of high school and in your twenties, what did you hope to be someday?"

"I never thought about that question."

"I don't understand, Larry."

"It's just not a question I ever thought about. When I graduated high school, I went to work. That's what guys like me did back then. You didn't have dreams of what you'd do in some glorious future because you knew what you were going to do in the future. A guy either went into construction, like I did, or worked as a teamster at the port, maybe joined the Army, or moved to Flint or Detroit to work in a factory. I didn't see the point in thinking about other things."

Anna tries to sit up while I say this, and if her face wasn't so horribly bruised, I would think she was giving me a quizzical look. She makes it to leaning on her good elbow while facing me.

"You can't mean that literally. Everyone dreams of being *something* when they're growing up."

"Well, I dreamed of being a baseball player, I guess. A few scouts came to watch me play my junior year, and a few more at the start of my senior year. But I hurt my throwing shoulder partway through my senior year, and that was the end of that dream. The scouts stopped showing up when they saw I couldn't throw the ball or hit it very well anymore."

"You were a good enough player that professional scouts came just to see you, Larry?"

"A handful of 'em, yeah."

"That had to be a lot of fun. At least, until you got hurt."

"It was, yeah. I think being seventeen was the most fun I've ever had in life."

"But you never dreamed of being anything besides a baseball player?"

"No. Playing ball was all I cared about back then. Well, besides chasing girls and working on cars sometimes."

"So, you could've helped me install the car battery if Rickey hadn't have been there that day last year?"

"Absolutely. That's part of why I volunteered to go with you. I wasn't sure if you knew how."

"I don't, so thank you for your kindness, even if it was a while ago."

"Don't worry; you paid me back."

Anna again looks like she's trying to make a surprised face at me.

"At the football game in November. You bought me that Coke, remember?"

"Oh, yeah, I did. I'd forgotten all about that. It looks like having a good memory is another one of your useful traits."

I'm not sure whether having a good memory is a skill or something a person's born with, but I know Anna means well, so I take it as a compliment once again.

Still sitting halfway up, propped on her good elbow, she continues. "But I still can't believe you didn't dream of being something amazing or famous after you finished playing baseball. I thought everyone did that, at least a little bit."

"Maybe now they do. I don't know. But when I was young, there just wasn't any point in dreaming. It wasn't going to happen, so why waste your time? I did what guys like me did in the sixties. You'd graduate high school, get a job, and work to support yourself. A lot of guys just did whatever job it was their own dad did."

"Did you?"

"No. I never knew my father. He died in France fighting the damn Nazis."

"My goodness, Larry! Your mom raised you all by herself?"

"Yeah. She was a secretary during the day, and sometimes she'd wait tables at restaurants in the evening, too, just so my sister and I could have food to eat and decent clothes for school. That's another reason I went to work right out of high school. She'd supported me long enough, and it was time I stopped being a burden on her. So, I took the first decent job I came across."

"She must be an amazing woman to have done all that herself. And very proud of you, too, for taking in your nephew."

"She was amazing, yeah. But she's been dead for several years now."

I'm not sure why I'm telling Anna all these things. When I agreed to bring her to my house, I meant to find out why her injuries were so bad and see if her boyfriend roughed her up last night like I suspect. Domestic abuse is serious. But instead, she's turned the tables, and Anna's been asking me about myself. I don't talk about my feelings often, mainly because I hang out with the same few people all the time and they already know my story, so I don't have to. Still, something in me feels good about saying these things because for the first time in years I'm saying them to someone who doesn't know all about me and might have a different response than I'm used to hearing.

Part of my brain tells me I shouldn't say anything more about myself, however. Anna's a stranger, and while I doubt she has any side motives behind her questions, still, I barely know anything about her, and she won't be able to change any of the choices of my past, anyway. While I think this over, I realize she's resumed speaking.

"My opinion might not count for much, I realize, but it looks to me like you deserve a lot of credit. You've got a house, a truck, and you take care of what family you have. And to go with all of that, you're a kind man who helped a stranger he barely knows when her day got off to a horrible start."

"About what happened to you, Anna. Is there anything more you can tell me about why your injuries are so bad? I'm no doctor, but they look very serious. Maybe serious enough that you should see a real doctor."

"I told you what happened. I'm just clumsy and took a real bad step on my way to school and locked myself out of my apartment while I was at it. I'm sure I look awful, my hair's a mess, and you're worried about me, but spending part of the day here helped a lot. There's quite a bit of pain still, and there will be for a while, I suppose, but I'm not as bad as I look."

Anna tries to smile again before remembering how much that hurts, so she ends up wincing instead.

"Are you sure, Anna? When Nick and I helped you into the cab of our truck, the effort brought tears to your eyes. I'm worried. Plus, you haven't moved your left shoulder without flinching or biting your lip since you got here. I don't think—"

Before I can say anything more, the honk of a car's horn interrupts as Nick pulls into my driveway. I stand and walk to the front door to hold it open for Anna but see Nick running to the door instead.

I poke my head out. "It's okay, Nick, no need to run. Unless we're in trouble for me missing the rest of my shift?"

"No, we're not in trouble, Larry, but you'd—"

Just then I hear my phone, its shrill ring piercing the quiet house.

"You need to get that," Nick says quickly between rings when I ask with my eyes if it's as important as his news.

I take three strides across the linoleum floor and pick up in the middle of the third ring. There's a dispassionate voice on the other end, speaking calmly, asking questions.

Am I the guardian of Anthony Maddox? it asks.

"Yes," I say.

A pause while the voice speaks again.

"I see," I whisper while my eyes widen.

When the voice talks for the third time, my knees buckle, and I grab a kitchen chair, so I don't fall over. Still, I'm down on one knee on the floor by the time the disembodied voice on the phone finishes.

"I'll be right there, of course," my cracking voice manages to get out before the anguish wells up inside. I hang up and put my face in the crook of my elbow.

"What happened?" Anna wonders from the couch. I can hear the concern coursing through her voice even though I can't see her.

"Anthony and his friend Timmy were in a car accident just now. The nurse on the phone said Anthony's in serious condition but stable. Timmy may not make it."

XI

For the second time in recent months, I'm in a hospital room, except this time I'm not the one in the bed with the white sheets staring out at the white walls. Anthony's there, sleeping calmly, although his breathing seems shallow to me. Maybe it's because I'm worried and I fear the worst. Or it's because he's got a cast around his chest and left arm, which the nurse on duty tells me he's broken, along with some of his ribs.

The nurse also mentions that when the ambulance arrived to get Anthony, he was conscious long enough to tell them I was at work and that I worked for the City, so that's why Nick knew before the hospital called my house. Nick rushed me to hospital and then took Anna home afterward. We both tried to convince Anna to let someone at the hospital check her injuries, too, but she refused. Adamantly. So, we let it drop. I didn't have the heart to argue when I just needed to get to Anthony.

I haven't found out yet who is at fault for the accident—Timmy or the other driver. But I know Anthony is in the hospital, and it's mostly my fault.

I think now my whole approach to raising him these last few months was wrong. He had too much freedom and wasn't ready for the responsibility. Even though we agreed that when he made a mistake he had to act like a man and own up to it, he isn't doing any better than before. He still spends too much time with his friends playing Atari and acting out his wizard. My biggest mistake, though,

I can see now, was to let him ride with Timmy when Timmy has only had his license a few weeks.

It meant so much to Anthony, though. He hated walking to school on the cold, dark mornings. Said it was slow, and that everyone else he knew had a ride to school, and he liked being able to get a burger and a milkshake with Timmy after school. So, I agreed he could ride with Timmy until I got my license back and could take him in the mornings again.

Hell, who am I to talk to Anthony about safe driving, though? The whole reason he's in a hospital is that I let down my guard, got drunk, and lost my license for six months. A real man should only talk if he walks the walk, and I haven't done that. I've got no right to say anything about his choices. Just one more way I failed him that night.

Still, as I stand looking down at Anthony, I feel a tear form. It's not for me, though; it's because I want so badly to trade places with him. I'm getting old and washed up. He's young and still has a future. Or, at least, he would have a future if I was a good enough parent to get through to him and teach him anything. But things aren't going to change for me. I'm going to kick around at boring jobs, so I can pay the bills until my number's up. Anthony has a chance for more, though. I'd gladly switch spots with him to give him that chance.

A nurse comes in to check on Anthony. "Is he going to make it okay?" I ask her. "I'm Anthony's guardian, Larry Edwards."

"Yes, Anthony will recover. Don't worry about that. He's going to be in pain for quite a while, however. Just breathing can be painful when you've hurt your ribs. So, we have him on some painkillers. They help him sleep."

"I thought he was in serious condition. That's what someone told me on the phone."

"He is."

"I thought serious was the worst condition."

"No, Mr. Edwards. Critical is the worst condition. And, in fact, the only reason we listed Anthony as serious is that we feared he might have internal injuries and bleeding when we admitted him. It appears he got lucky and didn't sustain any internal trauma, so I'd imagine the doctor will upgrade him to fair condition soon. He'll be sore for quite a while, and his arm will need about two months to heal fully, but there's no reason to expect anything other than a full recovery, given enough time."

"What about his friend Timmy? Is he in serious condition, too? I'd like to check on Timmy and talk to his parents if Anthony's gonna be asleep for a while."

"There hasn't been anyone admitted to this wing of the hospital named Timmy today that I know of. If you'd like, I'll call around and see if I can find him."

"Yes, please. Thank you. Oh, Timmy's last name is Jenkins."

After a few minutes the nurse returns. "Timothy Jenkins is in the intensive care wing of the hospital and is in surgery as we speak. We won't know how bad things are until the doctors have finished operating on him."

"What are they operating for, nurse?"

"You'll have to ask the people in intensive care. I just know they took him into surgery as soon as the ambulance arrived."

"Okay. I'll come back to check on Anthony soon. Maybe he'll be awake then."

I walk across the hospital in the direction the nurse indicates and before long come to the intensive care area. After inquiring at the nurse's station about Timmy, I make my way to the waiting room outside the surgery room. I find Timmy's parents, Bill and Connie, seated there with a slew of used tissues all around them. It looks to me like they've come straight from work—Bill is in his suit from the bank, and Connie wears a long-sleeved dress. I think she's a secretary at one of the local elementary schools.

Bill comes over to shake my hand, eyes red. After we shake, he wraps his arms around his body, even though it seems warm to me in this part of the hospital. Connie stays seated, swaying slightly while looking at the wall in front of her.

"How's Timmy?" I ask, barely more than a whisper. Somehow, regular voices seem out of place when talking outside a surgery room.

"I don't know," Bill stammers while raising one arm and rubbing his temple. "An assistant came out a while ago and said they're doing everything they can."

"I'm so sorry about this. I don't know what else to say, Bill, but I'm so sorry this had to happen."

Suddenly, Connie blurts out, "They weren't wearing their seatbelts. I just know it. That's the reason Timmy's in there."

Bill rubs his hand on his wife's shoulder. "Now, honey, we don't know that. We've got to give the doctors a chance. There'll be time for questions later."

"But I just know it! The speed limit isn't high in that part of town. Why else would Timmy be hurt so badly?" Connie's voice breaks as she finishes the sentence. Bill hands his wife yet another tissue.

"Should I come back later?" I say to Bill.

"No, it's okay. What do the doctors say about Anthony?"

"They worried he might have internal, what's the word, internal trauma. Bleeding on the inside. But right now, they say they don't think so. He's got a broken bone in his left arm and his upper body's in a hard cast, just to make sure, but they say he'll be okay in time."

"I'm glad he'll be okay. That's good to hear. Anthony's always very polite when he comes over to our house, and I'd hate to know something permanent happened to him, too."

I shake Bill's hand again in appreciation of his concern. He and I haven't done too many things together, so I can't say we're truly friends, but he's always considerate when I pick up Anthony from his house. Even though he lives in a much nicer part of town than I do, he's never said anything condescending to me like a few parents at Anthony's schools have done over the years.

Then, something registers with me. It's the way Bill just finished his sentence. "Wait, Bill, why did you say 'too'? What's happened to Timmy?"

Bill lowers his voice a little more. "One of his lungs may be punctured. And his right leg is smashed to pieces. Maybe other things. We don't know everything yet."

Suddenly, a doctor emerges from the surgery room, removing his white mask in the process. He looks exhausted, and he isn't smiling.

"I'd better go," I say while giving Bill one last handshake. His arm quivers so much he almost misses when I reach for his hand.

XII

I take Friday off from work and then spend all day Saturday watching Anthony, too. Even though I haven't been on the job long enough to earn a vacation day yet, another guy offered to trade with me, and the boss approved it willingly. Anthony's doctor tells me they're slowly lowering the dosage of pain medication, and tomorrow he'll approve Anthony's discharge.

It's hard to understate how much I hate hospital rooms. The antiseptic smell, the bare white walls everywhere, and the shuffling feet of people constantly coming and going. Although everyone's polite enough, you know it's just courtesy because for people who work at the hospital, it's their job. I know they probably want the people in their care to get better, and hope that they do, but they're paid the same regardless of how quickly patients recover. Not only that, but hospital workers get tired and irritable at the end of a tough shift just like anyone else does, and they can't afford to form too many personal connections with their patients because the emotional strain is so great. That's how it seems to me, anyway.

Then there's the food. The hospital has a cafeteria downstairs, but I barely go in except for an occasional cup of coffee or an apple now and then. My stomach growls frequently, but I prefer that to the so-called ham sandwich I got on Thursday evening. Whoever made it spread the mayonnaise on so thick, I swear I can still taste it somewhere in the back of my mouth.

Plus, there's so little to do. Anthony rests quite a bit, so I spend far too much time watching pointless game shows on television while he drifts in and out of consciousness. If I'm ever invited to be a contestant on *The Price is Right*, I'll have a good idea what a sofa set is worth, at least.

Several of my friends have come by to check on Anthony, and his friends that he plays games with visit, too. Brad, Wally, and Sammy have all stopped in earlier today. Wally made Anthony's day when Wally gave him a chocolate bar and joked how it was probably the only food he'd want to taste all day. I just wish he'd brought me one, too.

Now, however, Anthony's fully awake, so we can talk a bit.

"How you feel today, buddy?"

"Almost the same as yesterday. Really sore."

"Can you breathe okay?"

"Sort of. That part's getting a little better. Do you know how Timmy's doing yet?"

I've been avoiding that question for the past two days, saying I wasn't sure or that I didn't know yet, but I decide I'd better come clean this time.

"Timmy's hurt really bad, Anthony. He's alive, and his doctors don't expect him to die, but he'll never be the same person again."

"What do you mean, he'll never be the same person?"

"His right leg got cut all to pieces in the crash, and the collision also hurt his spine. It's doubtful he'll ever walk again. When he gets out of the hospital, he'll need to have a wheelchair."

"Timmy has to be in a wheelchair forever?" Anthony's voice rises, and I see his good arm start shaking.

"It looks like it, yeah. I'm really sorry, Anthony."

"But that's not fair! The crash wasn't Timmy's fault! The other guy swerved into Timmy's lane and sideswiped us! I saw it!" I see the boy's eyes tearing up.

"I know that, Anthony. The police report says the same thing. It was the other guy's fault. But that can't change what happened to

Timmy." My own voice starts cracking, and I barely get the whole sentence out. I struggle to look Anthony in the face while I say it.

His mouth opens and closes, but Anthony can't seem to put any words together. He's crying like I've never seen him cry before, and I can't blame him. I can blame myself, though. If I hadn't lost my license last November, I could have picked him up from school. He never would have been in Timmy's car. If he hadn't been there, maybe Timmy would have seen the other driver just soon enough to avoid the collision. If, if, if. If only I hadn't failed so badly, maybe this whole situation never happens. I put my head in my hands, on the verge of sobbing, too.

Dimly, I'm aware that Anthony's started speaking again. He's saying, "I never want to drive in a car again. I never want to drive in a car again."

I look up at him. He goes on. "All cars do is hurt people I care about. First Mom, then you, and now Timmy."

"Anthony, those were all accidents, but they aren't your fault. You aren't responsible for any of them."

"I'm a curse on people who drive in cars. That's it. I'm bad luck. Maybe I just need to stay away from people, so they won't hurt themselves anymore because of me."

"Anthony, maybe this is something we need to talk about later, but you're not a curse. No one is. You can't make other people do things just by knowing them or thinking about them."

"But now I'm scared, Lawrence. What if Timmy blames me? What if he can't even remember what happened because he's hurt so bad? What if he doesn't want me as a friend anymore because of this?"

"I can't answer those things. Maybe we should worry about one thing at a time, okay? Like getting you feeling better, so we can take you home where you belong, all right?"

He nods weakly.

"Tell you what, I'll go find a vending machine and see if I can get you another chocolate bar, okay?"

Anthony gives another nod, accompanied by half a smile.

I have no idea where a vending machine might be. I never use them, so I never look for them or remember where I've seen one. So, it takes a good while before I return to the boy's room. When I do, he's fallen asleep. Can't say I blame him. Right now, his dreams must seem better than reality. Perhaps he'll dream about wiping out some orcs or goblins or something else that makes him happy. I decide to eat half the chocolate bar and leave the other half for him when he wakes up.

At that moment, I realize I'm as exhausted as Anthony is. I let out a huge yawn and consider that maybe it's time I go home and get a real night's sleep tonight. There's nothing more I can do for Anthony right now, so I write him a note telling him I'll be back to check him out of the hospital as planned tomorrow.

I'm almost ready to leave the note when I sense someone at the door. Assuming it's the nurse, I finish scribbling my message. After a couple more moments, however, I realize the person isn't coming inside like a nurse would, so I look up. It's Anna, carrying a small bouquet of flowers. I know nothing about flowers, so I can't say what kind they are, but the bright yellow, vibrant orange, light red, and soft purple petals look very pretty.

Conveniently, there's an empty vase on the counter by the sink. I suppose it's natural to bring flowers to someone resting in a hospital, so the hospital staff has vases in each room. Anna inserts the flowers and then turns on the faucet, filling the vase partway before setting it on the rolling table next to Anthony's bed.

Turning to me, she says, "They're for both of you. A 'get well' gift for Anthony and a 'thank you' gift to his wonderful guardian who was so nice to a clumsy wreck on Thursday."

"Those are beautiful, Anna. I'd ask how you knew where we are, but Port Huron doesn't have that many hospitals."

"Not to mention I was with you when Nick dropped you off on Thursday," she adds with a big smile.

Anna's face looks a little better today, but it's partly because she's wearing heavy makeup to cover some of her bruises. Still, it's nowhere near enough makeup to cover all of them, and I'm guessing she's still in considerable pain. I also notice she hasn't moved her left arm since she came in. Anna held the flowers, turned on the faucet, and carried the vase to Anthony's bedside all with her right hand.

Still, despite everything wrong with her physically, there's something graceful about Anna, although I can't pin it down with any better word than that. Her smile is brilliant. Somehow, it seems to me that light just radiates outward from her face when she flashes a full smile like she just did.

"Cat got your tongue?" she asks playfully.

"Yeah, I guess so," I finally stammer. "I wasn't expecting to see you again, least ways not this soon, and not with such incredible flowers."

"I wanted to stop by yesterday evening, but I just couldn't bring myself to leave the apartment."

"How're you feeling today?"

"Better. I know I still look awful, but the pain's gone down some."

"What about your shoulder?"

"It's better, too."

"Anna, come on. You haven't moved it since you came in the room. That isn't good. Are you sure you're okay?"

"Yes, I'm okay!" she snaps, and her smile disappears. "I came here to say thank you, not to get a quiz about my life."

"I'm just worried that—"

"Yeah, too worried about me. I'm not as helpless and weak as you think, Larry, and I don't need you or anyone else looking out for me all the time."

I have no idea what brought on this sudden change in Anna. I meant to be helpful, and I thought she liked that. So, I don't know how to reply. While I try to think of something, she says, "Maybe I'll just go now. Enjoy the flowers."

Before I can get a word out, she storms past me and, for all I know, out of my life for good. I stand there looking at the door for several moments, dumbstruck about what just happened. At least Anthony kept sleeping and didn't hear anything.

When I sit down to gather up my coat and go home, another person walks into the doorway. For the second time in about five minutes, the surprise takes me aback.

"I see you still have a way with women, just like always," the new woman in the doorway tells me.

"Hi, Shawna. Did you hear that whole exchange?"

"Most of it, yeah."

"What the hell did I do wrong for her to lose it like that?"

"Don't know, Larry. I was hoping you could tell me. Who is she, anyway? She didn't look your type."

"What do you mean, my type?"

"When a woman I've never seen you with before brings flowers to the hospital and says they're for both you and Anthony, I assumed she was your girlfriend."

"Girlfriend? Anna? That's nuts."

"I don't know," Shawna answers in a tone that I know means she's half teasing and half serious. "The look on her face when she hurried by me wasn't anger, for sure. She was practically tearing out her hair, and she started sobbing before getting ten feet past me. Like someone who just made a big mistake, knew it, and was already having regrets."

"That's not the person who was in this room just a minute ago. She looked mad as an angry hornet when she stormed out. That's a little cliché, I suppose, but she did."

"Well, maybe. I'm just telling you what I saw. What was she doing here, then, if she's not your girlfriend?"

Still seated, I tell Shawna English about my series of random meetings with Anna Nicholson over the past several months. When

I finish, Shawna sits down next to me, gives an amused chuckle, and puts her arm on my shoulder.

"Maybe all these chance encounters are fate trying to bring the two of you together."

"Don't be silly, Shawna. I think she's fifteen years younger than I am. Something like that. I'm still nervous, though. Do you agree with my theory that her boyfriend's probably the cause of her injuries? I can't help but care about someone who's getting beat on by a man, even if she did just burst out of here like she never wants to see me again."

"I've never met her, so I can't say very well, but I trust your judgment, Larry. If that's what you think, you're probably right. But, if she continues denying it, or won't even talk about it, I'm not sure what you can do unless you catch the guy red-handed."

"Why would she deny getting hit by her boyfriend if it's causing her so much pain? That doesn't make any sense."

"It doesn't to you or me, no. But I think I read once about how that can happen. Something about how some people won't leave a bad relationship because their fear of the unknown is greater than the pain the relationship causes."

"That doesn't sound right to me, Shawna, but maybe you're correct. I've hardly read a book in years, so you'd know better than I would. I knew someday you'd move past celebrity magazines," I chide her, my shoulders finally slumping. Until that moment, I hadn't even realized how much my neck muscles were cramping, but now I feel it dissipate thanks to a little humor and Shawna's laugh.

"You've always trusted your gut, Larry."

"I'm thinking about trying some books, though, believe it or not."

"I don't believe it, but go on."

"Brad tells me his wife reads books on how to be a parent. I'm thinking I should get hold of some of those. No matter what they say, I can't do any worse than I'm doing right now."

"You shouldn't be so hard on yourself, Larry."

"Why not? I'm a lousy dad, or guardian, or whatever you wanna call me. None of my decisions turn out right when Anthony's involved."

"You aren't blaming yourself for this, surely?"

"Why not? If I hadn't lost my license, I might have picked him up from school on Thursday. Then, he wouldn't have been in the car with Timmy, and then—"

Shawna puts her index finger to my lips. "Larry Edwards, stop trying to put the world on your shoulders! You always try to take personal responsibility for everything, and one person just can't do that. It a great trait sometimes, I know. You're responsible, honest, and you never duck the tough situations. But don't let it twist you. Don't take so much responsibility that you forget you're human, too."

While Shawna says this, I feel my cheeks flush, and before she's done, I'm standing up and about ready to dismiss what she says or give her an angry denial. But just before I open my mouth to shout at her, I look in Shawna's face. There's no anger there, no challenge. Just compassion for a friend.

Slowly, I run my right hand over my eyes and slump back into the stiff plastic hospital chair at the foot of Anthony's bed. I just sit there a moment, elbows on knees, trying to knead the tension out of my forehead.

Shawna squats down next to me, her long brown hair almost touching the floor. "Just think about what I said, okay? I know you've got so much on your mind right now, but consider that being able to forgive yourself means just as much as anything else sometimes, all right?" She's got her arm around my shoulders and gives me a side hug. "It's how I finally snapped out of that phase I was in while we dated. I finally accepted that I can't change yesterday, so I might as well concentrate on today."

"I don't know if I can do that."

"Like I said, think about it. That's all I ask. For an old friend who wants to see you happy."

With that, Shawna squeezes me in another hug and then stands up and heads for the door. Like usual, I'm left there on my own, trying to figure out what to do now.

XIII

The following Wednesday, I'm sitting at home in my faded blue armchair after work, trying to help Anthony with his math homework. He can't go back to school until his injuries heal up more—the doctor was worried other kids might jostle him and that sitting at desks all day would compress his injured ribcage. So, I'm trying to help him with the work his teachers sent home.

"Lawrence, what does it mean to isolate the variable? The book says you have to do that to solve equations. Look." He points to the first example problem in the book.

"I'm looking, Anthony. Isolate means to put something by itself, right?"

"That sounds like what Mrs. Wilkinson says, yeah, but I don't get how."

"Um, let me see." I scan the book for something I recognize that'll help. "Okay, look here. It says to isolate the variable by putting all the numbers with variables on one side of the equation and all the numerals on the other."

"So, then, the Xs go on one side, and the numbers go on the other?"

"Sounds like it."

"But, how?"

"Well, Anthony, let's look at this sample problem. That's what they're in there for. It says that $4x + 5 = 13$. So, that means we need to get the numbers all on one side of the equation."

Peering intently, he replies, "Okay, the next line in the example shows that we subtract five on both sides of the equation. How come we have to do that?"

"I think because if you have five and you take away five, you end up with zero. Then there's no more numbers on the left side of the equation. Only variables."

"So, then, Lawrence, if it was 4x - 5 on the left, then we'd add five, because minus five and plus five make zero?"

"That sounds right to me."

"So, now we have 4x = 13. What's next?"

"Now we have to divide by the number in front of the variable, just like in the sample problem. Your book says that you do that because dividing the numerator by the denominator equals one, so there's only one X left, and that's the answer we're looking for."

"Why does math have to have so many special terms, Lawrence? That always confuses me. Like this. Numerator and denominator. Why not just say divide by the number in front of the variable to get the answer? That'd be so much easier."

"I don't know, Anthony. But, anyway, let's finish the problem. So, if we divide by four, we get one X on the left and thirteen over four on the right. It's a fraction. Do we have to simplify the fraction?"

"Wait a minute. The book says the answer is two. That's not a fraction. What'd we do wrong?"

Biting my lip, I scan the example problem for our mistake. This seems like it should be so easy. Why can't I get it right?

"Oh, here it is," Anthony points to a spot on the page. "We didn't subtract five from both sides of the equation. Only the left side. If we subtract five from both sides at this step right here, we get 4x = 8. Then, if we divide both sides by four, we get two on the right. That's what the answer's supposed to be."

"Right, right. You always do the same thing to both sides of the equation. I forgot about that."

The Long Way Home

"Okay, well, what about this sample problem?" Anthony indicates the next one in the book. It reads: -3x + 7 = 4.

"Step one is to isolate the variable, right, Anthony? So, how do you do that?"

"We subtract seven from both sides. Let me see, four take away seven is . . . um, it's, oh yeah, minus three. So, we have -3x = -3. Now, we just have to divide by minus three. What happens when you divide by a negative number? I don't get that."

"Shoot, I don't know, either. You don't have to divide by negatives when you work at a hardware store."

"So, what're we doing this for, then, Lawrence?"

What do I say to a teenager who asks why math is important when I can barely do math myself? I'm sure it helps and it's worth something; otherwise, Mrs. Wilkinson wouldn't ask students to learn it. But, about the only math I really know how to do is to figure out batting average and earned run average in baseball. I know those by heart and have for as long as I can remember. But dividing by a negative number? Who does that? A baseball player can't have negative at bats or negative innings pitched, so I have no idea what to say.

I'm about to stammer some nonsense when the telephone rings. "Keep checking out the example problem, Anthony. Maybe you can figure out what to do from there."

While I walk into the kitchen to answer the phone, all I can think of is what kind of lousy parent tells his kid something like that to cover for the fact he doesn't have an answer. I should've just admitted how stupid and useless I am at math.

"Hello, this is Larry," I say into the receiver in a dull monotone.

"Larry, this is Anna. Please don't hang up," she says rapidly. I'd already moved the receiver halfway back to its cradle on the wall when I heard Anna's voice, but she sounds earnest, so I bring it back to my ear. I probably would have hung up anyway, if not for what Shawna said to me on Saturday afternoon.

"Yes?" I say noncommittally.

"Larry, just don't hang up. I want to talk about the hospital the other day."

"How'd you get my phone number?" It comes out a little harsher than I meant it to.

"I went into Wally's Bar last night and asked him for it. I told Wally I was worried about Anthony and wanted to check on him."

"And are you?"

"Yeah. I hope he's doing okay."

"I'm trying to help him with his homework right now. What else do you want to talk about?"

"I want to apologize really badly for running out on you. I overreacted, and I know it. I'm so sorry that happened."

"It's okay. I always feel a little out-of-sorts when I'm in a hospital, too."

A short pause follows, as if Anna's taking a deep breath on the other end of the line. "I wanted to say more than that, though, Larry. You deserve better after taking care of me all afternoon last week."

"I think we're about even, Anna. You brought those pretty flowers to Anthony. It was a thoughtful gesture, even if things went badly after that. He's got them in his bedroom right now."

Should I ask Anna about her shoulder today? It's tempting, and the concerned, pragmatic part of me tells me I ought to, but I decide not to risk ruining another conversation by setting her off again.

"To me, I still think I owe you. It just wasn't polite to rush out like that. I also want to explain why I did it."

"You don't have to explain if you don't want to. It happens."

"Still, I think I should."

"Go ahead, then." I try to say it in an encouraging tone, but who can tell if that's how it sounds on the other end of the line? I've never spent too much time on phone calls, so sometimes I have no idea if what I mean really comes through to the other person.

"I think it'd be better said in person. Can I meet you after work tomorrow at the café down the street from my apartment complex? The one with the 1950s theme?"

"Sure, I know that one. I guess Anthony'll be okay on his own for an hour or two. I'll see if he wants a friend to come over."

"Thanks so much, Larry. See you at 5:30?"

"Sure."

I hang up the phone and stand for a minute. *Why did I just agree to that?*

Meeting Anna at 5:30 gives me plenty of time to wash up after work. For a garbageman, the day starts early so that we'll be off the streets and out of the way in the afternoon when people start coming home from work. I even give myself a second shave to look more presentable. We aren't on a date, obviously, but I try to keep up a little pride in my appearance, and I've never thought brown stubble with a hint of gray looked very attractive.

I'm still trying to figure out why I agreed to meet Anna again. To try to get more evidence about my suspicions, I guess. And because she asked nicely and thought it was important. Still, even if I'm right and Rickey roughed her up last week, what does it matter? Like Shawna said, if she denies it or won't talk about it, I can't prove anything. And I promise myself I won't try to pry anything more out of her than she wants to say. Eating dinner on my own doesn't sound very fun.

Donning dark slacks and a white polo shirt, I head for the café. They're about the nicest clothes I have, save the suit that I wear to weddings. My plan is to get there early, around 5:20, because I've always taken pride in being on time. Besides, I've been to the place a few times, and they make a pretty good go of simulating a 1950s atmosphere. Their floor is a black-and-white checkerboard, you eat from black-leather barstools or sit in booths, and the place has all kinds of photos of 1950s movie stars, musicians, automobiles, and so forth around the walls. The jukebox only plays fifties tunes and the waitresses wear ankle-length baby blue skirts to complement their white sweaters, bobby socks, and white shoes with black saddles. I didn't even know stores sold bobby socks or saddle shoes anymore, but apparently some stores still do.

I'm shocked when Anna's already there, sipping from an iced tea. She's got on a stylish purple blouse, and today she's gone light on the makeup. The left side of her face still looks in sad shape, but some of the bruises stand out a little less. Although I can't believe she beat me here, I recover from the surprise and join her. "You mean this place serves more to drink than milkshakes?" I try to joke.

She laughs. "I was gonna order you a beer but didn't know what kind you drink. Or maybe a Coke. What'll ya have?"

"I might just go for a coffee tonight. What kind of iced tea is that?"

"A Long Island Iced Tea." There's that radiant smile again as Anna slowly stirs her drink. I notice a light perfume, although because I'm a single man, I have no idea what it's called.

"Ah. I shoulda thought of that."

"Where's your truck? This place isn't that close to your house, Larry."

"About that. I'm not driving these days." I feel some red creeping into my cheeks.

"Why not? Don't tell me you're on a fitness kick," she chides gently while wrapping both hands around her drink and leaning forward a little. "You look great."

"Well, I'd say I don't wanna talk about it, but I don't want to repeat what happened at the hospital, so I'll just tell you straight."

"Yes?" Anna says when I pause for a moment.

The pause continues. I just can't make myself say the words and admit it. Finally, though, it comes out. "I lost my license, Anna."

"Lost your driver's license? How?"

"The same night Eddie laid me off from the hardware store, I just got angry and drank too much. Then, I got behind the wheel of my Cheyenne and went to Wally's to drink some more."

Anna's eyes grow wider, and I notice she's backing away from me ever so slightly. But, having started, I might as well finish, so I take the plunge and give her the rest of the story.

"Wally only gave me one drink before he realized that even that was too many. He tried to stop me from driving home, but I punched him and stormed out. I hadn't been on the road long before I ran a four-way stoplight and was in a collision. So, they took away my license for six months. I've got about two months left before I get it back."

Anna looks down at the table, hands not moving. I'm prepared for her to just get up and leave now that I've shattered all her images of what a quality person I am. In the momentary silence, I feel my pulse accelerate as I prepare for another rejection because of my failures.

Instead, she starts sniffling. I just stare at her beautiful face while she raises her hands to rub her forehead. At least she's moving her left hand a bit today.

"Anna, I know I just ruined whatever picture you had of me as a good person, but please don't cry," I start to say.

"It's not that," she says, her palms muffling the sound.

"What did I say wrong this time, then?"

"I know you didn't mean to, but you just reminded me of how awful and pathetic I am."

I'm unsure how to respond. What did I say to make her feel so bad? I'm the one who screwed up. Why is she almost crying? I decide to wait until she's ready to continue.

After a few more seconds and a few more sniffles, Anna says, "I'm just such a rotten person."

When I see the waitress approach with pad and pen to take our order, I wave her away for a moment. "Anna, what on earth are you talking about?"

Finally, she looks up and looks me straight in the eyes while inching backward in her booth until she's sitting perfectly straight against the backrest. "I keep asking you these hard questions, and you always give me honest answers. Like just now. You probably didn't want to admit that, but you did it anyway. And I've been scared to tell you things and misleading you ever since last week. I just need to get myself together." Anna's eyes start darting back and forth, as if she expects the people around us have been listening in.

It's been a long time since I've been in this position—sitting across the table from a woman who's scared and vulnerable. In fact, toward the end of my relationship with Shawna was probably the last time, and that was five or six years ago. I'm trying to remember something wise to say that'll calm Anna down when she takes several deep breaths, puts her palms on the table, and refocuses on me.

"Okay, here's the truth. I owe it to you." Another deep breath. "When you found me last Thursday morning, I didn't lock myself out of my apartment, and I didn't fall down the stairs. I was late for school, but that was the only truthful thing I said." All this comes out quickly, but after it does, Anna shoulders relax, and her eyes become steady again. "All the rest was just an excuse because I've been so frightened ever since Wednesday night."

"What happened on Wednesday, Anna? Wait. Tell me when you're ready. Do you want to order our food before you start?"

A sigh of relief, and Anna nods. I make eye contact with the waitress, a dark-haired woman who appears about my age, and wave her over. I already know I want fish and chips, anyway, because they have good fried fish here, and after a moment, Anna asks for a regular hamburger with onion rings.

As the waitress departs with a plastic smile and a twirl of her long blue skirt, I look back at Anna. "Are you sure you're ready to go on?"

"I think so. Hard as you may find it to believe right now, I'm really an honest person. It's just that I didn't know who else to tell this to."

I pat her once on her hand, very gently.

"It's Rickey. We've been dating for over three years, and for a long time everything was good, but suddenly, he's changed, and I don't know what to do."

Sadness wells up inside me. While I'm a little pleased I put the clues together properly to figure out what happened, I'm devastated that a person could harm anyone else so violently, let alone a girlfriend who trusts him and lives with him. I nod, hoping it shows how sympathetic I really feel, and wait for Anna to continue.

"You see, after high school Rickey went to play college football because being a pro football player was his dream. But he couldn't make the grades in school his redshirt year and dropped out after one semester."

"That happens to lots of people. Did you already know him at that time, Anna?"

"Yes. We went to high school together, and we had a bunch of friends in common. We still do. That's part of why I'm telling this to you. I'm scared to tell our friends because then they'll have to choose sides between us, or maybe they won't believe me, or they'll tell me he doesn't really mean to hurt me, and I want to believe that's true, but I'm just not sure I can trust them to tell me the truth. Does that make sense, or am I just crazy?"

"It makes a lot of sense, Anna."

Anna's shoulders, which had tensed up again while she spoke, relax once more. Her beautiful light-blue eyes focus back on me. She gives a sigh of relief.

"I'm so glad. I just think I'm losing my mind sometimes because everything is so confusing right now."

"How long did you say you two have dated?"

"Over three years. One day we talked for a long time at a party at a friend's house and started going out. Rickey's always been one to do a bit of drinking, but it was never that bad. We argue sometimes, but every couple does that, right?"

I nod again. My own history says she's spot-on with that statement.

"I thought I was in love with him, but now I'm not sure I ever was. I mean, we've dated for three years and have so many happy memories together. I don't want to lose all that and throw it away. For a long time, he was really good to me. He'd take me shopping sometimes, or we'd go to the movies together, things like that. He even bought me this nice necklace I've got on." She holds it out for me to see. It's a thin silver chain with a simple heart at the end of the chain.

"I never noticed your necklace before. It's beautiful."

"And he was fun for most of that time. We'd go to the beach at the lake, or watch sunsets, visit the county fair in the summer, all those fun things that people do together. He even got me interested in watching sports on television."

I smile at that. If it wasn't for sports on television, mine wouldn't go on very often.

"But a few weeks ago, things changed between us. Or, I should say, Rickey's behavior changed. One day, several weeks back, he told me he wanted to play football again and that he'd decided to join the local semipro team, so he had to hit the weights hard. I was happy he was going to go back to doing something he used to love."

"But things didn't go as planned?"

"He joined a local gym a few years back, and he's always been a big guy who stayed in good shape, but lately he's been working out for hours each day. Even after his construction job. However much time he spends at the gym, Rickey just doesn't seem to get tired. At night, he does pushups while we're watching TV. But that's when he started acting different, when he decided to go back to football. He's become this whole new person lately, and I'm terrified."

"Do you have any idea why he's changed, Anna?"

We pause a moment when the waitress arrives with our food. Although I toy with the fries on my plate, my eyes stay fixed on Anna, hoping that gives her confidence to continue. Once the waitress departs, Anna gives a deep sigh and runs her right hand through her blonde hair.

"I don't really know why Rickey's become so different. The only thing is that when I went into our bathroom the other day, I saw him swallowing some pills. He said they were for his nausea, and it's true he's had some trouble with vomiting lately, but the bottle didn't have a label, and it didn't look like it came from a drug store. He said not to worry, that it was just an old bottle that lost its label, but I think he made that up."

"That doesn't sound like anything I'm familiar with. I'm not sure what to tell you about that."

"But then, then the worst things started happening just last week," Anna says, and she's on the verge of tears again. She picks up her hamburger but sets it back on the plate without taking a bite. "One day Rickey took off his shirt, and I noticed fresh needle marks on his left arm. When I asked him where they came from, he started saying crazy things, crazy things about me." She's not even looking at her food anymore.

"Like what?"

"Like that I was cheating on him with other guys, and that I'm getting fat, and other weird things. Just crazy stuff. I never did any of the things he claimed. That's when he shoved me down, and I smashed my face on the kitchen floor. Even though I tried to get up and run away, Rickey caught me, and he's just so strong. He picked me up and threw me at the door because he thought I'd been cheating on him. When I crashed into the door is when I hurt my shoulder."

I wince several times while Anna speaks. "My God, Anna! Things are worse than I thought, then."

"What do you mean, Larry?"

"When we picked you up in the alley last week, I was pretty sure you'd been in a fight. I've been in a few myself over the years, so I know the look. But I just figured you'd had an argument. This sounds way worse. What are you going to do? You can't go back to this guy and risk all this happening again."

"But the next day, in the morning, he called me from work and apologized, just begging me to forgive him and saying how sorry he was and how he just lost his mind without knowing why. I'm not sure if I should believe him. That's what I was thinking about in the alley when you found me. Rickey's been staying at a friend's house since that night, but I'm thinking of calling him and telling him to come back."

"You can't be serious. After all this?" I motion up and down her face where the bruises are.

"But we've had so many good times together. What if he's really sick and he needs my help to get better?"

I don't know anything about psychology and why Anna would even think about seeing someone again after he'd thrown her into a door and almost broken her shoulder. I would've called the police on the spot if it'd been me. There must be something, though, because she's not stupid, yet she still can't decide what to do about Rickey. I decide I need to tread carefully.

"Have you tried mentioning any of this to your parents, Anna?"

"I can't."

"How come?"

"Because if I do, they'll rush over to check on me like I'm some teenage girl who can't handle herself. And then they'll start judging me, asking me why I don't do this or that, and telling me what I should do. That's why I stayed here when they moved to Chicago. I had to get away from all of that. They don't respect me and won't treat me like a grownup, so I'd rather they stayed in Chicago and didn't have anything to do with me right now."

The more she speaks, the more compassion for Anna I have. Regardless of whether she's exaggerating about her parents, her unwavering eyes say she believes everything she says. Combine that with her uncertainty about what to do with Rickey and how much support she might get from her friends, and her decision to meet me here makes more sense than I first thought. I'm about to tell Anna so when we both hear the café's door slam. Anna's looking over my shoulder, and I see her face blanch white. I turn to look, but I already know. It's Rickey.

XIV

Advancing toward our booth, Rickey brushes aside a waitress with one arm when she tries greeting him. It appears he's just come from a workout at the gym because he's wearing a plain white t-shirt and black cotton gym shorts. His full, dark brown beard can't hide the angry contortions of his face, and even from here, I can see blue veins sticking out of his forearms as he clenches and unclenches his fists.

"You!" he shouts, stabbing his right index finger at Anna. "I knew you'd be here, whoring around behind my back! I come home early from the gym to see you, and you ain't even there!"

I look at Anna. She's trying to back away, but that only means scrunching her body into the corner where the backrest of her booth meets the wall. "No! Rickey, let me explain!" she cries hysterically.

Rickey's halfway to our table, striding quickly, by the time I've wiggled out of my own booth to stand up and face him. He sneers. "This is who you're sneaking around with? Some old used-up piece of shit? Can he even get it up to fuck you right?"

Part of me is aware that everyone in the café is staring at me to see what I'll do, but that's peripheral to the fact that Rickey's only a few steps away and seems bent on pummeling me into pulp with his meaty fists. Vaguely, I hear the café manager calling out "Sir, sir!" in his useless effort to dissuade Rickey.

I step back with my hands up, palms out, and try saying, "Whoa now, buddy, let's just calm down, okay?"

From the corner of my eye, I see Anna put her hands over her mouth to cover a gasp. "No, don't!" she screams.

"I'll calm down when I have my girl back," Rickey snarls while drawing back his right fist to swing at me.

I know it's coming, but I'm not the athlete I used to be, so my dodge-and-duck move only results in Rickey's uppercut connecting with my left shoulder rather than my face. Damn, he's strong. The blow spins me one hundred-eighty degrees, and my stomach collides with our table, knocking my plate to the floor and taking some of my wind. I see Anna's face, eyes wide in fear as she screams again.

By the time I can get a breath and turn around, Rickey's left fist pounds my gut, and I stumble backward, falling on my butt. The force of the blow also makes my head slam into the metal pillar holding up a table, so I sit there stunned, blinking while trying to figure out where the stars in my eyes came from.

Dimly, I hear my adversary growl, "Fuckin' pussy. It's like fightin' someone from the old folks' home." He turns to Anna and shouts, "Come here, slut! We're leaving."

As my vision fades, I hang on just long enough to hear Anna scream again and see her kicking backward uselessly in her booth while she extends her arms and waves her hands wildly. Rickey grabs Anna by her legs and yanks her to the edge of the booth. Grunting, he puts his right arm around her waist, hoists her over his shoulder, and carries her to the door. Anna doesn't fight back, but the last thing I see before the darkness takes me is her face looking back at me, eyes bulging while her entire body shakes.

I can't tell for certain how long I'm out, but I doubt it's very long because when a woman and her husband shake me back awake, the café's still in an uproar. I just lay back as the manager presses ice wrapped in a kitchen towel to the back of my head where it connected with the table support. A few other customers gather around me, exclaiming variations on the phrase "Are you all right?" as I blink my eyes open.

"Where's Anna?" I stammer through the haze in my mind. "Is she okay?"

"We've already called the police, sir, and I got the license plate of that brute who just barged in here, so it shouldn't be hard for them to find your date."

It wasn't a date, but after everything Rickey said, I understand why the manager thinks so. I let it slide.

"Are you okay, mister?" a gray-haired woman asks me. "That man said so many vile things to you I'm sure you must be terribly insulted."

"I think my shoulder and head hurt more than my pride, but thank you."

"It may not be my business, sir, but do you have any idea what all that was about?" the manager asks me. His nametag identifies him as Dale. "I only ask because I'll have to make a report to the owner, and maybe give a statement to the police, too. It'd be nice to have some information beyond that a very large and strong man burst into the diner, hit one customer, and carried away another, all over . . . what word should I use? Jealousy?"

"Yeah, that's a good word, I guess. Use that one. The guy who hit me is out of his mind, for sure, but I can't tell you why with any certainty."

"You don't know the man who attacked you?"

"Barely. We met once. I don't think I said ten words to him. I think he would've gone after anyone who was in my place. But, like I said, I don't know anything for sure. There's nothing more I can tell you, Dale. You'll have to get any more information you need from the police if they show up to ask people what they saw."

"Do you need more medical attention? Should I call for an ambulance?" Dale questions. "I probably should've thought of that first, but it's not every evening this happens, you know?"

Smiling weakly, I reply, "I'm not sure. I hope not. Let's get me on my feet and see how that feels."

Slowly and shakily, I rise, leaning on a nearby table for support. A few diners clap when they see me get up.

"I want to pay for this man's meal," the gray-haired woman calls out. A few other customers offer to chip in and share the cost.

"Nonsense," Dale calls to the group. "This man's dinner is on the house. His next two dinners will be, too. It's the least I can do for him."

"I appreciate your generosity, but I don't hold you responsible for what just happened. What I need to do is get out of here and go help Anna," I say to Dale.

Normally, I don't enjoy being the center of attention, especially not after someone just wiped the walls with me, and I want to get out of here before more people decide they need to talk to me.

"Please, sir, just stay here where it's safe. The police will handle your girlfriend's abduction. I'll call them back, so they can assure you themselves, if you'd like."

I try to go to the door but stagger, only regaining my balance by leaning on an empty table. Apparently, that was too fast, because I feel a head rush and lots of dizziness. Dale puts an arm on my shoulder. "Please, sir, just sit down and rest."

"Gotta get out of here. I don't want to talk to people," I mumble back while the floor spins.

"Will you sit down for a few minutes in the kitchen, then?"

"Yeah, I guess so. But wait. First, you gotta call the police and tell them Anna's address." I tell Dale what it is, and then we walk to the kitchen.

I sit in a metal-backed chair in the kitchen, holding the towel full of ice to the back of my head. One cook brings me a plate of fries, which, once the immediate fear wears off, I gobble hungrily.

About an hour later, I'm still sitting there, eyes closed and half asleep now that the adrenaline of the moment has worn off and the situation is out of my hands. I'm startled awake by approaching footsteps, however, and I see Dale approach with a smile.

"Good news, Mr. Edwards. Your girlfriend is safe and unharmed. The police found Mr. Bradley at their apartment, like you suggested, and convinced him to give himself up voluntarily. It seems that whatever made him so angry doesn't last indefinitely because he was quite calm and remorseful when he surrendered to law enforcement."

As if I care what happens to Rickey at this point. I'm just relieved that he didn't hurt Anna any further.

"Where's Anna?"

"At home, I'd imagine. Can I call you a cab to take you there? On me, of course. A policeman showed up to take statements, but, given that dozens of customers all gave him the same description of what happened he saw no need to interview you and disturb your rest. The officer did, however, leave his card, so you can talk with him if you're interested in pressing charges."

"I never even thought about charges. Right now, I just want to check on Anna. Yes, a cab sounds good. Thank you."

Anna's apartment is only a few blocks from the café, but I accept the ride anyway. My unsteadiness and dizziness are gone, I notice, as I walk up the stairs and to her door. After knocking, I call out, "Anna? It's Larry. Can I come in?"

No noise comes from behind the door but in a few seconds, I hear the lock click, and it opens. Anna's there, now dressed in gray sweatpants and an orange sweatshirt, her wavy hair falling wildly over her shoulders. Her eyes are shot through with red, and I can see the streaks of drying tears on her face. Lots of streaks.

"I'm so glad you came over," she says while embracing me. It's not a polite hug or a friendly hug. Anna gives me the intense hug of someone who thinks she's just lost a best friend only to discover that person's still alive, after all. I wince when she squeezes my left shoulder, but I vow I won't let Anna see the pain. She doesn't need more worries right now.

Finally, she lets go and turns to go sit on her couch. It a dull gold color with plenty of padding showing through thin spots and holes in the upholstery. The springs creak when she sits down. Since there's nowhere else to sit, I join her. "You didn't call anyone to come over and stay with you?"

"I'm too scared. What would I tell them? They wouldn't understand what just happened. My friends would probably say I was exaggerating, if I could even find the right words to say to them."

"Well, we know about two dozen witnesses at the café who'll back your story if you need to convince anyone."

I keep my hands in my lap. Should I offer another hug? I've never been very good at comforting people, even under better conditions. Unsure, I ask, "Do you feel any better now?"

"A little. I just don't know what I should do."

"Do about what?"

"I can't stay here, for sure. I've got to find a new place to live, away from Rickey. Whatever those pills are doing to him, after tonight, I'm too scared of him to be around him ever again. But my lease goes for three more months. And I haven't been to school in almost two weeks because I didn't want anyone to see my face, so I bet I'm failing my classes now, and my professors probably think I've given up on school. If my parents ever see my grades, they're going to lose it, and they'll never trust me again. And how will I find a new place to live, all by myself, when I can barely afford this one with a roommate? Everything's just falling apart."

Sliding closer, Anna buries her face in my chest and sobs. I put my arms around her shoulders, being careful to touch her left shoulder very lightly.

"Tomorrow'll be a better day."

"No, it won't," she says into my shirt. Pulling her head out, Anna looks me in the face, right hand brushing her wavy blonde hair from her eyes, and asks, "How will anything be better tomorrow? None of those things will be different in the morning."

"No, they won't be different. But you will. You've had so many things happen to you today, I'm sure it seems like the world's ending right now. But in the morning things'll look different, and you can figure out how to tackle your problems one at a time."

Sitting up again, she asks, "Will you stay with me until the morning? I really need some company. I'm just terrified right now, and I'm scared to trust anyone else."

In this moment, Anna sits perfectly still, bent forward just slightly. I can almost swear I see her mouth the word "please" while she waits for me to respond. So much of me wants to tell her yes, after what she's been through today, but I know she's in shock and not thinking clearly. Right now she needs someone better than me, someone less likely to fail her. Leaving Anna alone tonight would be a very bad idea, but maybe I can help her find someone she trusts who can help her better than I can.

"Is that a good idea, Anna? I feel crushed after seeing everything that happened to you this evening, and you know I want to help you if I can, but I'm not very good at this sort of thing. I'm scared I'll make things worse instead of better. Do you have at least one friend you can call? Someone who's been your friend for a long time and knows you better than I do? I think they'd know how to help more than me. Don't you?"

She shakes her head while she draws back, scooting away from me on the couch. Her chest starts heaving, and she sniffles, "You're going to leave me too, aren't you? Why did you come over, then, if you're just going to leave me alone when I need you!"

I take a deep breath. I've got to get this right, and not fail for once. The next words must be the right ones. "Anna, I'm not going to leave you alone. You shouldn't be by yourself tonight, and I'm not going to walk out on you. Do you believe me?"

Anna's breathing slows a bit, and she nods, but very slowly, as if she's not quite sure. So far, so good.

Another deep breath. Looking her in the eye, I say, "But here's the thing, Anna. I don't know the best way to help you. I'm not good with words at times like this. That's why I suggested calling a friend to come over and stay with you. I'm not going to abandon you, but

I don't trust myself to say smart things to make you feel better. Does that make sense?"

Her shoulders slump, and Anna nods again.

"Larry?" she says in a very small voice.

"Yes?"

Very quietly, she tells me, "Don't leave me right now. You don't have to say anything smart. Just don't leave me. You always follow through and do what you say you'll do, and you're honest with me. That's what I love most about you. Right now, that's what I need. Someone I can trust not to hurt me. Can I trust you?"

Love? Did she really say that? I guess her shock hasn't worn off yet. But Anna's looking up into my eyes, perfectly still again, waiting for me to respond. Somehow, despite her bruises, despite the trauma and all the tears of this evening, she looks as beautiful now as I've ever seen her. Anna's face is so serene, her blue eyes steady, there's just no other word for how she looks. Once again, I have one chance to get this right and avoid another failure.

"I'll never hurt you. And I'm not going anywhere tonight. I can't promise much more than that, but I can promise you those two things."

Anna falls forward into my arms, her body practically melting into mine as she embraces me. "Thank you," she tells me, smiling even as more tears begin. "Thank you, Larry."

It seems like I should say more comforting things to her, but I just don't know how. Still, I've got to try. "After you left the hospital, I figured I'd never see you again. But I'm glad that isn't true."

"I'm glad, too," Anna says into my shoulder. "The moment I stormed out I was horrified at what a stupid thing I'd done. I was sure you'd hang up when I called you yesterday."

"I almost did. It all makes sense now, though. You were scared to reveal where your injuries came from, right?"

"Yes. I didn't want to admit to myself how much Rickey's changed. Part of me feared that people wouldn't believe me, or they'd think it was partly my fault."

"I don't think you need to worry about that anymore. Everyone in the café this evening saw the change with their own eyes."

"Thank you for standing up to him tonight."

"That's not what I was doing, Anna. There's no way I could have won a fight with him. Even when I was younger, there's still no way."

"But you didn't run away and leave me on my own. That's what I meant. I'm not used to that."

"What do you mean you aren't used to that? Did he threaten you other times, too?"

"Yes, but he never got rough until last week. Sometimes, though, when we were around friends, just having drinks and watching sports, or if we were at a bar, if someone tried to argue with Rickey, he'd get raging mad and get in their faces. They'd always back down or leave. That's why I told you I can't trust my friends right now. They either take Rickey's side because they're scared of retaliation, or they just clam up, so he won't get upset at them. Or, they've stopped hanging out with us altogether because he frightens them with his mood swings. It seems like I was the last one to open my eyes all the way and see what a monster he's become. I just couldn't believe he could change so much from the guy I started dating three years ago. I wanted it to be a phase he'd snap out of, and be normal again, but now I'm just so scared."

"That makes a lot of sense now that you say it. So, his anger's gotten worse and worse over time?"

"I think it's whatever pills he's taking that are doing this to him. Even though I never want to see him again, I hope he gets help because he's so dangerous right now."

While Anna's speaking, I give her good shoulder a reassuring caress. "I know you probably won't believe me, but I think you have a lot of strength and courage, Anna."

"Why do you say that? I've spent most of tonight either crying or on the verge of it."

"It's a strange thing to say, I know, but hear me out, okay? I admire your loyalty. Even though it didn't work out well in this case, you stuck by someone you cared about instead of running away at the first sign of things getting tough. Not everyone does that."

"I have to admit I never thought of it that way, Larry. I wasn't trying to be tough."

"Maybe not. But, that's one way to show toughness. And just now, you showed empathy that most people wouldn't have shown. Even though I agree that you need to stay away from Rickey after everything he's done to you, still, you just told me you hope he gets help and gets better. Most people would be cursing him and hoping he dies a painful death right now."

"I guess you're right," Anna says while looking up into my eyes.

"The point is, Anna, even though today has to be one of the worst days of your life, you didn't change from who you are. It's like what one of my baseball coaches told me once. He said something like, 'True courage is not the absence of fear, but moving on with dignity despite that fear.' He never said that you can't cry or be sad. But real courage is the ability to move forward even when things are going badly. And I think you've got a lot more courage than you think you do."

"That means so much to me. Thank you. But I need to ask you one thing, Larry."

"What's that?"

"Why did you lie to me a little while ago?"

"I lied to you?"

"You said you didn't know any smart things to say to help me feel better. That was a lie. You just said a whole bunch of smart things."

As Anna's eyes drift closed and she lays her head back on my chest, I can't help but smile. Maybe Anna's right. Maybe, just once, I didn't fail at something important.

After a few moments of silence, Anna snuggles further into me, if that's possible, her right shoulder leaning in as she rests her eyes and breathes deeply. Not knowing exactly what to do, I wrap my arms around her shoulders again and hold her there. Eventually, however, it occurs to me I need to call and check on Anthony. He went over to his friend Blake's house for dinner, and he's probably still there, playing wizards and dragons.

"Anna?" I whisper. No response. She's asleep in my arms, a gentle smile on her face, breathing deeply at last.

Slowly, ever so slowly, I disengage and stand up. Somehow, I do it without waking her. First, I walk to Anna's bedroom to get some sheets to lay over her, before realizing the apartment only has one bedroom. Will she want the same sheets she and Rickey have been sleeping in together? Hard to say, but I wouldn't, so I decide to play it cautious and just drag the comforter off the bed. It's navy on the top and solid white underneath. Ah, there's a closet. Luckily, it has some fresh linens, so I grab one and let it settle over Anna's body. She murmurs something incoherent but doesn't stir. Next, I add the comforter. Hopefully, that'll be enough.

Next, I find the thermostat and turn it up a couple degrees for my own benefit. Finally, I tiptoe back to the bedroom, where I noticed Anna has a telephone, close the door, and sit on the bed while dialing Blake's house. His mother picks up.

"This is Larry Edwards," I say as softly as I can while trying not to sound as nervous as I feel.

"Larry, you sound a little quiet."

"Okay, I apologize. It's been an unusual evening. How're things with Anthony and Blake?"

"Oh, just fine. They're listening to music and playing their game. Right now, I'm popping popcorn, so they can watch a movie on television. Is everything okay? You said things were unusual."

"Crazy, to be honest. Look, it's a long story, and I'll tell you about it next time we meet, but can I ask a huge favor?"

"What is it?"

"Can Anthony stay with you tonight and go to school with Blake in the morning?"

"Oh, now I see what you mean by unusual."

Even hearing it over the telephone makes me blush. "No, it's not like that at all. Like I said, I'll tell you all about it soon. Some weird things happened tonight. A friend had a really horrible day, and it'd be a bad idea to leave them right now."

"I was just kidding with that last remark, Larry. It's none of my business, anyway. Of course, Anthony can stay here. The boys'll be thrilled, I'm sure. What should I tell him if he asks why you're not picking him up this evening?"

"Just what I told you. A bunch of weird things happened, a friend needs me, and I'll explain the rest as soon as I see him tomorrow."

"Sounds good, Larry. Don't worry. Anthony'll be fine. Duane and I are taking good care of the boys."

"Thanks so much, Diana. We'll talk soon."

That mission accomplished, I open the bedroom door and step lightly into the living room. Anna's still asleep on the couch, breathing softly. Fast asleep, with all the tension and fear gone from her face, I'm struck again with how naturally beautiful she is. It's not the perky cuteness that so many teenagers have but lose when they hit their twenties; rather, it's the true beauty of a woman who's in the prime of life and is comfortable with the fact.

Or should be comfortable with it, if she could only have the chance to relax and set her fears aside for a while. I wonder how long it'll take before she can do that again? For that matter, I also wonder if I should even be thinking about Anna in terms of her beauty. In my defense, it's hard to miss because it's right there every time I look at her. But doing that also begs the question of what our relationship will be after tonight. The fact that I'm in an apartment right now with an emotionally devastated young woman sleeping right in front of me isn't something I know how to deal with. Maybe no one else does, either, but I sure don't.

The more I think about it, the more I realize that everything's that's happened is nuts. Through a series of chance events in both her life and mine, most of them negative, Anna and I are together right now. I don't regret being here because I'm helping a young lady who's scared and needs help badly. However, what'll happen after tonight I can't say. It'll take care of itself, I suppose, but I don't want Anna to depend on me. I'll only find a way to screw up and fail her just like I do in every other phase of my life.

Grabbing another set of linens from the closet, I lay the fitted sheet on the floor. You can never tell what shape these bland, gray apartment carpets are in, so I figure I need a sheet beneath me. Next, I turn out the lights. In the darkness I fumble to get the top sheet unfolded and covering my body, but eventually I figure it out and drift off.

XV

Suddenly, I jerk awake. Anna's living room is still dark, lit only by the streetlight filtering through the blinds of the living room's one window. I try to get a look at my watch in the gray half-light, but I can't make out what it says. The time matters because it's Friday, and I have work today. Then, I look behind me at the couch. Anna's gone.

In the stillness I hear a dim humming noise. Who runs a vacuum at this time in the morning?

Heartrate accelerating, I throw off the sheet and jump up, or try to, but my back barks at me to take it easy. I'd forgotten how long it's been since I slept on the floor, and every muscle is stiff as can be. Despite the soreness and dull pain, I stagger to my feet to figure out what's happened.

That's when the humming noise stops, the bathroom door opens, and Anna emerges wearing a sky-blue t-shirt and black jeans. When she sees me awake and turns on a light, her blond hair looks slightly damp, and I finally get it.

"What's the matter, Larry? You look like you've lost something important."

"A heard a strange humming noise and couldn't find you. For a minute, I thought you'd left."

"I just needed a shower after everything yesterday, and I needed to blow dry my hair."

"Yeah, I get that now. I don't own a blow dryer, so I didn't recognize the sound, but it makes sense. What time is it?" I ask while flipping on the living room's overhead light. "Oh, 6:15. I've got a little time before work starts at seven."

"Let me make you some breakfast, and then I'll take you there."

"You don't have to, Anna. I'll be okay."

"Larry, I'm not letting you leave until you eat some food. Now, let's see what I've got."

Anna walks to the kitchen and opens the white refrigerator door, gazing in. "We've got, hmm, we've got orange juice. A couple eggs . . . umm," Anna finishes, standing back up. "We've got orange juice and a couple eggs. I hope that'll be enough. Oh wait, we're okay. I forgot. There's some pancake mix in the cupboard. How does that sound?"

It isn't worth it to argue, especially not after last night, so I say, "That sounds wonderful, Anna. Thank you."

Looking around and seeing no kitchen table, I assume that Anna just eats from the coffee table near the couch, so I sit back down on the couch after moving the comforter aside. Once the pancake batter is on the griddle, Anna comes and sits next to me.

"Sorry, I don't have a lot of money for things like tables and chairs," she says.

"It's okay. It takes time."

"Thanks again for everything last night, Larry. You helped me in so many ways. I'm not sure how I would've managed if you hadn't knocked on the door."

"I just did what any person would have done. It was nothing special. I wanted to make sure you were safe."

"And I was safe, thanks to you."

I feel some color in my cheeks and put my head down.

"I still feel safe with you, Larry, even this morning after I've had a chance to calm down and sleep. You know why?"

"No."

"I thought of this while I was in the shower. A lot of guys, including some of my friends, I bet, would've tried to take advantage of me last night. But you never even thought about it."

"That's crazy. What kind of a man would do that to you, Anna, after all you went through?"

"More of them than you think, in my experience."

Anna gets up for a moment to flip the pancakes, then returns.

"Well, they aren't really men, then," I say when she sits down again. "Just scum. No real man treats a woman like that."

"Maybe I need to spend more time with real men like you, then. I seem to know too many of the other kind."

"I'm surprised you thought a guy my age might try to take advantage of you. I mean, look at me, Anna. I'm not exactly in my prime anymore. Even if I wanted to, I think my days of being able to take advantage of women are just about over."

"Can I ask you something?"

"Yeah, I guess."

"How come every time I try to compliment you, Larry, you want to deflect the compliment and try to pretend you aren't as good as I think you are?"

"How do you mean?"

"Well, take last night, for example. You claimed you didn't know anything to say to help me feel better, but you did. And just now, you started talking like you're all old and worn out, but you don't look like that to me."

"That's because you can't feel my back after sleeping on your floor last night," I say with a laugh and a smile.

Anna laughs, too, while returning to the kitchen. After a moment she brings back two plates of pancakes and two glasses of orange juice. "Don't dodge my question. Why is it that whenever I say something nice about you, you want to act like it isn't true? I admire modesty as much as the next person, but why do you pretend that even with the obvious things?"

I think a moment before trying to answer. "I'm not sure exactly how to answer that, Anna. But when you get to be my age and look back on everything you've failed at, and you see all the mistakes you've made along the way, all the things that might've been good but didn't turn out that way because you did something wrong, then you'll understand."

"But surely, you've done good things along the way too, right? I know you must have some successes to balance out the mistakes. Everyone does."

"I'll let you know when I think of some," I say while looking down just a moment, shoulders sagging.

Anna frowns. Well, it's not a frown so much as the half-smile of someone who wants to see the best in something but can't quite do it. She reaches her right hand out to touch me on the shoulder but pulls her hand back and wrings it in her left hand instead.

After an awkward pause, Anna speaks. "Here's what we're going to do, then. From now on, you're going to feel better about yourself. After last night, you have one good thing to start balancing out the mistakes. And the next time you do something good, think of me and know you have two good things. Then it'll be three, and four, and before long you'll realize you've done a lot more good than you think you have. Deal?"

By the time Anna finishes, her radiant smile is back, and I do feel just a little better. "Deal."

Our pancakes are about half gone, and I know I need to leave soon, but I want to ask Anna a couple more things.

"Do you plan to go to class today, Anna?"

"I don't think so. Remember my list of issues from last night? I think I need to work on those a bit this morning."

"You do seem like you're feeling a little more optimistic this morning. I told you that would happen, didn't I?"

"You did, Larry, and you were right. Well, what do you know? We're already up to two good things." We both give a little chuckle.

"Well, for what it's worth, can I at least suggest you check in with your professors today and let them know what's happened to you recently? Maybe stop by to see them in the afternoon after you've done those other things you need to do? I have no idea how college works, and if professors will cut you any slack when you've had as many shocks as you've had lately, but it's worth asking them about, don't you think?"

"That might be a good idea. I don't know what they'll say, either, but for sure bad things will happen if I don't ask, right?"

"That's my thought, too. Besides, as hard as it might be for you, the evidence is there for them to see."

"Yeah, I suppose so. I never wanted anyone to see my bruises out in public, but I guess now that I'm done with Rickey I shouldn't feel as bad about that."

Now it's time for the question most on my mind. "Can I ask you one more thing, Anna? Don't answer if you're uncomfortable, but it seems to me like it's important."

"What is it?"

"When are you going to tell your parents about everything that's happened to you? I know you told me you're scared of their reaction, but don't you think they'll want to know?"

Anna sighs deeply. "I don't think we have enough time right now for me to explain about that."

"But you'll tell me when the time is right?"

"Yes. I promise I will. When are we going to meet again?"

"You wanna try the café again tonight? You can tell me how your day has gone and what you learn about school. Besides, I have two free dinners coming."

"Two free dinners?"

"Oh, yeah, you missed that part last night. After Rickey took you away and some of the customers picked me up from the floor, the manager offered me two free dinners to make up for what happened. He thought we were on a date. After everything Rickey said to me, I guess that's understandable."

Anna giggles. "Free food? Those words are magic to a college student. See you at 5:30 again?"

"How about 6:30? It was unlucky to meet at 5:30, so let's try another time, okay? Plus, it's probably a good idea I spend some time with Anthony this afternoon. He's not gonna believe everything that's happened since I saw him last."

"Got it. Okay. Now, let's get you to work, Larry."

As we head for the door, Anna gives me another deep hug, and I give one back. I don't know where things are going, but I hope the worst of the drama is over.

XVI

Nick drops me off at home after work. He knows a little of the story between me and Anna, so I told him most of the rest while we drove our route.

"You want me to keep this under wraps and not tell everyone?" he asks when I'm getting out of his car. Nick drives a 1983 Toyota Celica coupe with metallic gray paint that his parents gave him last year. How someone who lives in Michigan can drive a foreign car and maintain his self-respect is beyond me, but now probably isn't the time to give him grief about it.

"Yeah, that'd be good. The last thing I need is for someone like Chris or Cedric to hear this story. They'd never stop asking me why I didn't score when I had the chance."

Nick laughs. "Yeah, sounds like something they'd say. Those two act about half their age. Well, see ya on Monday, Larry."

"Right, Nick. Just stay sober this weekend, okay?"

Nick laughs again while he drives off. I'd bet Nick's never touched alcohol in his life other than the wine he drinks at Communion.

Turning around to unlock my front door, something about the house seems off. Anthony isn't home yet, although he will be soon, so it's nothing he's done. Then, I notice. The screen door covering the front door is ajar. I always close it completely when I leave. Maybe Anthony just forgot when he left for school yesterday.

I shrug and put my key in the lock to the front door. It's already unlocked. Even Anthony never forgets that. The hairs on my neck rise, and I feel a tingle in my nerves. Did someone break in? Are they still inside? I've never owned a gun and never want to, but I do have a blackjack I keep in the dresser in my bedroom, and a baseball bat in the kitchen. Neither do me any good, however, if I'm at the front door and an intruder stands between me and them.

"Yogi, come inside, man! It's just me," a voice booms out from the kitchen.

My heart drops until a moment passes, and the voice registers. Crab. Great. I push the door open.

"Larry! Dude! Good to see ya, man!" Crab Parker hops up from the kitchen table, the flaps of his stained and threadbare fatigue jacket flailing in the process. He slaps my shoulder and then heads for the refrigerator. "I brought some beer with me, brother. Let me get you one."

Crab Parker is the younger brother of Todd Parker, a friend I played baseball with in high school. His real name is Alan, but he always thought his name sounded too wimpy, so he goes by his nickname. I can barely even remember how he got the nickname, except I think it had to do with him walking really bow-legged as a youngster and having eyes that seemed small, like a crab's.

Crab and Todd both volunteered to fight in Vietnam as soon as Crab graduated high school in 1965. Sad to say, Crab made it home, but Todd never did, and Crab hasn't been the same since. He's hooked on alcohol and marijuana, and maybe harder drugs that I don't know about. I can never be sure when he'll turn up, if he'll be sober when he does, or how clear his mind will be. It's a tragedy because he was such a promising kid. Before 'Nam, he was smart, athletic, funny, and generous with his friends. Whatever happened to him there after his brother died, though, he's never pulled out of it, even twenty years later.

Today, however, he doesn't look too bad. Crab's eyes have focus, he's trimmed his beard and his hair recently, and, unlike many times we've met, it's clear he's bathed within the last twenty-four hours. While he hands me a PBR, I ask, "How'd you get in, buddy? This is my house. Did Anthony forget to lock the door or something?"

"Sorry about that, dude. I came by yesterday afternoon when I thought you'd be off work, but no one was here. So, I let myself in." He extracts an item from his fatigue pocket that looks vaguely like a Swiss army knife but that I assume is a lockpick, holds it up for me for a minute, and then puts it away. "When it got to be, like, seven, and I could see no one was comin', I just decided to camp on your couch for the night and watch the place for you. I've been guardin' your perimeter ever since, dude."

"Anything to report, Crab?"

"No, sir. Quiet as a mouse in your yard last night. You gonna crack that beer or what, Yogi?"

"Not this time, Crab. I'm meeting someone tonight."

"Oh, that's right. You got busted and lost your license, man. That sucks, dude. You ain't no drunk, unlike me, and you're the one who gets busted. God bless the USA, Yogi." With that, Crab cracks my beer since he's already finished his.

Crab likes to call me Yogi because he thinks I'm named after the baseball player Yogi Berra. It's true that Yogi Berra's given name is Lawrence, like mine, and that my dad was a Yankees fan. However often I try to tell Crab I was born in 1942, though, and Berra didn't even come up to the Yankees until 1946, he still says it, anyway.

"How'd you get the beer, Crab? You workin'?"

"Same way I got into your house, Yogi, if ya know what I mean."

"Right. Where you stayin' these days?"

"Down by the waterfront, mostly. Sometimes I camp out in Danny's backyard, though, and he lets me freshen up a bit. I'd like to get some work, but, dude, there ain't many places hirin' these days, man."

"I know it. That's why I'm workin' for the City right now, Crab. There just ain't much out there."

"You got any around-the-house stuff that needs fixin'?"

"We'll see. Let me think on that one, buddy."

"Doin' something constructive beats drinkin'. Well, no it don't, but I gotta find me some work if I can, get some cash. You let me know if you hear of anything, all right, man?"

"Got it. You gonna drink one for Jackie Junior today?"

"Of course. The next one's for Jackie. And the last one's for Todd."

Strange as it seems, Crab has more of a connection to major league baseball than I do. When he served in Vietnam, he ended up in the same unit as Jackie Robinson, Jr., the son of the famous black baseball player. His unit was a strange mix of working-class guys like Crab, some laid-back guys from Southern California who got unlucky and got drafted together, and a few young black men like Jackie. To this day, Crab's speech remains a mixture of all three influences. Crab says Jackie Junior was a good man, however, and went into a streak of depression, even for Crab, when he learned that Jackie died in a car crash in 1971.

Anthony knows who Crab is, of course, although I don't think he understands fully why Crab behaves so erratically. Although I try my best to show courtesy to Crab and give him a little help when I can out of respect for his brother Todd, I don't want him hanging around Anthony too much if I can help it. Knowing that Anthony'll be home any minute, I need to think of a polite way to make Crab disappear before Anthony arrives. One day, I need to give Anthony the full explanation of why Crab acts the way he does. Anthony should know it isn't all Crab's fault that going to Vietnam and seeing his brother die messed him up in the head.

I'm not ready to do that today, however, so instead I say, "Crab, you think about tryin' to get on at that new garage downtown? You clean yourself up a bit, maybe they'll give you a shot. You learned how to repair stuff when you were in 'Nam, right?"

"Yeah, I'm a pretty fair mechanic, brother."

"You might just go down there and give it a look. It's Friday afternoon, maybe someone just quit, and they need some help. You never know, buddy."

"Can I borrow a toothbrush? Get the beer off my breath before I go?"

"Sure, I'll see if I have a spare."

A few minutes later, I'm watching Crab walk down the street toward downtown. I feel sorry for him in some ways. Lots of ways, actually. He and his brother volunteered to serve their country, and all they got for it was one brother dead and the other with mental issues. I know Crab's parents tried everything they could think of to get him straightened out, but none of it worked, and after about five years, they didn't have anything more to try or any money left to pay for more ideas. Crab's only a few years younger than me, but I expect to see his obituary in the paper any day, saying he died of an overdose of something or other. Seeing what's happened to him is one reason why I plan to discourage Anthony from joining the military in two years when the recruiters start calling. The country isn't in a big war right now, but as long as politicians are running things, that could change any day.

Only minutes after Crab's departure, Timmy's parents drop Anthony off in the yard. I walk out to thank them.

Once they've driven off, I say to Anthony, "Hey, buddy, I thought you were at Blake's house last night?"

"I was, but today at school Timmy told me he wanted me to have his bike."

"He's giving you his bike?"

"Yeah, he said he can't use it now, and since mine has flat tires, I should have his."

"That was really classy of Timmy. I hope you thanked him a bunch of times."

"I wanted to hug him, but I can't do that until next week when the chest cast comes off."

"Well, that was still something special on Timmy's part."

"So, where you been, Lawrence? Blake's mom just said a bunch of crazy things happened to you yesterday."

"Yeah, they sure did. You wanna hear about them?"

"Sure. If it's a good story, that is."

"Well, Anthony, it involved me getting in a little fight of my own."

His eye light up a bit. "Yeah, I wanna hear about that, for sure."

"Can we talk about it over some crackers in the kitchen? I know they're not your favorite thing, but it's Friday, and I'll get some more groceries tomorrow."

"I suppose. I am a little hungry."

While we eat some soda crackers, I tell Anthony about finding Anna in the alley, how she came to see him in the hospital but he was asleep when she ran out, our dinner last night, the lightning-quick fight with Rickey Bradley, why I decided to stay with Anna last night, and how we're meeting again this evening.

"Holy sh—, I mean, you're crazier than I thought, Lawrence. Ronnie Bradley's one of the most popular kids in school, and he's so good at football, and you got punched by his big brother?"

"Twice. Who's way bigger than Ronnie is, let me tell you."

"All to save this girl you just met by chance?"

"Well, I failed at saving her, but I guess you can think of it that way."

"So, is she your girlfriend now?"

"No. Why would you say that, Anthony?"

"You just told me you two are having dinner again tonight. That sounds kinda like a date to me."

"No. I'm just checking with her to see how things went today. Anna told me she doesn't have much trust in her friends right now, so I'm being her friend until she's squared away again."

"What happens after she's squared away? Then are you gonna ask her out?"

"I don't think so, Anthony."

"Why not? I mean, if you like her. It sounds like she likes you, bringing flowers to the hospital and all. I always wondered where those came from. I thought maybe the hospital just gives them to all the patients."

"Why not ask her out? She's about fifteen years younger than me, for one thing."

"Yeah, I guess that might matter."

"And for another, Anthony, we aren't in the same place in life. She's just finding her way, going to college, and all that. Anna told me she wants to work with children when she's done with college. My path in life is set. I don't know if I'm all the way over the hill, but I'm getting there. I can't imagine she'd ever be interested in someone like me."

"Maybe you'll know after tonight."

"And here's one more thing, Anthony. A real man doesn't take advantage of women. Even when they're vulnerable. It'd be wrong for me to ask Anna out right now because she's just been through a bunch of tough times and isn't her normal self. Try to remember that."

"I thought you weren't giving me advice on life anymore. You said you weren't any good at it, so don't say that to me," Anthony stands up straight and thrusts his chin forward. But then, he breaks into a big smile and relaxes. "Just kidding, Lawrence."

"Geez, kid, you almost had me there. I know I said that, but this is an important lesson that I don't want you to learn the hard way. Okay? Because if you have to learn it the hard way, it'll mean that you hurt someone who didn't deserve it."

"Right. Except, what am I gonna do tonight if you'll be at dinner? Can I go see Timmy?"

"I think that's a great idea, if his folks don't mind picking you up again."

"I can't just ride Timmy's bike over?' he says with another laugh.

"It's gonna be dark soon, Anthony, and for sure it will be before you come home. How about if you ride tomorrow, instead?" It feels so good to just say absurd things to Anthony for once and have him take things as intended. He's not riding anywhere with his injuries, and we both know it.

"Oh yeah, that makes sense. Well, I think I'll go give them a call. Have fun at dinner tonight."

I don't know if fun is the right word for my plans tonight, but I'm anxious to speak with Anna and find out what happened today.

XVII

My slacks and polo shirt remain wrinkled after sleeping on the floor at Anna's apartment, so tonight I go with a gray-and-white checkered sweater and some blue jeans. Although I've never been a fan of sweaters, it just seems classier than a Michigan Wolverines sweatshirt that's seen a few too many washes. I get there at 6:15, determined to be first this time, but Anna walks in just a few seconds later, smiling and looking relaxed. Tonight, she's got on a purple dress that highlights her neck and shoulders. Her soft skin looks a little pale, but then again, who doesn't in Michigan in late February?

"You look amazing. Even more than usual," I tell her with a grin. "What's the big occasion?"

"Seeing the man who helped me through the worst day of my life."

"You put me to shame, I'm so underdressed."

"I'm not complaining, Larry."

"In my self-defense, working at a hardware store or as a sanitation worker doesn't require a shirt and tie too often, but maybe I should have dug mine out for tonight."

"I'm still not complaining."

"You sound like today went okay, Anna. Want to talk about it right now?"

"Let's order first. I don't anticipate anyone carrying me from the booth again tonight, so I think we can take our time, don't you?"

When the waitress arrives, I request the fish and chips again. "I thought you believed in bad luck," Anna chides. "You're going to eat the same meal as last time?"

"It's still the best food on their menu. I just hope I can finish before getting punched tonight. What about you?"

"You told me it's on the house, right?"

"Sure is, sweetie," the waitress tells us. "I was here last night when things got crazy, and Dale's on shift again tonight, too, right over there. We remember what happened, and I'm glad you're still in one piece. Both of you. So, what'll it be?"

"I want to see if Larry knows the menu as well as he thinks. I'll have the fish, too."

"You got it. Thanks for coming back," the waitress tells us as she turns to head for the kitchen, white skirt flaring as she does so.

The food ordered, I ask Anna, "Well, what happened today?"

"To start with, the police came by to get more information about Rickey's behavior a little while after I dropped you off at work. I told them everything that'd happened before last night. After that, they took me to talk with the apartment manager and told him that Rickey was under a restraining order and wouldn't be staying with me anymore."

"That's good news, right?"

"Sort of. The apartment manager agreed to terminate the old contract that Rickey and I signed months ago. He looked shocked when the police described the violence and he saw my face. But the thing is, if I'm going to stay there and sign another lease, I need to find another roommate because I can't afford the rent all by myself. The manager said that he'd give me next month at a lower rent while I found another roommate, but after that I had to either pay full rent and sign another lease or move out."

"Well, that could've been worse, I suppose."

"Yeah, I've got about five weeks to find another person to live with."

"What are you going to do, Anna? Do you trust any of your friends enough to invite them to stay with you?"

"I'll have to think about that. I don't know. Some of my friends are married, and most of the rest already have apartment leases of their own with their boyfriend or girlfriend. I may have to advertise and live with someone I don't know too well. Except, after living with Rickey for most of the past year, I don't know if I'm comfortable with that. It's a little hard for me to trust people right now, especially strangers."

"A solution will present itself in the next five weeks, I'll bet."

"I hope you're right, Larry, and you probably are. You have a good feel for these things." Anna's face has its glow back while she gently bites her lip.

"You're trying to get me up to three good things already, aren't you?"

"Maybe four, if we talk long enough," Anna replies with a smile and a laugh.

"So, Rickey's under a restraining order. You think he'll observe it? I worry about that. About you."

"He'll be breaking the law if he doesn't."

"Do you think that would've stopped him last night?"

"Well, when I told the police I thought the pills were the cause of Rickey's change, they asked to look through the medicine cabinet. I agreed and showed them the ones I saw Rickey take. They told me the pills are probably steroids."

"I don't know much about steroids, Anna. What do they do, besides enrage the person who takes them?"

"The police told me steroids are a drug they're seeing more often the past few years. The way they explained it, steroids help people grow their muscles bigger and recover from exertion faster. But they have side effects, and, sometimes, sudden anger is one of them."

"That certainly sounds like what you told me last night."

"I hope, though, that if Rickey doesn't take them anymore, he won't get angry, and I'll be safe."

"Keep your door locked all the time just in case, okay?"

"The officers said to do that, too."

"Well, Anna, that means one of your big worries is taken care of, for now at least. What about the second one? Did you speak with your professors today?"

While I ask, the food arrives. It looks like the cooks fried up an extra piece of fish in this order, just for us, and they've stacked the fries high. I tell the waitress to pass along our gratitude.

The waitress winks and says, with a touch of southern drawl, "We all just felt bad your first date ended like it did. Everyone hopes the second one goes better and ends with you two walking out of here together."

I blush. Anna does, too, although neither of us bothers to correct the waitress. Given the beautiful dress Anna has on, the waitress probably wouldn't believe our denials, anyway.

When left to ourselves again, Anna says, "I'm taking two classes because I can only afford being a part-time student. I spoke with both my profs, and they said they're quite willing to let me make up what I missed."

"That's wonderful!"

"It is, except, well, I wasn't doing all that great even before I missed the last two weeks. I missed some other classes along the way, too. Even if I do okay on the tests I have to make up, I'll barely be passing, and the semester's not far from ending."

"That's something I don't think I can help you with, Anna. School isn't my thing."

"No, it's my fault for not being a more consistent student. And because I have to work to pay for both my rent and going to school."

"Where do you work? You've never told me that."

"At the grocery store by my apartment complex. I work the night shift, sweeping floors and stocking the shelves. That's part of the reason I've missed some classes at school. I work at night, so I can go to class during the days, but sometimes, I'm just so tired after work that I don't make it up in time."

The Long Way Home

I nod gently while biting into some fish. It's as good as ever, steaming and hot. A little too hot, so I go to the fries after one bite. I also think it's time for the big question, and I must be careful.

"Anna, is now an okay time to ask whether you've told your parents anything?"

"Yes, you can ask. It's probably time I told you that story and why I've not tried to contact them yet."

"You're sure? I don't want to pressure you. Tell me if you're ready."

"I'm ready. And you're such a good listener, Larry, that maybe you'll know what I should do next."

Although I doubt that, I decide to hold my tongue and just listen to what Anna says. When she hasn't said anything after a few moments, I try to help her out.

"You said your parents are from here but moved to Chicago, right?"

"Yeah, my dad, Benjamin, owns a construction company, and he believes that business is better there."

"He's probably right."

"Anyway, they moved several years ago, the year I graduated high school, and I've lived on my own ever since."

"Did it anger your parents that you didn't want to move with them, Anna?"

"A lot. They are, oh, what'd be the right word? Very conservative and old-fashioned when it comes to family values. They didn't think it was proper for a teenage girl just out of high school to live on her own. And my dad is nothing, if not stubborn," Anna finishes with a little laugh while shaking her head. "You see, he was a mid-ranking officer in Korea, so he believes that superiors give orders and subordinates take orders."

I've gone back to the fish now but nod as Anna talks. Would my father have been the same, if he'd come back from France?

"Anyway, I was eighteen when I graduated, and you know how teenagers are at that age, wanting to establish their independence and all."

I give a big smile. "That may be the one thing in our life stories that's exactly the same. Except my youthful rebellion, if you want to call it that, lasted until I went to work. After that, I didn't have the time, or much energy, for rebelling. Besides that, I didn't see much to rebel against. I was on my own, and I thought times were good."

"That's exactly what my father called it, a rebellion. He always had a military expression for everything, it seemed like. Dinner was 'chow,' he told me to 'fall out' after I finished my chores, and so forth. He'd write down a schedule on a notepad every day. And since he woke up at 5:30 for breakfast, he wanted lunch at exactly 11:30 and dinner at precisely 5:30, or 17:30 as he called it, so that everything would be symmetrical, six hours apart. Oh, and you should have seen the look on his face when I got a C grade once in intermediate school. At first, I thought he might lock me in my bedroom all day just to teach me a lesson."

"Wow, Anna. I think I'd a been ready to get away from that, too."

"You wanna hear more? I could never watch more than one hour of television in a day. Unless it was a TV movie, then I could watch one movie. The rest of the time, I had to read if I wanted entertainment. My lights had to be out at 9:00 every night. Until I got to high school, and then it could be 9:30. I couldn't ever keep a boyfriend very long because he scared all of them to death, until, eventually, no one would even date me."

At first, Anna sounded lighthearted when talking about her relationship with her father, but now, she's stopped eating and seems to be looking past me, rather than at me. Her eyes have narrowed, and she's tensed her shoulders.

"And my mom, Georgia, always took his side. Said I should be grateful to him for providing for us and working so hard. The one time I tried playing sports, he quizzed me so hard about every mistake I made that I forgot I was playing a game. All I wanted was not to make a mistake, so he wouldn't get upset."

"Can I ask what sport it was?"

"I played softball when I was eleven and twelve, and that's the last sport I ever tried. What's sad is that I like watching baseball on TV now, so I think I probably would have liked softball a lot if my dad had treated it more like a game and less like a job."

"At least you picked the right sport to try," I tell Anna, trying to lighten the mood. It works, a little. She brings her eyes back to mine and gives me a tiny smile.

"Sorry, Larry, I just get so frustrated thinking about it, even now. I was just a young girl, but I felt like an employee at my dad's company most of the time growing up. After I gave up softball, he said I had to do something constructive with my time. So, I learned to play the violin. That turned out a little better. I liked music a lot, and still do today, and since my dad didn't know anything about playing violin, I didn't get quizzed after I practiced in my bedroom."

"Last night in your apartment, I noticed you don't have many books besides a few college textbooks, but you have a big stack of cassette tapes. Now I know why."

"Yeah, I guess I'm still rebelling a little bit in that sense. I don't read much anymore, and I can't afford many books, anyway, so on the rare occasions I want one, I get it from the library."

"Are you an only child, Anna?"

"No, I've got an older sister. Laura. She was the perfect daughter to my father. Never did anything wrong, perfect student in school, tall, beautiful, and she followed everything he said. That's why he paid for her to go to college and learn to be an accountant, so she can manage the finances for his construction business. She's married now and has two children of her own."

"Wait a minute. Your dad paid for your older sister to go to college, but you have to work a job at night to pay for your education?"

"It's the price I've paid for defying my father's wishes, Larry."

"He's not forgiven you, even after ten years?"

"We had a big argument the night I moved out, and he said that was it. My father thought he could cow me into doing what he wanted, like he always could with my sister, but I'd just had enough, and I decided to go my own way. He's so stubborn that he won't change. Even now."

"Do you ever speak with him anymore?"

"A few times a year. He'll call on my birthday, and every now and then just to 'check in,' but even still, I feel like he's quizzing me most of the time."

"Let me guess, Anna. He treats you like you're still a teenager, even though you're almost thirty and you've been living on your own for a decade, and you resent that."

"How did you know?"

"He isn't convinced your friends are a good influence on you either, is he?"

"My father doesn't know them very well, but he says they must be too satisfied with mediocrity since hardly any of them have gone to college or opened a business. He never really approved of Rickey the handful of times they met at the holidays, even when Rickey was normal. He got even more upset when he found out we'd gotten an apartment together."

"I'll bet he thinks it's childish you still play games, too, because that's not how grown women are supposed to behave."

"Larry, how do you know all these things? It's like you're reading my mind. Or maybe his."

"Well, I know the last thing because I was at your apartment last night. When I rummaged through the linen closet to find the sheets, I saw your Dungeons & Dragons books stored in there."

"How do you know what those are? I can't believe that you play."

"I don't, but Anthony plays the same game. All the time. Too often for my tastes," I reveal with a laugh. It works, as Anna shakes her head lightly and sits back in her booth, cracking a full smile for the first time in several minutes. "Although, if Anthony knew you played, too, you'd probably be his hero. They'd make you queen of their game, or something."

Anna laughs again, this time a bubbly laugh of real enjoyment.

"I guessed on the other two. My friends, like Wally and Brad, have kids who are hitting their twenties, or are in their twenties already, and we talk about it sometimes. I think that a lot of parents worry about things like if their kids truly are ready to be adults and if they spend time with the right people. Most parents just do a better job of letting go than your father, it seems. But, here, Anna, why don't you take a minute to just eat a bit? You haven't gotten very far on your food while telling me your story."

She nods and digs in. After a few bites, however, she says, "I'm glad you just let me talk, though. It feels good to say all of that to someone who hasn't heard it a hundred times before, you know?"

Working on my own food again, I don't have the heart to tell Anna that I've thought about conversations like this many times over the years. What I'd say, and could I get the words right. Granted, in my mind I was speaking to my own kids about these things rather than to a woman I'd only met a short time ago, but I find myself telling Anna many of the same things I'd envisioned saying to my own grownup children I'd hoped to have someday.

Looking up from her fish with a smile, Anna tells me, "You know, Larry, you're on at least four good things now. Maybe five. Somehow, you just have a knack for saying things in a way that makes sense to me. Part of me was worried that you'd think badly of me for being twenty-eight and working nights at a grocery store, and not having a college degree, and being basically a failure. I didn't want to tell you about my family, either, because I was nervous you'd think I'm crazy. But you're so patient and understanding. I'm thankful for that."

"Well, Anna, maybe we're more alike than I thought. I never knew my father at all and never had any relationship with him, so I know how it feels to be out there on your own. People make mistakes, and life has a way of not going how you plan. If you wanted to hear about even a small portion of the big mistakes I've made, we'd need another order of fish. That's how long we'd be here. I know it isn't quite the same as your situation, but I'm starting to understand why you avoided the question about your parents with me for so long. Do you think anything'll ever change between you and your father?"

"I don't know. It just seems like, no matter how old I get, I'm still seventeen in my father's mind. His little girl in need of help and guidance. I think that until I prove myself in a way that he approves of, it'll always be that way. Maybe that's why I want to learn how to be a teacher or open my own day care for kids. It's possible he'll finally approve of me if I can do that. It just seems so far away, though. I've only been in school for two quarters so far, and only part-time, at that. There's so far to go, just to get an associate degree from a community college, and it doesn't seem as if I'll ever get there."

"You'll get there, Anna."

"How do you know that?"

"Because your other choice is giving up, and you don't look like a quitter to me."

She blushes a little but smiles warmly. "Now you're on five good things, for sure."

"I may be on five good things, but I don't know that I'm going to make it to six tonight, Anna. We've been here almost an hour and a half, and after all the drama yesterday evening, I'm just tired. I don't regret staying with you last night, but my back regrets having to sleep on your floor, if you know what I mean."

"It was a crazy night, Larry. I only have one bed in my apartment, and neither of us ended up using it," she giggles.

"I'll tell you what. Here's my phone number." I reach for a napkin to write it on.

"I've already got your phone number, Larry, remember? That's how I roped you into that mess last night."

"Oh, yeah, that's right. Well, after I gave you my phone number, I was going to ask you to call me in a couple days. Let me know how things are going, make sure you're feeling okay, and so forth. Sound good to you?"

"Absolutely. I won't forget. Larry, our situation is a little unusual, I know, but in a way I'm glad it happened. You're so easy for me to talk to, but you're also a real adult."

"What do you mean, a real adult?"

"Well, that's not the best word for what I'm thinking, maybe, but most of my friends, if I try talking with them about my life, they just nod and agree with me, or it's like they're only partly listening, and whatever they say, when they say anything at all, doesn't really help. With you, it's different. Last night was horrible, but between last night and this morning, you gave me good advice and smart ideas that worked when I tried them. That's what I meant by saying you're a real adult. I guess I don't have many of those in my life, so I'm grateful that I found one in you."

I give Anna a smile that I hope appears reassuring. "Tell you the truth, I'm not quite sure what to make of things either, Anna, but I'm glad I've met you, too. If I tell you something, will you promise to just take it as an honest compliment?"

Anna perks up and tilts her head to the side. "I'm listening."

"You have the most dazzling smile I've ever seen. I'm sure people've told you that before, but you do. Just seeing it makes me more hopeful. When you really want to, you can light up the room with it."

After a moment in which Anna does exactly that, I continue, "See? There's proof. I rest my case. I bet the people three tables over feel better now, too."

We both just laugh, Anna shaking her head playfully. As we gather our things to leave the café, she asks, "How do you do it, Larry?"

"Do what?"

"How do you know just the right time to say something to make me feel good?"

"I have no idea, but if you figure it out, will you tell me? I don't have much luck doing that with Anthony. Maybe my talent only works with adults."

"Maybe, but I'll bet you mean more to Anthony than you think you do."

"I don't know about that. After all the mistakes I've made with him, I just hope I haven't screwed him up too badly."

"Will you tell me about it next time we get together, Larry?" Anna asks while giving me a long embrace at the door of her car.

"Yeah, I'd like that."

XVIII

I spend Saturday at my kitchen table trying to help Anthony catch up on his math, although I can't say how many problems we've done correctly. Too few, I suspect. On Sunday morning, we go back to the hospital and Anthony's cast comes off. The doctor gives him a sling for his left arm and warns him to take it easy. Then, we head to Timmy's house. It's an important day—the first time Timmy's had friends over since the accident that put him in his wheelchair. We walk briskly. It's a nice early spring day, mid-fifties and clear. I hear a few birds singing, although it beats me what kind they are. The cement sidewalks look just a little less gray in the sunlight.

"I'm always ready for the first days of spring. How about you, buddy?"

"I guess so, yeah. I don't like walking to school in the morning when it's dark outside. This is better now that it gets light a little earlier."

"Speaking of that, how've Timmy's spirits been at school, Anthony?"

"Not bad, most of the time. I think he feels strange, though, a little uncomfortable, because now he's different from everyone else."

"Anyone givin' him trouble for bein' in a wheelchair?"

"Some, yeah. I don't see why kids can't just leave him alone. Don't they know it wasn't his fault?"

"They probably don't know. I think you'll understand more about this in time, Anthony, but some people don't need a reason to be mean to others. They feel better about themselves by making other people feel worse."

"That's stupid."

"Sure is, but some people, it's all they've got. They want to feel like they're better than someone, but they ain't worth shit, so they try dragging other people lower than they are. Have I ever told you much about my friend Sammy?"

"Not really."

"But you know who he is, right, Anthony?"

"Yeah. We ate at his restaurant one time, and you introduced me to him. You've had him over to the house a few times, too."

"Sammy's a good man. He's funny, and kind, and when we played ball together, he was one of the best athletes I knew. Sammy's smart, too. Smarter than me, at any rate."

"Sounds like he'd make a good person to run a restaurant."

"He is. Probably, he should've been a manager a long time ago, but I suspect that the old owner of his restaurant didn't like him because of his color. I noticed that he only got promoted after a new person bought the place and saw how good Sammy is with the customers."

"That's stupid, too, Lawrence. If he's good, he should be in charge, right?"

"I always thought so, and I'm glad you agree."

"What's this got to do with Timmy, though?"

"The point is that some people hate other people for being different. With Sammy, it was his skin color. With Timmy, it's because he needs to be in a wheelchair now. Did I ever tell you I had to fight a few times when people tried to pick on Sammy?"

"Yeah, once or twice."

"I'm not happy I had to do it, but it wasn't right to see people give him a rough time just because of his color."

"But I'll be in big trouble if I fight anymore at school. How can I stick up for Timmy, then?"

"I know. Times have changed some, Anthony. People get more worried about fights at school than they used to. I'm not sure what to tell you."

After walking in silence for a while, Anthony's head perks up. "I just thought of something. What if I learn how to do weightlifting? If I get big and strong, maybe I can stand up for Timmy without fighting because no one will mess with me then."

When Anthony says this, I can almost feel my chest expand. Although I doubt he understands how much weightlifting a person must do to achieve a muscular physique, the fact that he wants to stick up for Timmy so badly makes me as proud of him as I've ever been.

"I think that's a great idea, Tony."

Anthony stops midstride. "Wait, what did you just call me? I thought you were never gonna call me Tony."

I stop, too, and face him. "You earned it. Sticking up for your friends is what a man does. If you follow through, I'll call you Tony more often."

"Really?"

"Sure. You remembered your gift for Timmy, right?"

"Yeah."

"What'd you get him? Looks like a cassette tape, since you've got it in your pocket."

"I got him the latest Mötley Crüe tape, *Theatre of Pain*."

The names of bands these days.

"Well, tell you what, Tony," I say with a little laugh. "If you decide to try weightlifting and really get into it, just stay away from steroids, okay?"

"What're those?"

"They're what almost got me knocked out at the café on Thursday night."

"I thought it was Anna's old boyfriend who hit you."

"Well, yeah, it was, but the police told Anna they think he was using pills called steroids to help get stronger. I'd never heard much about them, either, but she told me they help people gain muscle but can also have bad side effects, including anger. I don't need to get knocked on my rear again for a while." We both laugh.

As we walk along, we both spend a lot of time stepping over cracks and pitting in the sidewalk where the cement's nearly disintegrated. The dandelions and other weeds are starting to emerge from the cracks again, too, now that it's spring. The sidewalks of Port Huron have seen better days, for sure. At least the leaves on the trees are coming out. I always feel good when I see that. Even though I don't play ball anymore, it means baseball season isn't that far away.

"Speaking of Anna, Lawrence, you gonna see her again?"

"Yeah, in a couple days, I hope. She's gonna call and let me know how she's doing."

"How about after that?"

"I don't know. She's a nice young lady but her life and mine are in very different places, Tony. I'm not sure what's going to happen after her life calms down and she realizes she doesn't need me anymore. If she ever needed me."

"You stayed at her apartment overnight. I'd say she needed you if she asked you to do that."

"Well, that one night it was important that someone stayed with her, and I was the one available, so I did. But I'd imagine that before long she'll go back to her friends, start spending time with them again, and in a few weeks, she'll realize that our lives don't have much in common. It's just how life goes sometimes, Tony. Circumstances bring people together, but then, when the circumstances are over, people get back to their regular lives."

We get to Timmy's driveway as I say this to Anthony. It's a nice house. Two stories, with a coat of dark gray paint and a paved driveway flanked by hedges. The second story has one of those large windows in the upstairs living room that lets the people there see the whole street. The front yard isn't much, but I know the back yard is bigger. Anthony told me Timmy's parents planted apple trees in the back and that Timmy loves to throw the ball for his dog. I wonder how much he can play with a dog now. Just the thought that maybe he can't makes me shake my head.

Anthony knocks on the front door, but before he finishes, we hear Bill's voice call out, "Come around back."

Skirting the house and passing through a wooden gate in the chest-high privacy fence, Anthony and I find some people gathered in the back yard. The privacy fence encloses a large yard with grass so well-maintained I think Bill must've cut it this morning. The house is to the left, several rose bushes on the right as Anthony and I pass through the gate. Around the perimeter of the yard, I see rhododendron bushes and other flowers. I'm not so good with identifying flowers, but I think I see daffodils and a few other kinds. Three apple trees are near the far end of the yard.

"Hi there, Larry," Bill calls to me. "It's a nice, sunny day, so Connie and I decided to barbeque the hamburgers instead of cooking them inside." To my relief, I see that Timmy can still play ball with his dog. Timmy has a large golden lab that returns a tennis ball by dropping it in his lap on the wheelchair. It's not much, but it's a small victory for the kid.

"I brought a gift for Timmy," I hear Anthony tell Connie. "Should I put it inside?"

"You didn't need to do that, Tony," Timmy's mother tells him with a warm smile. Connie has short, blonde hair, and today she's wearing another of the long-sleeved dresses she seems to like, light red in color.

"But, Timmy's my friend. I thought I should do something for my friend."

While Connie gives Anthony a big hug, Bill motions me over. He's got on slacks and a white polo shirt, which seems about right for the casual attire of someone who works at a bank.

"Everything's taken care of with the hospital bills for Anthony. It was the other guy's fault, and my lawyer says we'll get compensation for the injuries and hospital time for both boys. It won't undo what's been done, but it's something."

"I'd give it all back if it meant Timmy could stand up and be himself again."

"I know you would, Larry. So would I."

"Is there any hope that he'll recover at all, Bill?"

"Not much. It's the damage to his spine. It resulted in Timmy losing feeling in his legs. Not many people walk again after that, the doctors tell me. Connie and I will get him all the help we can, but there may not be anything that will give him his full life back."

I put my head in my hands and rub my face slowly. "It ain't right, Bill. Your boy ends up like this, and the guy who caused it all has a broken leg and nothing else." Shaking my head slowly, I repeat, "It just ain't right."

"The other driver wasn't even drinking. Just didn't see Timmy's car somehow when he switched lanes."

"How're Timmy's spirits?"

"Up and down. Connie's been a stay-home mom until the last couple years, so she's good at taking care of him, but he gets so frustrated at not being able to do what he used to do."

"I can't even imagine what that'd be like. If only I had something I could do for the kid."

"There's one thing you can do, Larry. One thing we can all do."

"What's that?"

"The doctors told us that one of the best things for people in Timmy's condition is to keep doing as many normal things as possible. Even though he'll have to do them differently because of his wheelchair, just making sure he keeps as much of his old life as possible will help him feel better and cope with his new one more effectively."

"That makes a lot of sense. I'll try to think of ways to do that whenever Timmy comes over."

"We all appreciate that, Larry."

"You know what Anthony told me on the way over here?"

"What's that?"

"He said he was thinkin' about takin' up weightliftin', just so he could watch out for Timmy and make sure no one gave him a hard time at school."

"That's amazing. Especially considering he says he doesn't like sports. I'm touched, Larry." Bill chokes up just a bit. "Thanks for suggesting that to him."

"I had nothin' to do with it, Bill. He thought it all up himself."

"I'll be darned. Do you think he'll follow through?"

"Don't know. It's easier said than done. His heart's in the right place at least, though."

"I'm gonna go throw on an extra burger for him, then," Bill says. "You gonna stay for a while? At least have a burger yourself, Larry."

"I'll have one, I suppose, but I'm kinda waitin' on a phone call at home, so I should get back pretty soon."

"No problem, Larry, we'll just throw something on for you. And Connie'll drive Tony home afterward."

I've been home about fifteen minutes, long enough to change clothes and grab a drink. Standing by my couch, I'm looking down at the creased paperback book resting on my coffee table. I shift my weight from one foot to the other and scratch my head, considering if I should open it. Partly because it's been years since I read a book, but mainly because of the book. Yesterday, Brad stopped by and offered me one of his wife's favorite parenting books, *The Mother's Almanac*. He told me it was mostly for kids younger than Anthony, but still had some good advice that might help, according to his wife, because it was full of everyday stuff that regular people can do. I took it, and now, I'm even thinking about reading a chapter or two.

Just as I reach for the book, the phone rings like I expected. Anna is supposed to check in today. Hopping up from the couch, I lift the receiver. "Hello?" I try to say it with a smile.

"Larry, it's Shawna. How are you?"

"Oh, hi Shawna. I wasn't expecting to hear from you today."

"I just wanted to know how things were going. Especially for Anthony. But for you, too."

"Anthony got his cast off today, so he's feeling pretty good. As for me, you won't believe it, but I was just sitting down with a Pepsi to do a little reading."

"I don't believe either thing, Larry," she says with a laugh. "You never cracked a single book while we dated that I remember. And when did you start drinking pop?"

"I told you that you wouldn't believe me. The book is from Brad's wife. One day a little while back I asked him what he did to help his daughters turn out so well. He said his wife reads all kinds of stuff about good parenting. So, I asked for a book. Couldn't hurt, I figured."

"You mentioned that when I met you at the hospital the second time. I'm happy you followed through. Maybe you can pass it along to me when you finish reading it. My little boy is nearly six, and he's a handful. So much energy in that little guy."

"Well, the title is *The Mother's Almanac* if you want to buy a copy."

"But Pepsi, Larry? What's that all about? Do they have a new whiskey-flavored type of Pepsi that isn't in stores in Lansing yet?" We both laugh.

"Something happened to me after Anthony went into the hospital."

"Was it the woman who brought the flowers?"

"No. Anna has nothing to do with this. Although I'll give you the rest of that story in a minute."

"You mean I was right about her? I knew it!"

"Like I said, I'll get to that in a minute. But here's the deal. The boy who was driving Anthony, Timmy, he's probably going to be in a wheelchair for good."

"Oh, my goodness. That's terrible news, Larry."

"It is, yes. I feel so bad for the kid. The accident wasn't his fault, but now he's going to miss being active during the best years of his life. It's horrible."

"What does that have to do with you, though?"

"Just a little while ago, I took Anthony over to Timmy's house. It was the first time Timmy has had people over since his injury. So, I'm looking at the kid playing ball with his dog from his wheelchair, and I'm thinking how unfair it all is. He and I have both been in accidents in the past few months. My accident was my fault, and even though I had injuries, I'm fine now. Timmy's accident wasn't his fault at all, but he'll never walk again. That isn't right."

"But like I told you, Larry, you can't change that. Your accident was just one bad night where you made a mistake and got unlucky. Every day, thousands of people do just what you did, and it doesn't always end with a traffic accident. I hope you aren't still blaming yourself for Timmy's collision?"

"Well, I'm not blaming myself directly, no. But it struck me today that if I give up drinking, there'll be less chance an accident could happen involving me in the future. Besides, Anthony's still scared by the idea of driving a car. He turns sixteen in May and hasn't even applied for his learner's permit yet. I think I need to do something to help him feel better about driving. This is how I'm going to start. I want to give up drinking, so Anthony'll know I'm trying to be safer."

A pause for a moment, then Shawna says, "That's wonderful, Larry. I'm so proud of you, trying to set an example for Anthony like that. And I'm glad you've forgiven yourself a little bit, too."

"How come you paused?"

"I never thought I'd hear you say you planned to stop drinking. It just took me a minute to think of something. I really am proud of you, though. What'll the guys at work say?"

"Don't care. I guess I'll just spend more time with Nick."

"Who's that, Larry?"

"The other guy at work who doesn't drink. Religious family."

"You going to join him in the pews, too?" she jokes with a laugh.

"Doubtful." I can't remember the last time I saw the inside of a church other than to see someone get married.

"Okay, maybe that'd be too much change all at once. My husband Vernon's a highly religious man, too, as you probably remember. So, I go with him most Sunday mornings. I don't know if I'm a true believer yet, but Vernon is very rigid about proper family values. He takes it seriously. Maybe too seriously sometimes."

"Well, you know how I feel about all that. If other folks want to go to church, fine by me, but it ain't my thing."

"You know I never cared much for it either, Larry, but my therapist says that a little sacrifice for family harmony is a smart move."

"You know how I feel about that, too. About seeing a therapist, that is."

"Of course." Knowing this is a dead-end conversation topic with me because I believe most therapists are frauds, after a short pause, Shawna asks, "What about the young lady from the hospital? You said her name's Anna? What happened with her?"

Briefly, I tell Shawna everything that Anna and I experienced since last week.

"You did the right thing again, Larry. I'm glad you helped her. What happens with her now?"

"I don't know, Shawna, but I don't think anything happens with her now. The plan is I'll keep checking in with her to make sure she's doing okay, but I don't think there'll be much more to the story than that."

"Sounds like there might be to me."

"How do you mean?"

"You think she's seen the end of her old boyfriend?"

"Can't say. I hope so, though. Anna says he was normal until he started using those steroid pills to gain strength. If the guy stays off the pills, hopefully that'll be the end of it."

"Hopefully, yeah. But what do you think, Larry? You have a good feel for these things."

"I don't know. The only part of Rickey I've met up close is his fist, and I didn't enjoy that an awful lot."

"Well, you know her, and I don't, but I just have a feeling she's going to need you again at some point."

"You were right last time, Shawna."

"Like I told you in the hospital, maybe this is fate trying to bring you two together."

"I think that's nuts. Have you been reading some crazy New Age philosophy books or something?" I ask with a laugh. Shawna laughs, too.

"Nope, and I'm not checking your horoscope, either. You make it sound like she trusts you, though, and has confidence in you, and that's the start of a good relationship. Put it this way: If things were different, and you were ten or twelve years younger, would you want to see her then?"

"Probably. Anna seems like a nice lady with a good heart and good intentions in life. And I think she's got more courage than she knows. Her smile is contagious, and she's beautiful, too. Not runway model beautiful, maybe, but just everyday beautiful, even when she isn't trying. But it doesn't matter. I'm not ten years younger. I'm forty-three and feeling older by the day. It'd never work."

"Well, don't shut that door until you have to, okay, Larry? You're probably right, but don't close your mind and make things a self-fulfilling prophecy. Even if you two just end up as friends, it never hurts to have one more friend you can trust."

"Shawna, I think you need to quit your job at the beauty parlor."

"Why?"

"I think you should quit and become an advice counselor for couples or something. Go into the therapy business for yourself. Everything you've told me has been right so far." We both have a good laugh.

"Then why won't you listen to me when it comes to Anna?" she asks over the phone as the laughter fades away.

"I just don't think it's gonna work out that way."

XIX

A week and a half later, Nick and I drive our usual Thursday garbage route. The weather's been superb for early March, several sunny days in a row with temperatures in the upper fifties.

"Just think," Nick says. "In another month, we'll get to take turns driving. You almost have your license back."

"Yeah, I'm getting there. I guess that whole situation just goes to show how one night of bad judgment can screw up your life. But I've sworn off drinking, so it shouldn't happen again."

"You have?"

"Yeah. Partly to help Anthony get his confidence back, so he'll want to get behind the wheel. I understand why he's scared, but he can't go his whole life without learning to drive."

"Can you take him to practice right now?"

"Not until I get my license back, but he's never even mentioned wantin' to get his permit, and that's strange for someone who's almost sixteen, isn't it?"

"I think so, yeah. I couldn't wait to get mine. Did Anthony follow through on his plan to become a weightlifter?"

"Sort of. He went after school last Monday to work out, and he said his muscles ached for three days after that. No one told him you gotta take it easy the first couple times and let your muscles get used to it." We both chuckle. "But he went back on Friday, Monday, and plans to go again today, so who knows? He may just stick it out."

"Was weightlifting in that parenting book you told me about?" Nick says with another laugh.

"I can't say. Haven't opened it yet. You see—"

"What's that up ahead?" Nick interrupts while scooting forward in his seat and craning his neck. "Is that a fire?"

"Yeah, I think so," I reply while doing the same.

Suddenly, I realize we've driven into the apartment complex by the community college. The one where Anna lives.

In a moment we're forced to stop driving because the fire engines surround a charred building, and we can't finish this part of our route. A crowd of people have gathered to watch, of course, pointing and gesturing as a side of the building collapses. Since it's the wall facing me, I can see the fire's gutted the entire place.

Nick says it first. "Isn't that the building where we found Anna?"

"Yeah," I respond slowly. "I'm sure she got out. She's probably at school."

"What do we do?" Nick wonders. "I don't think we're gonna do this part of our route today."

"Can you stop for a minute? I just want to see if she's here."

"Yeah, I'll try to back up and turn around while you look for her. Meet you again in fifteen minutes?"

"Sounds good. Thanks, Nick."

Hopping down from our garbage truck, I wander across a lawn that has some bare spots where the grass is absent, frantically looking this way and that to see if Anna's anywhere at the scene. It looks comical, I'm sure, to see a man in a garbage collector's uniform dodging through the crowd but I don't mind.

I don't find Anna.

Just as I give up the search and head back to our truck, I see her pull up in her beige Honda Accord. She runs toward her former home but stops short when she can see everything's gone. Then, she just stands and stares for a while, finally putting her head in her hands. Although I'm behind her, from the way her shoulders are heaving, it's clear she's breaking down.

I go and stand beside Anna, but I'm not sure what to say, so I wait in silence while trying to think of something. It takes several moments before she notices me. The tears are fresh on her cheeks when she turns and realizes it's me.

"How'd you get here, Larry? It's totally gone, isn't it?"

"It's Thursday. Your complex is on my route. But yeah, I think everything burned up. I'm so sorry, Anna. I'm just glad you weren't home when it happened."

She stares a while longer, cheek twitching while she runs her hand through her hair several times. Finally, Anna looks back at me and asks, "Now what do I do? Everything I own just went up in flames." It comes out as a sniffle, and I think the tears are about to resume. She turns and stares at the building once again.

Rubbing my cheeks, I find I'm just staring at the grim scene, too. The firemen have done their job, and the fire's nearly out, but they couldn't get here fast enough to save much. There's a shell of the outside walls left, but the wall facing us collapsed entirely and most of the inside looks charred. It takes a moment but soon the obvious answer comes to me. "You're welcome to stay at my house until you figure out something better."

Anna turns to me like she just awakened from a nightmare, eyes frantic and darting around. I take her by the arm to try to calm her. After a few moments, her eyes come back to me. "You hear me, Anna? I said you're welcome to stay with me for a while if you need to."

"I'm sorry, my mind just started racing. I was trying to think about the things that were in there when the fire started. Most of it was second-hand stuff, but at least I had something." She sits down cross-legged in the sparse grass, head in her hands. "Oh, Larry, what do I do? My whole life is gone, just like that."

"Did you hear what I said to you?" I ask, squatting down beside her.

"No. What did you say?"

"You should stay at my house until you have somewhere else to go."

"Really? That's asking a lot, Larry. Are you sure it's okay?"

"Where else are you gonna go? You have a Plan B?"

Anna turns to me, and she pushes a lock of golden hair from her face. She opens her mouth to respond but closes it before speaking. Finally, she stammers, "I don't know what to say."

"Say yes. I'm happy to help you until you figure out what to do."

She still doesn't respond. While I wait, I wonder what personal items Anna just lost. I hope there aren't that many, though, since her boyfriend is out of the picture and she talks to her family so rarely. All the while, she sits there, looking off again.

"Anna?"

"Yes," she whispers, then just stares ahead at the destruction of her old life.

Maybe there's something to Shawna's idea about fate bringing us together, after all.

"Well, this quarter at school sure is a washout," Anna tells me over coffee at my kitchen table that evening. "Both of my professors said they'd give me a withdraw grade from their classes. I'll take them again spring quarter and maybe, just maybe, I can concentrate and do better." She runs her right hand through her hair, closing her eyes momentarily and sighing. "I think maybe I need to take a withdraw from my life for a while and try to start over."

"Did you salvage anything from your apartment this afternoon?"

"No, it's all gone. I have renter's insurance, so I'll get something back for what I lost, but who knows how long it'll take for that money to show up? Right now, I've got nothing except the clothes on my back, my Honda, and the schoolbooks and other things that were in my car."

"You've also got my roof over your head for as long as you need it, Anna."

"I can't say thank you enough times, Larry. I'm gonna ask for more hours at work since I don't have to go to classes for the next few weeks. That'll keep me busy and out of your way, I hope."

"What if I don't want you out of the way? I just want you to have a safe place to gather yourself and get your energy back, so you can go on with life as normally as you can. Believe me, even though it's been a while, I haven't always lived by myself. I've lived with a few girlfriends for a short time. I knew what I was getting into when I asked you if you want to stay here."

"You have? Lived with other women, I mean." Anna stops her coffee mug halfway to her mouth for a split second.

"It's been years, but there've been a couple, yeah."

"I'm sorry, I probably shouldn't have said it that way. It isn't my business to ask about that. I'm just so frazzled right now."

"Don't worry about it, Anna. Like I was saying, you're welcome to stay until things calm down for you."

"You've got to let me do something, though, to help a little bit."

"I wasn't going to insist on it. But, if you are, what're you good at?"

"Not cooking, that's for sure," Anna says with a laugh. "The only reason you didn't see all the frozen sandwich wrappers in my apartment is that I took out the trash the day before you stayed the night."

"I've got an idea," I say, slapping a palm on the table. "You're in college. And I'll bet, with your dad being as strict as he is, you were a good student in high school too, weren't you?"

"Most of the time, yeah. I'm good at school when everything else isn't distracting me."

"What if you helped Anthony with his homework? Are you good at algebra?"

"I was an A student in math, even though I didn't like it that much."

"That's where he needs help the most. That, and history. I don't suppose you're taking a history class at the college?"

"No. I'm taking Intro to Psychology and Intro to Sociology. I don't know how much history I remember from high school."

"Let's start with math, then. I'm useless at math and Anthony needs help, but he's afraid to ask his teacher at school because he says she doesn't like him."

"I doubt that's true."

"So do I, Anna. I think he just says that to cover for the fact he's afraid to ask for help in front of his classmates. But, true or not, if you tutor him with algebra, maybe he'll do better. He's practically failing right now, and he can't afford to fail his classes."

"Deal. I'll also work on keeping your house clean, handling the dishes, and things like that. It's the least I can do."

"Plus, if I'm allowed to say it, Anna, I have a feeling Anthony'll listen better to you than he does to me."

"Why is that?"

"Well, if you were fifteen and someone with movie star looks offered to help you with your schoolwork, wouldn't you pay attention?" I say with a grin.

"Don't tease me like that, Larry. No one's ever gonna cast me for a movie because of my looks, silly. You're just trying to get me to feel better."

"Let's just see what happens when Anthony gets home from weightlifting after school today, and I tell him you're his math tutor. You'll see."

Looking me straight in the eye, Anna asks, "Larry, do you believe in fate?"

"No. Not really." Despite what Shawna keeps telling me, I don't.

"Why else does everything that happens to us just bring us closer together, then? Every time I need help, somehow, you're there to help me. I can't imagine where I'd be without you," she says, taking my hands in hers, still looking me in the face.

I should pull my hands away, but I don't. Somehow, at this moment, it just feels right, so I leave them.

"I don't know what else to call it," Anna goes on. "What is it, then, if not fate?" she asks while leaning over the table.

I'm not going to take advantage of her. I pull my hands back and look down for a moment to break the spell, although it takes all my willpower to look away from her crystal-blue eyes.

"Chance. Bad luck. Living in a modest town like Port Huron. There's a lot of explanations more logical than fate, aren't there?"

She slumps back into her seat at the table and takes a sip of coffee. "Maybe you're right," she says, dropping her head as a vacant look enters her eyes.

Then, like a rubber band snapped somewhere inside Anna, she just puts her head down, cradling it in her arms, and her upper body goes limp. "Larry, what's wrong with me?" comes the muffled question. "What have I done to deserve all these things going wrong all of a sudden?"

"I don't think there's anything wrong with you, Anna. I know things seem awful, but remember that they aren't your fault. You didn't ask for Rickey to take steroids and become an angry, raging monster. You didn't burn down your apartment building, either. None of these things are because of you."

Slowly, Anna raises her head, and I can see she's on the verge of tears, but she's trying to fight them.

"Can I ask one more thing, Anna?" I say carefully.

"What's that?"

"Promise you won't get upset? If now's not the time, it can wait."

"You're going to ask about my parents, aren't you?" she says warily, although without anger.

"I was thinking about them, yeah. Don't you think they'd let you stay with them for a while, given that you lost your home and it wasn't your fault? I mean, you said your father's stubborn and all, but won't he understand that?"

"I talked to him two nights ago."

"And?"

"And for once, he seemed happy when I told him Rickey and I aren't together anymore."

"You mention why?"

Anna looks down. "I'm not ready for that conversation yet. I'm not sure if I'll ever be. I told him Rickey's behavior had changed for the worst, and that I'm not seeing him now. Dad approved and said I'd done a good thing by standing my ground."

"Will you call him again, though? Let him know about losing your apartment?"

"I'm thinking about it. But I'm not ready yet."

I pat Anna on the shoulder when I stand up to start dinner. "Give it time, Anna. Maybe someday the time'll be right. It's been another long day for you, and you probably feel buried by an avalanche of disaster, but you'll bounce back."

Anna looks up, a touch of hope in her eyes. "I'm trying. It's just so much at once."

"Remember when we had dinner together, and I told you I know you'll be okay?"

"Yes."

"I still feel the same. Your only other option is quitting, and you still don't look like a quitter to me."

Anna smiles and then sets her jaw. "No, I'm not ready to quit yet."

XX

The next morning, Friday, I'm just getting downtown to start my Friday shift when, of all people, Crab Parker meets me at the glass door to the sanitation building.

"Larry, dude, come over here a minute," Crab says while motioning around the corner to the back of the building. At most times, I'd be suspicious he's done something illegal, but he's got on a work shirt from Greg's Motors garage and looks fully sober, so I decide to follow.

"Crab, buddy, you're looking pretty good."

"Yeah, brother, I got a job, just like you said. How'd you know Greg was hirin'?"

"I didn't. Lucky guess."

"Well, it was a good guess because I've got steady work now, and I'm stayin' clean, so I don't lose it."

"That's great, Crab, but what are we meeting behind the building for? You don't need to hide the fact that you've got work now. You should be proud."

He motions me in close and says in a quiet voice, "You hear about that fire yesterday near the college?"

"Yeah, the apartment complex is on my Thursday route. I saw the fire firsthand."

"I've got the dope on how it started, man."

"I heard it was an electrical fire, Crab. That's what the newspaper said this morning."

"Nah, Larry, that's just a fake, dude. That ain't what happened."

My eyebrows perk up. "I'm listening, Crab. What've you got?"

"It was arson, Yogi. And I know who started it."

Now I'm looking around, too, as if the walls could record what Crab tells me. "Who?"

"Man, you remember Chet Barry?"

"Of course. How could I forget the guy who sat on the bench of our high school baseball team for three years because I was better than him? I'm pretty sure he's hated me ever since, too."

"Yeah, that dude couldn't hit a curveball to save his life, but he's got money now."

"Only because his father died and left Chet his real estate development business."

"See, that's the thing, brother. That's why the fire started."

"Chet started the fire?"

"Nah, he's too smart for that. He wouldn't risk gettin' caught. It was his younger brother, Paul."

"How do you know that, Crab?"

"Our garage is right next to Ted's auto parts store. Convenient if we ever need supplies in an emergency, right? So, anyway, I go in there to say hey to Ted before work, show him I'm cleanin' up, and what do I see but Paul buyin' a gas can and payin' in cash. I played ball with Paul, and he weren't anything better than Chet at baseball, but Paul used to lie like crazy."

"That's a good clue but doesn't prove anything."

"Not by itself, no. But you forget, Yogi, I know the streets, and the people of the streets know me."

I nod, waiting for Crab to continue.

"One of my friends comes down to the garage after work yesterday. Never mind which one; you don't know him. He tells me he was sleepin' off a hangover in the alley behind the apartment when he sees this guy drive a nice car into the alley, get out, and start toyin' with the electric meter outside the building. I gave him Paul's description, and he tells me, yeah, that's the guy he saw. Then he says Paul looked around and opened his trunk, quick as lightning, then turned a key to a door and took the gas can inside. And—"

"And the sparks from the electric shortage ignited the gas," I finish Crab's thought for him.

"Damn straight, Yogi."

"How'd he get a key to the building, though?"

"I'm thinkin' the owner gave him one. You think the owner was in on the scheme? Have a fire, collect his insurance money, and then sell the land to Chet's company and have him develop it, all for a cut?"

"I've heard of stranger things, Crab. That might be true. Except, wouldn't the fire department figure that out? Be able to detect foul play?"

"Not if they're in on it, too, brother."

I nod while biting my lip. "What're we gonna do about it, though, Crab? The word of a drunk in an alley isn't going to stand up to the money Chet and Paul have, 'specially if the fire chief backs them up."

"You want I should look into it a little more, see what else I can dig up, Yogi?"

"Can I count on you, private?"

"Yes, sir. I'm on the job. After my day job," Crab finishes with a wink.

"Dismissed. Good luck, Parker," I say and give Crab a salute.

He salutes back and marches off. What'll I do, even if he finds out something? I'm not sure what I have to gain or lose by looking into things, but I figure it can't hurt to know more. It's true Chet resented me back in high school, but I've probably only met him once or twice since then, and nothing happened between us. As far as I know, I was a small fish, and he thought he was swimming with the big fish, so I wasn't worth his time. I don't think there's any way that the fire had anything to do with him hating me back in high school.

But, if someone planned to burn down the apartment building, well, arson's against the law. So is the insurance fraud they'd be committing if the apartment owner is in on the plan, although I can't say I have much sympathy for any insurance company. More important to me, the fire forced a couple dozen people out of their homes, including Anna. And it destroyed their property and complicated their lives in a hundred other ways.

All this makes me very curious if there's more going on than meets the eye. Not to mention that anything that keeps Crab occupied and away from booze is probably for the best. Unless it gets him into a new kind of trouble.

XXI

Early Sunday evening I am, of all the things I couldn't imagine I'd be doing a month ago, sitting on the couch watching a basketball game on television with Anna after dinner while eating chocolate ice cream. We ate early because her night shift at work starts at six.

"Did you ever play basketball, Larry?"

"Not much. I've always liked it okay but stopped playing when I hit fifteen or so. That was about the time I knew I'd never be seven feet tall, so I couldn't play basketball, and I also knew I'd never be seven feet wide, which ruled out being good at football. Baseball's about the only sport left for normal-sized people."

She giggles. "I love baseball, too, but I like basketball a lot. I can't stand football, though."

"Too rough?"

"Well, kinda, but more than that it's the machismo that goes with the game. It's like the players can never be big enough or tough enough, right? It's always a race to be bigger, faster, and stronger than everyone else. And even if you win, it's only a little while before someone else bigger, stronger, and faster than you comes along."

I'd never thought of it quite that way before, but she's right. I wonder how much of that has to do with dating Rickey for three years?

"It's good to see you feeling better today, Anna. You sound like your old, more confident self again."

"It helps to have something secure to come home to. You've given me a chance to get my feet under me again."

Next, I ask a question I've been wondering about all day. "You changed your hair today, Anna. How come?"

"I had an appointment for a trim, yeah, but I decided to get rid of the waves and just have straight hair for a while."

"You gonna keep it tied in a ponytail, or just let it hang free?"

"I'm not sure. It's been a while since I had straight hair. I used to have a ponytail in the back when I was a teenager, but maybe that's a look for young people now, and I need to try something that looks a little more grown up."

I just laugh.

"What, you don't like it?" Anna starts fingering her new hairdo while looking at me.

"No, it isn't that. You look beautiful no matter how you have your hair. I just couldn't help it when you said you were getting older and needed to look more grown up."

"Well, I am getting older. I'm twenty-eight. Thirty isn't that far away, you know."

"Don't be in a hurry to feel older, okay?"

"Part of me wonders what'll happen when I do hit thirty. Will people respect me more because I have experience, or just look at me as a has-been?"

"Trust me, Anna, no one will look at you as a has-been if you look anything like you do now. You remember that morning after I slept in your apartment, when you got out of the shower and mentioned that some of your friends might have tried to take advantage of you that night?"

"Of course."

"I could never excuse it if they did because taking advantage of vulnerable people isn't right, but a small part of me understands the temptation."

"So, what are you saying, Larry?" she asks me, suddenly holding still and looking at me intently.

"Just what my eyes see. When you decide you want to date someone new, guys'll line up for a chance to take you out."

After a few moments of silence, Anna runs a hand over her head and leans in a little. "Can I ask you something kinda serious, Larry?"

"Yeah, I guess." It occurs to me I haven't looked at the television in several minutes and can't even say which team is leading the game anymore.

"Are you sad that you never had any children of your own? Do you feel like you missed out on something important? I know the question's coming out of nowhere, but I've been wondering that for a while."

"That's a hard question, Anna. I haven't thought about it much since Anthony came to stay with me." I pause to think for several moments.

"It's okay if you don't want to talk about it."

"I'm just trying to figure out how to answer. I guess, well, I think the answer is yes, I've missed out. For a long time, I was okay that I didn't have any kids, even after my friends started having them. Wally married his high school sweetheart just two years after we graduated, and Brad just a little while after that. Most of my other friends got married by their mid-twenties. When they started having children, it felt like I was missing out a little, but I didn't worry too much because I felt like I still had lots of time. Plus, I told myself I wasn't ready for fatherhood, anyway, and that was probably true at the time," I finish with a weak attempt at a laugh.

Anna nods and waits patiently for me to gather my thoughts and continue.

"By the time I hit my thirties, though, things started feeling different, like I was doing something wrong, or that I had some fatal flaw other people could see that I couldn't. Even though I never stopped dating women altogether, it was like I started every new relationship waiting for it to fail because all the other relationships had. I don't know how much that showed on the outside, but it's how I felt on the inside. Which isn't good, I realize, but how often can you fail at something before you throw in the towel?" My voice cracks just a little at the end.

Anna slides closer and puts an arm around my shoulder. "It's okay to stop if it's too painful."

"It's just admitting the truth. I wasn't good enough, and I failed. It's just that so many things I see around me remind me of everything I've missed. Like when I see young kids riding their bikes down the street in the afternoon. I hoped that someday I'd teach my son or daughter to ride, and I'd be able to watch with satisfaction when they realized they could pedal on their own without falling. Or when I used to go to Brad's house to watch a ball game and I'd see the art his daughters made for him posted on his refrigerator. I can't even remember what weekend of the year Father's Day is because it's never mattered for me. So many afternoons I've stared out the window, wanting a son to play catch with, or maybe take him to his first Tigers game. Hell, I was even looking forward to scaring my daughter's first date by shaking his hand with my right hand and holding a baseball bat in my left." Again, I hoped that might be humorous, but all I can manage is a rueful smile and a couple shakes of my head.

"Maybe it was the wrong time to ask, Larry."

"No. Why would it be the wrong time? A real man admits his failures. He doesn't hide or make excuses. In the end, I just wasn't good enough. I never quite figured out how to make women happy enough to stay with me."

"You're going really hard on yourself. I know you don't believe it's fate, but maybe it's just bad luck you haven't met the right woman? Or sometimes you meet the right person but just at a strange time, you know?"

When Anna says this my thoughts drift to Shawna momentarily. The handful of times we've talked recently, I've been amazed with how much she's grown up and what a woman she's become. But she's married. Another failure on my part. I'm the one who left that relationship, after all, because I didn't have enough patience.

Realizing that Anna's looking at me and expecting a response, however, I say, "Can I ask why you're curious about that?"

She bites her lip for a moment and then replies, "It's just something I've been thinking a lot about recently. The idea of having children, that is. I believe I want to have them someday, but I'm scared what'll happen if I do."

"Why are you scared? You're smart, you're caring, and you've got a good head on your shoulders. There's no reason you wouldn't make a good mother."

"No reason except that I'm nearly thirty, I'm practically broke, I've lost my apartment, and the only education I have is about one quarter's worth from a community college. How can I support kids and take good care of them when that's all I have to show for the first twenty-eight years of my life?"

Neither of us says anything for a while, perhaps because there's nothing comforting to say that won't sound fake and contrived. Finally, though, I break the silence. "We're a strange pair, Anna, you and me. Every time I try to tell you how great you are and how much you have to offer, you have a hard time seeing it and believing me."

"And the same thing happens when I talk about you," she replies. "I think you're a terrific man, but you seem to always think about your mistakes instead."

"That's what I mean. I can't understand why you don't have more self-confidence. You're intelligent, and level-headed, and you care about others. I know you've had some bad luck lately, a few setbacks, but that doesn't change the core of who you are. You're gonna be fine, Anna. Someday, you'll be my age, happily married to a great guy, watching your children run through your house, and the parents of all the little kids in the class you teach will be telling you how glad they are that their kids have you for a teacher."

She blushes at first, but then replies, "And someday you, Larry, will understand that you've done way more good in the world than you realize. You've made some mistakes, sure, because we all have, but someday you'll look back and see Anthony grown up into a healthy and productive young man with a family of his own, and then you'll have a chance to do all those things you just told me you missed out on with your own kids. Plus, you'll know that when I needed help the most and was in real trouble, you did everything right."

With that, Anna gives me a deep hug, stands up, and takes our ice cream bowls into the kitchen. Now the basketball game is over, and I have no idea who won.

When she comes back from the kitchen, Anna stands in front of me, smoothing her plain yellow cotton t-shirt repeatedly.

"Larry, I just thought of something. When I called my manager at work today about changing my hours for a while and told him what happened at school, he suggested I look at working during the day instead. He said I should learn to be a cashier because I'm responsible and dependable, and that's a bit of a step up from people who can only stock shelves."

"What about going to school?"

"The college offers night classes. Not for all the courses, but for ones that lots of people take, like psychology and sociology, they have classes in the evening for people who work. I'm thinking about that."

"That's great, Anna. If you can make more money or move up at work that's a step forward, especially if you can keep up your studies at the same time."

Anna pauses for a moment and runs her hands over her shirt again. "I want you to take a night class with me."

"Wait, what?"

"I want you to take psychology with me at the college."

"What on earth would I take a college class for? That isn't gonna help me."

"Not as long as you collect trash, no. But come on, Larry, that isn't the job for you. You've told me a couple times how unreliable your back can be. What'll happen next time you strain it hauling garbage? What if you decided to get a college degree, so you could get a desk job someday that isn't so hard on your body? And I think it'll help in other ways, too, besides maybe getting you a better job someday."

"What other ways?"

"Well, I've heard you say lots of times you don't understand why Anthony does things."

"Yeah, I say that a lot. So?"

"That's what you learn in psychology. You learn why people do the things they do. If you really want to know how to help him better, maybe a psychology class will give you some clues."

I run my hands over my cheeks a couple times, not saying anything. Anna's got a point when it comes to Anthony. But I know I don't belong in college.

"Anna, I graduated high school twenty-five years ago and haven't set foot in a classroom since. I'd have no idea what to do."

"I see quite a few adults like us in my classes, Larry. It isn't all twenty-year-old kids in a community college. Some of 'em have been in the military and are going back to school. Others want to get training for a new job. You won't be as out of your element as you think."

"I doubt they'd even let me in. That's why I need you to help Anthony in math instead of doing it myself, remember?"

"It's an open-enrollment school."

"What's that mean?"

"It means they'll let you enroll in school, although you have to take some tests to see where you place, but they won't turn you away or say you can't take classes."

"There's no minimum requirements for going to community college?"

"Not at their school, no."

"I'll be darned. I never knew that. Still, I just can't see myself in college. Besides being lousy at math, I haven't cracked open a book in a couple years at least."

"The new quarter begins in April. You've got until then to think it over. They have people who specialize in admissions if you want to talk with someone about how college might help you. Maybe you'll tag along next time I go and talk with my advisor? I'm not saying it'll be easy, but remember what you told me once about moving forward with dignity despite your fear?" Anna's face is smiling, and she has her hands just below her chin, palms together, like someone praying.

"It's true. I did say that, I realize. I don't know about college, though. It's never even crossed my mind before."

"Like I said, you've got a little time before you have to decide. I'm gonna go get ready for work, but I've thought about that a couple times lately. I think it'd be good for you. You might even learn to not beat yourself up so often."

XXII

The following week, on Thursday, I come home from work later than usual because we had a meeting. Apparently, some residents complained about someone throwing their trash cans all over the place, but it wasn't on the routes Nick and I cover, so we're in the clear. My guess is that Chris and Cedric drank a little too much at lunch one day. Although I suppose I feel bad for the residents who had to walk all the way across the street to collect their empty trash cans, I only partly blame Chris or Cedric. It isn't as if collecting trash is very stimulating work. Still, it means I'm home about an hour later than usual.

Walking in the door, I hear the music coming from Anthony's room. At least, I think it's coming from his room, except it doesn't sound like his music. Instead of electric guitar, this music features keyboards and a woman singing. Pop music. Maybe Anthony's time working out is paying off, and he's found a new girlfriend?

After pulling out some breaded chicken patties from the freezer and turning on the oven, I'm about to go check on Anthony when the phone rings. "Hello," I call into the receiver.

"Larry, buddy, it's Wally. You haven't stopped by in forever, so I thought I'd check on you and make sure everything's okay."

"Wally, good to hear from you. Yeah, things are going okay. A little strange, but okay. Nothing to worry about."

"What do you mean, strange? I don't think I've ever heard you say that before."

How long has it been since I've spoken to Wally? I can't even remember, so I forget how many of the recent things that've happened he knows about. The last time, I think, was when he came to the hospital to check on Anthony, so I decide to start there.

"Well, not all the news is good. Did I see you last at the hospital?"

"Yeah, it's been that long. That's why I called, Larry. I started gettin' a little worried."

"So, you know that Anthony's friend is stuck in a wheelchair now."

"It's a tragedy, that happening to someone so young like that. But I knew that was probably gonna happen when I left the hospital. Not to sound insensitive to what happened to the kid, but I called to check on you. Did that woman ever call you? The blonde one who came in that second time and asked me for your number? I almost didn't give it to her, but she sounded sincere. Or maybe she just flashed me that big smile she has. That's kinda persuasive, too."

"She's living with me now, Wally."

"Now I know why you haven't been by in a while. Nice going, Slugger! I told you that you still had it in you, remember?"

"No, it ain't like that, Wally. That's the part that's strange."

I go on and tell Wally everything that's happened with me and Anna.

"That's some story! You wanna come in some night this weekend and give me more details?"

"That's a good idea, except there's one other thing that's happened recently."

"What's that?"

"I decided I'm done with drinking, Wally. After watching what happened to Timmy, and knowin' that beer caused my own accident that's set me back so much, I think it's time to stop. You wanna meet somewhere else, so I can avoid the temptation?"

There's just a moment of extra silence on the phone before Wally says, "Well, I'll sure miss you as a customer, but I'm your friend even more than that, and I think you're doin' a good thing, Larry. All of it. The girl, the beer, everything. I'd still like to see you, though. Maybe Sunday afternoon before I come in to tend bar here? There'll be tournament college basketball on TV. You still watch, or did you give that up, too?" he says with a laugh.

"No, I'm still good with basketball," I reply, sharing the laugh. "I'll be there. You want me to bring somethin'? Some chips or anything?"

"Sure, chips're always good to have around. See you then, Larry."

"All right, thanks for calling, Wally."

After hanging up, I decide to check on Anthony and see why he's playing new music while the oven finishes warming up. Will he want t-shirts and cassettes of a whole bunch of new bands now?

I hear a cheer go up from inside just as I'm about to turn the door handle. I recognize Anthony and Blake, but the third voice is female. Must've been right about a new girlfriend, I guess as I go in. My jaw hangs loose when I open the door to find Anna, Anthony, and Blake in the middle of a game of dragon warriors. They're high fiving each other as they turn to look at me.

"Lawrence, Anna's character just killed the march warden of the hobgoblin tribe! A double-damage backstab!"

"Even now, he's spasming in his blood-stained chain mail, clawed fingers twitching," Blake adds with gusto.

"Okay . . . nice work, I guess? But what's going on?"

Anna looks up at me with a bit of a sheepish smile. "I promised Tony, or should I say, Halmar of Solburg, that I'd join his noble band of heroes if he got an A or a B on his math test on Monday."

"I did it, barely. Eighty-two percent," Anthony proclaims. "Which is good because now we have an elven thief in our party, and we needed a thief to help us sneak into the hobgoblin lair."

"You're a thief?" I ask Anna, eyebrows going up even farther.

"I only use my skills to steal from the bad guys."

"Oh, right. Of course. Obviously."

"And Halmar is a human paladin," Anthony adds.

"I thought you were a wizard with fireballs, Anthony."

"That's in our *other* game, the one we play with Timmy."

"Yeah, we elected Timmy permanent Dungeon Master," Blake adds.

Blake is a pudgy kid with heavy glasses and thick brown hair that he parts on the left, and he always wears solid-colored sweatshirts or sweaters with a collared shirt underneath, top button undone. If ever someone needed a model of a nerdy kid, it'd be Blake. I'm confident he gets the best grades of any friend Anthony has, too. Nerdy or not, though, he's exceptionally polite whenever he comes over, he looks me in the eye when he shakes my hand, and I'm also confident he's the least likely to lead Anthony into trouble of all Anthony's friends. Not only that, his parents are wonderful people and live just a few blocks down the street in a house they bought after moving to Port Huron two years back. If Anthony had a dozen friends like Blake, I'd feel great.

"Our guys are too advanced for a brand-new character in that game, so we started a new one with Anna," Anthony explains patiently. "I decided to be a paladin, so I could dedicate myself to protecting her."

"I'm glad you did better in math this week, Anthony, or should I say, Tony. That's terrific. Anna, you want to get the fruit salad ready for dinner? I've got some chicken about ready to go in the oven."

"Sylvia the Stealthy will rejoin your righteous quest to infiltrate the hobgoblin stronghold at a later time," Anna says to the boys in a mock British accent as she stands up to follow me. "Just be sure I get an equal share of the loot from the hobgoblins, or else I'll just steal my share from you." All three of them laugh.

"Of course, m'lady," Anthony replies with an even worse British accent.

As we walk into the kitchen, I ask Anna, "So, you bribed him to do better?"

"I did. You told me once that if I offered to join their game, they'd make me queen, so I decided to try it and see."

"I'm not sure if I like that or not."

"What's wrong with it? My plan worked, right? How many other times has Tony got a B in math?"

"I'm really pleased you helped him do better, don't get me wrong. I just don't like the idea of bribing someone to do something they should be doing anyway. That won't happen in a couple years when he graduates. Besides, I think Anthony'd do anything you asked him to. How many teenage boys would ever turn down a suggestion from a beautiful grown woman?"

Anna gives me a smile while opening the fridge to get the fruit out. Not her best smile; more of a sarcastic smile reminding me I don't need to call her beautiful every time.

"I don't know if I have *that* much influence on him."

"You want more proof? Whose music were you listening to in there? It didn't sound like something Blake would play, and I know I've never heard Anthony listen to that stuff before."

"Oh, yeah. A couple of my cassettes didn't melt in the fire because I had them in my car that day. So, we made another deal. Tony got to play one tape of Heart, and then we had to listen to my Stevie Nicks tape after that."

"Isn't she the lady who used to sing with Fleetwood Mac?" I ask.

"Yeah. I like her better as a solo artist myself."

"So, you agree that Anthony'll do whatever you ask him to, though?"

"I don't know if I'd go that far."

"I've tried my best to teach him that a man should do certain things just because it's the right way to do them. I'm just not sure that bribery will be helpful if he gets too used to it. That makes sense, doesn't it?"

"Yes, those are good points, Larry, but he did do better. You want me to stop offering rewards, anyway?"

"I don't know. Let me think on that."

She's arranging the fruit out on the cutting board—apples, bananas, and strawberries—when I remember to ask Anna about work this week. "How'd your discussion with the store manager go?"

"Really well. He wants me to learn to be a checker who works the cash register."

"Does that pay more?"

"Not really, but he also said that in a couple months the person who runs the seafood department is probably going to retire. He's going to have that person train me to be the new seafood department head."

"And does that job pay more?"

"Sure does," she says while slicing a peeled banana into thin discs.

"That's wonderful, Anna. Maybe you can save enough to take more classes and speed up getting your degree or find a place of your own to live."

Did Anna's slicing pause for a split-second when I said that?

"Oops, that part about finding your own place again just slipped out, Anna. I'm not trying to get rid of you. Honestly."

She nods, returns my smile, then says, "Well, whatever happens, it's several months away, I think. Who knows? With my luck, the seafood manager will decide not to retire after all," she replies with a hesitant laugh.

"You have plans for tomorrow night?" I ask Anna.

"Maybe."

"What's that mean, maybe?"

"Well, they maybe involve you, Larry. If you'd like, I was thinking we could get some pizza and watch the NCAA tournament games tomorrow. I'm not working. Maybe the TV'll show the Michigan game against Akron."

"That's right, the tournament started today. Who do you think'll go farther this year? Michigan, or State? They're both in the field of sixty-four."

"I've always been more of a Spartans girl. You?"

"Hmm, just don't let Brad or Wally hear you say that. They've always been Wolverines guys, and I guess I have, too."

"Friendly bet, then, Larry?" Anna inquires while topping the strawberries.

"What're your terms?"

"If State goes farther, you let me keep rewarding Anthony for doing well in math. If the Wolverines win more games, I'll stop the bribes, and we'll see what happens that way."

"And if they go out in the same round?"

"I don't know," Anna giggles. "That didn't occur to me. Flip a coin?"

"You're on."

XXIII

Friday evening comes, and Anna and I are watching the Wolverines on television. The Spartans won yesterday, beating the University of Washington 72-70 in their first-round game, so the Wolverines must take care of business against Akron today for me to keep up in our bet. I feel good about their odds, though. They're the number two seed and have been in the top ten of college basketball every week of the season, getting as high as number two in the country for several weeks. Akron is a number fifteen seed, so they're supposed to be weaker.

"Where's Anthony tonight?" Anna asks. It's been a warm day for mid-March, so she's wearing a dark green Spartans t-shirt to go with blue jeans.

"He rode over to Justin's house."

"Justin, is he the one—"

"Yeah, of all Anthony's friends, I think I trust him the least. Maybe because he's a bit too much like Anthony."

"In what way?"

"He just seems like a kid who's angry with the world. Way more than Anthony, even. I barely know his parents because he hasn't lived in Port Huron very long."

"Do you think that's his problem, then, having trouble fitting in?"

"Maybe. It just seems weird that people like Justin hang out with kids like Blake and Timmy who seem squared away, but I guess they really like that game they play. I just hope Justin doesn't turn into a bad influence on the others. Not saying that he will, but I just worry."

The game's winding down now with Michigan winning, but it's closer than expected.

"It looks like our bet will go at least two more days," Anna tells me. "The Wolverines look like they've got this one. You said they're a good team, though."

"I've only watched a couple times, but yeah, they have some players. The big kid, Roy Tarpley, is the best, but Gary Grant can play, too, and I just have a feeling that that freshman kid, Glen Rice, is gonna turn into a ballplayer before he graduates."

"Larry, does it bother you at all when I ask you about yourself?"

"Not really, no. It's just that when you've been living on your own for most of the last twenty-five years, you don't get a lot of practice at talking about your feelings. I guess I'm a little rusty."

"Brad and Wally never ask you serious questions?"

"They do, but they asked them years ago, and the answers haven't changed much since then, so they stopped asking a while back."

"Can I ask one more, then?"

"Is it another big one, Anna?"

"Yes."

"Okay. I'll try. Ask away."

"I realize I haven't known you that long, Larry, and the circumstances of our meeting aren't exactly normal, but there's something I don't understand. Just in the short time I've known you, I think you're twice the man compared to most of the people I used to spend time with."

"That seems a little generous. I'll settle for one and a half," I venture to try to lighten things up just a little.

"See? That's what I mean. You're secure enough and comfortable enough with yourself to say something like that. No bravado and no dumb remarks like asking why it took me so long to notice. You're responsible, honorable, you don't run away from challenges, you care about the people around you, and you're dependable. I can't say that about too many of the guys I used to spend time with."

It's true that since Anna moved in with me, I've barely heard her mention any of her old friends, but I never thought to ask her why. "Give them another decade of experience, Anna. Even if everything you just said is true, it's not as though I was born like that. Some of those lessons I've learned the hard way. It takes time, and it takes some people more time than others."

"There you go again. Deflecting compliments left and right. Most of my other friends are about my age, and it seems like twenty-eight years ought to be long enough to grow up. The thing I'm trying to ask you, Larry, is how have you gone through life without meeting at least one woman smart enough to marry you?"

For a moment the question just hangs there while I fumble for an answer in my mind. Anna looks at me with her impossibly blue eyes, leaning forward on the couch with her hands on her knees.

Finally, I stammer, "You weren't joking when you said it was a big question, were you?"

"No, I'm not joking at all. I can't understand how it's possible for you to go this far without someone seeing all the things I see in you and appreciating them the way they should."

"It's a moot question anyway, isn't it, Anna? That part of my life's in the past. It's over. I wasn't good enough, whatever the reasons, so I don't spend too much time thinking about it anymore."

"Oh, no. I'm not letting you off that easy. I can't understand it, and I can't believe you've given up on yourself like that."

"If I've given up on me it's only because other people gave up on me first."

"You're still dodging my question," Anna says quietly, averting her eyes, hands now folded in her lap. "I just don't understand, and I want to understand."

The Long Way Home

I realize my cheeks are flushing a bit, and I said the last remark louder than I meant to. Anna probably thinks I'm getting upset with her, so I decide to try something different. "Anna, I'm not mad, but I don't know what to tell you. I can't explain why women don't like me enough to stay with me because I can't read their minds. Maybe I'm not the great catch you think I am, though."

"Why wouldn't you be?" she wonders, meeting my eyes again.

"A single guy with a moody teenager is a lot of baggage. I have a house, but it ain't the nicest house, and my life doesn't consist of much more than goin' to work, watching a little sports, then saving my energy, so I can work again the next day. I couldn't tell you the last time I had enough money to go on vacation. I'm not sure I can even tell you the last time I left the state of Michigan for any reason. I've had nothing but dead-end jobs lately, and that doesn't seem likely to improve. And, let's face it, the older I get, the more wear and tear starts to show."

I pause to think of something else to say. When I do, Anna moves right next to me, takes my head in her hands, and kisses me. My eyes go wide for just a moment before I remember to close them, lean in, and enjoy it. Maybe I should have expected this when Anna started asking about marriage, but it's been a while since my last romantic kiss.

After a few moments, our lips part, and we sit there staring at each other. "I'm not giving up on you, Larry," Anna tells me, her eyes locked on mine. "If other women have, it's their loss, but to me, you're everything a man should be, and I'm lucky you found me. Let me be part of your life."

She leans in again, and this time we wrap our arms around each other's shoulders as our lips meet. I hadn't noticed Anna is wearing perfume until now, but there's just a hint of it. After a few moments of this, Anna leans backward, gently pulling me down on top of her. We kiss and rub for a while before she pushes me back up to a sitting position. Then her hands drop to her waist, grasping her shirt to take it off. My chest flutters, and my skin tingles watching her.

I drop my hands and hold her arms gently when she's got her shirt halfway up her chest. "Not now, Anna."

"You're right. Let's try the bedroom," she replies, breathing audibly.

"No," I say again, shoulders slumping as I exhale slowly. "I mean us doing this isn't a good idea right now."

Anna eases back as I release her arms. I can see the wrinkles of the grab marks on her shirt when she lets go of it. "Why not, Larry? You're not taking advantage of me. I kissed you because I wanted to."

"I know you did. And part of me wants to just as much as you do."

"What're you waiting for, then? What's wrong?"

"Nothing's wrong with you. That's what's wrong. This isn't the right thing to do because you're young, and beautiful, and smart, with your whole life ahead of you still. Your future isn't with an old guy like me whose best days are long gone. I don't want you to become another woman I couldn't make happy and have you go through life wondering why you wasted time on me."

When I look at Anna for her reaction, I see what I expected. She draws her arms to her body, and her blue eyes dull while she sits up. "I'm sorry I failed," she says flatly and quietly.

"You aren't the failure. I am."

"No, I've failed, too. I wanted to show you I don't care about what you did wrong in the past, and I don't care that you're older, or think you aren't who you used to be. I wanted to show you I love you for who you are right now, and that that's good enough for me. So, I guess we're both failures because I can't get you to see that." Anna stands slowly, arms still wrapped around her body, and walks silently to the guest room where she sleeps.

I stand unmoving for a few moments, just staring at the couch where Anna sat, not knowing how to respond. Nothing's changed a minute later when Anna reemerges with her coat and walks to the front door.

"Be back in a while," she says softly over her shoulder as she passes me. I still don't know what to say. Maybe there's nothing to say except the obvious: I've made another mistake.

After I listen for a while and don't hear Anna's car start, I realize she must've gone for a walk, so she really will be back at some point. Hopefully, I'll think of something to tell her by then. I just hope that our conversation will last longer than the word "goodbye."

XXIV

Anthony's home and in bed, and it's past eleven when the front door opens quietly and Anna returns, eyes red and baggy. I've spent most of the past couple hours right where she left me, staring at the walls and thinking.

"I'm sorry—" we both say simultaneously. She smiles while rubbing her hands on the legs of her blue jeans. For me, the empty feeling that's been building in my stomach gnaws away. I feel a little better just knowing that Anna came back, even though I thought, or at least hoped, she would.

"Was it too soon?" she asks hurriedly. "Did I take you by surprise when I kissed you?"

"A little, yeah."

"I thought so. I wasn't sure if tonight was the right time, but I feel so comfortable and relaxed around you that I decided to go for it."

I nod slowly, looking down just a moment before looking at Anna again and asking, "I jumped to conclusions too quickly, didn't I?"

"What do you mean?"

"About your intentions. I could have, probably should have, just enjoyed the moment with you, but immediately I started thinking a year down the road instead."

"No, not necessarily. I was sorta thinking that way, too."

My stomach churns again, so I decide to pose the critical question without waiting any longer. As calmly as I can, I ask, "And did you change your mind about me while you were walking?"

Anna looks me in the eye. It's probably only a couple seconds but seems so much longer. "No. I haven't changed my mind. I didn't come to this point in a couple of days, Larry, and it's not a teenage crush. I've done a lot of thinking the past couple weeks, and I hope I'm old enough to know what I want in life and what type of people I want to spend my time with. If you don't want the same thing, though, I understand. If I screwed things up tonight, I'll pack up my belongings and look for a new place to stay tomorrow."

Anna's face softens, and she sits down in my worn armchair, running both hands through her straight blonde hair. Then, she looks to me for my reply, eyes shining.

"No, Anna, I don't want you to go. It's just that, in that moment, I couldn't believe someone like you could feel that way about me. It's been a couple years since someone my own age felt that way, let alone a stunningly beautiful woman in the prime of life. Part of me has a hard time believing it now, even after everything you've said. It's just all the letdowns and mistakes of the past haunting me. And the fear that even if you feel that way today, you'll change your mind before long. That's what frightens me the most. Everyone always changes their mind and walks away eventually."

Anna comes to sit beside me and puts her index finger under my chin to lift it up. I hadn't even noticed I'd dropped my head. "Will I ever be able to help you defeat those demons, Larry? Can anyone?"

"I don't know. It's been a long time since I even tried."

She puts her left arm around my shoulders and gives them a gentle squeeze. "Will you give me a chance? Please?"

"I think I need to sleep on it."

XXV

I'm sitting at the polished wooden table in my kitchen, head down from fatigue after a very busy Monday, while TV dinners cook in the oven for Anthony and me. I didn't get a good night's sleep last night, for one thing. Or, maybe better to say I didn't sleep long. After both of us thought things over on Saturday and Sunday, Anna and I talked deep into the night about so many things that I'm not sure I slept more than five hours.

Against my fears, I finally agreed that we should try dating. Well, that's a harsh way to put it. Like I told her many times, Anna has so much going for her. Or at least she would have a lot going for her if she had more confidence and more help from the people around her. And I'd be lying if I didn't admit her attractiveness helped seal my decision.

Deep down, though, I think I know how things'll end. Eventually, Anna will get tired of me, tired of dating a man fifteen years her senior, and will go back to her own age group. At heart, I think she looks at me partly as someone to date but also partly as the father that her biological father will never be. Someone who encourages her to be what she's capable of instead of someone trying to box her in and make her what he wants Anna to be.

That feeling won't last forever, though. I've seen it, dated women with it, before, but I think it's a first for Anna to have an older man she's close to who cares about her the way I do. She may not call it a teenage crush, but it's the same thing, just updated for women who are nearing thirty and need someone whom they can anchor themselves to when life gets rough.

Truth is, though, that I don't mind being that person for Anna. Take away her physical beauty, and she's still a very thoughtful young woman without many personality flaws that I can see. Like I said to Shawna on the phone a while back, if I was ten years younger, I would jump at the chance to date someone like Anna. Hell, most men my age would think I'm nuts for even having second thoughts about it and would probably have spent all weekend in bed with her.

I didn't, though, and it's because I like her too much to do that. And she deserves better from me. She'll get better from me. All my good intentions won't change the fact, however, that I don't think our dating relationship can go that far.

Sitting there at my kitchen table, however, I make up my mind. Despite my misgivings, for once, I'm not going to let them sabotage things with Anna. It may be over in a month, or it may end in a year, but I'm going to act like things have a chance to last and try my best to believe they will. Might as well, I decide with a little laugh. It's not like I've got any better offers on the table. Or ever will get a better offer, for that matter.

At this point I hear Anthony's door open and his footsteps marching into the kitchen.

"I'm hungry," he announces, slumping down into a chair.

"Dinner'll be ready in . . ." I look over at the oven clock, "about six or seven minutes. You can wait that long, right, Tony?"

"Sure, I guess."

"How's the math homework going."

"Pretty good, I think. Anna promised me she'd play D & D with us again if I can get good grades on all my math homework this week. I'm sure glad you two made that bet."

"She told you about the bet, huh?" It's true. My bet with Anna has ended already, and she won. The Spartans beat Georgetown, 80-

68, in their second-round game while the Wolverines lost in an upset against Iowa State, 72-69.

"Anna told me about your new bet, too. If the Spartans get to the Final Four, you'll play one whole D & D adventure with us next time we start a new one."

"It's true, I agreed to that."

"What happens if they don't make it?"

"Then Anna buys my psychology textbook for the night class I'm taking with her at the college spring quarter."

"You're gonna go to college?"

"I'm going to try it once and see what happens, yeah."

"That's great, Lawrence. In a couple weeks, you'll have your driver's license back, too. Maybe if you go to college, you can get a better job and not be a garbageman anymore."

"It's just one class, Tony. The counselor I talked to says you have to take a bunch to graduate from college, so it doesn't mean very much and probably won't get me another job all by itself. Does anyone at school give you a rough time about where I work?"

"Not really. I don't think most people even know that's what you do."

"But you've been holding your temper and staying out of trouble?"

"Yeah, no fights for a while. Mostly because I'm busy helping Timmy get to his classes."

"That's great you've stood by Timmy and you help him. I'm proud of you for that, Tony."

"He can't wait to meet Anna and adventure with her this weekend."

"Is your game at our house this week?"

"It's supposed to be, yeah. Except, now that Timmy has a wheelchair, I think we'll need to play in the kitchen instead of my bedroom, Lawrence. Is that okay with you?"

"Of course, yeah. I'll find something to do. Like read about psychology, maybe."

The Long Way Home

"I know it doesn't count for too much, Lawrence, but I really like Anna. I'm glad you two are dating now."

"Yeah, I like her a lot, too, buddy." I want so badly to believe those words will last.

The next evening, Tuesday, I'm outside looking at my flower bed. Anna's already left for work, so the driveway's empty. I don't have many flowers in my garden because my thumb tends to black more than green, but I have two I always take meticulous care of. A white rose bush and a yellow rose bush. Wally and his family brought the white one to me after my mother died, so I've taken special care of it, and then he brought the other after my sister's husband killed her.

"Just make sure I don't have to bring Anthony a red one for you for a few years, okay, buddy?" he told me while helping plant the yellow rose bush two years ago. Coming from anyone else it would have been a little insensitive, I suppose, but that's always how Wally tries to deal with sadness, through humor. The tears in his eyes while he said it were real enough.

I've always felt having a flower garden was a little incongruous considering that the lot next to mine on that side of the house isn't much more than a junkpile. No one's lived there in years. Two steps leading to the front porch are gone, the awning over the porch has a big hole where the rain rotted everything away, and someone broke one of the front windows years ago. And that's just the front of the house that faces the street. The rest of the place isn't in much better shape. In the back corner of the lot, where that property meets mine, a rusted Ford pickup sits. Whatever color it was once, it's a dull, pitted orange now, with blackberry vines growing through the empty windows of the cab. I'm not sure how they can grow there, considering how much motor oil has probably leaked into the ground below that truck, but I guess blackberries'll grow just about anywhere.

I come out here occasionally, especially when the sadness over losing Samantha hits me. I still miss my mother, too, but her death was normal. She didn't live that long compared to some people these days, sixty-three years, but she worked hard and lived a full, active life to the end of her days.

Samantha is different. She was my older sister, but only by two years, so we were close. Not that we talked daily as adults, but the kind of closeness that comes from growing up together without many other family members around. We had that automatic trust that comes from knowing your sibling is on your side, no matter what. I think about Samantha often, even if the thoughts are just sadness that she isn't here anymore. Like Timmy, a car accident struck her down, right in the prime of life.

To this day, I have no idea why she let Anthony's father drive that fateful night. He'd been drinking, but she hadn't. Samantha rarely drank. She was the better driver of the two, anyway. More responsible in every way, for that matter. I just can't understand why she wasn't behind the wheel, but now I'll never have the chance to ask her.

So, for several minutes I just stand there, eyes closed, and breathe. I never had a chance to say goodbye to her. That's one of the worst parts about sudden accidents—you can't anticipate them, so there's no chance to tell someone how much they mean to you for the last time.

I open my eyes again when the wave of sadness passes. As I stand there looking forlornly at the two rose bushes, I think I hear a sound, a rustling, maybe, coming from behind my house. No houses stand behind mine—it's just lightly wooded land, mostly beech and birch but with a few dogwoods interspersed, choked by lots more blackberry vines and overgrown grass.

I walk toward the back of the house to look. There it is again. Definitely a rustling sound. "Come on out, Crab, I can hear you back there."

Moments later, Crab Parker appears. "Yogi, we gotta talk, brother."

"Heavy steps, Crab. I heard you comin' this time."

"Must be that job makin' me soft."

Which isn't a bad thing, I suppose. Crab still looks presentable—he's shaved his face to a neat beard, his eyes appear clear, and he's got new boots on his feet. The fatigue jacket's still on, though, which means Crab's here on business.

"What are you sneakin' around still for, Crab? It's okay to use the front door."

"Not today it ain't, Yogi. I know things. I've got more dope on that fire you wanted me to look into, and it's hairy, man."

With everything happening with Anna lately, I'd almost forgotten. "Let's go through the back door, then, Crab."

I thought Crab'd find my kitchen safe enough, but he draws the shades on the kitchen window. "Can't let no one see me here, dude."

"What'd you learn, Private Parker?"

"Here's the scoop, Yogi. My buddy, same one who was in the alley when the fire started, followed the Barrys one evening earlier this week and figured out they were eatin' at that nice Italian restaurant. You know the one?"

"Yeah, I know the one. Never could afford to eat there, but I know the place."

"Well, my man's hangin' in the back like he sometimes does. He went to school with the daughter of the owner, and she's one of the cooks, and she'll give him a meal every now and then if the restaurant's about to throw somethin' out and he's hangin' around."

"Wow, maybe there's something good about being from a town where everyone knows everyone after all. Anyway, carry on, Crab."

"Since he gets food there sometimes anyway, he don't attract no attention when the employees head out back to have a cigarette on their break. In fact, he knows some of 'em, and they share smokes."

"The employees told him stuff, Crab?"

"I'm gettin' to that, dude. Yeah, he asked if the Barrys were eatin' that night, and the guy who waited on their table said yeah, but they had an unusual guest. Wanna know who, Yogi?"

"That's why you're here, isn't it, Crab?"

"Take a guess."

"The apartment complex owner."

"Nope. Higher up than that."

"The mayor?"

"Not quite that high, but the fire chief."

"No shit. We were right, then. Looks like he might be on the take like we thought. Nice work, Private Parker."

"I ain't done yet, brother. Wanna know some more I found out?"

"I'm not sure. Do I?"

"Well, you asked for more dope, so you're gettin' it."

"Carry on, private."

"When I found out the fire chief is in on things, I went into motion myself. See, I know the sister of the chief's secretary. Never mind how."

I never ask questions when Crab says that. Usually, those words indicate illicit activity of some sort that I'd rather not know about, so I let him be. I shrug, indicating he can go on.

"So, I call her up, the sister, and ask if she'd like to get some drinks. She's feelin' a little depressed lately, so she agrees. That was last night."

"You didn't do anything underhanded, did you, Crab?"

"Nah, dude, I just bought the drinks and let the alcohol do the rest. It's crazy what you can do when you've got some money in your pocket and don't have to bum things off other people."

"Crazy, indeed. You like the feeling?"

"I just might get used to havin' work and havin' some cash, yeah. Anyway, here's the rest of my investigation. I know this girl's a lightweight with the booze, so after about three drinks, I start askin' her how her sister's doin' and all. Turns out, they've fought a fair amount lately, and before long she's goin' on about how the bitch is screwin' the fire chief."

"She know that for sure, Crab, or just sayin' she suspects it because she was drunk and her tongue was loose?"

"She claims she walked in on 'em one time. The chief bribed her not to say nothin', but a bribe's nothin' a healthy flow of alcohol can't overcome, right, Yogi?"

"What's that have to do with the Barrys, Crab? You thinkin' those bribes are drainin' the chief's bank account, so he's lettin' the Barrys bribe him to recoup the cash so that everything looks proper when his wife goes to write a check or gets a bank statement?"

"Could be, Yogi. That don't sound too far off, brother. That, or they know about his affair, too, and are usin' that against him."

"Maybe I'll do a little work of my own on this story. I work for the city. It should be easy enough to check some records and see where the Barrys buy property. Maybe that'll turn up a pattern that shows something. Maybe I'll also ask Brad. He knows a guy in the City Records division."

"I'll keep my ear to the streets and see what more I can learn, man."

"I don't know about this, though, Crab. I mean, what're we gonna do even if we find stuff out?"

When I look at Crab, he's got this look on his face I can't remember seeing in years. Rather than cringing or slouching like he usually does, looking off to the side and avoiding eye contact, he's sitting up straight and looking me in the face. His chin is up, his shoulders are square, and he looks confident, like he's got a reason for being here. It pains me to remember this is what he used to look like when I knew him as a teenager, back before he went to 'Nam and his life spiraled downward. Although he's looking at me, he hasn't answered yet. "What is it, Crab? You look different. Did I say something on accident?"

"I don't care what happens to me, Larry, I just want to do somethin' that's good for once," he splutters, suddenly breaking down in a way I haven't seen in almost two decades. I've seen Crab cry before, but it's always been the crying of someone in despair who feels life caving in on them and doesn't know what else to do. This time, though, I see the same expression and tears I remember seeing when Crab gave up a home run to lose an important baseball game in high school. The tears that someone cries when they think they've let down people who care about them.

"I don't get it, Crab. What do you mean?"

"How much money have you given me over the years, Larry?" he says while rubbing the moisture from his eyes.

"I don't know. I never kept count, and it doesn't matter to me."

"And how many times did you let me crash on your couch when I didn't have nowhere to sleep?"

"Beats me. Why does that matter now?"

"There ain't too many people who've treated me decent since I got screwed up in the head, Larry. I've done a lot of taking, and I ain't given much back to anyone. Now, I've finally been straight for a while, and it's because you helped me."

"That was just luck, Crab. I didn't know that job would be there. It was me bein' hopeful more than anything else."

"But you didn't give up on me, and you kept tryin' to help, Larry. There ain't many people who can say that. The rest all gave up on ol' Crab years ago. I can't really blame 'em 'cause I ain't good for much anymore, but you stuck with me more than most."

"I'm glad I helped. That's what a friend does. Both you and Todd were always good to me, and that means somethin'. But I still don't see what all this has to do with the fire and all this bribery."

"What I'm tryin' to say is, if things get hairy and you need someone to take the bullet for you, I'll be there."

"I can't imagine it'll ever come to that, Crab."

"Probably not, brother. And I know it sounds weird to hear me tell someone they can count on me because usually it ain't true, but I'm with you if you need me."

The Long Way Home

With that, Crab Parker stands up, clicks his heels to attention, gives a formal salute, and strides out the back door.

I have no idea what brought about this change in Crab. There's no way it's all because of me helping him get a job, I know that much, but I barely held back the tears myself when he looked like the teenage Crab for a few moments. It's strange how sometimes I just remember images from twenty years ago, but I recall the good times with Todd and Crab, hitting baseballs on the high school field together all Saturday long because we had nothing better to do and didn't want to do anything else. Then we'd toss back some drinks afterward and talk baseball into the night. Those were great times, times I'll never forget, but never again more than a memory. Vietnam made sure of that.

It occurs to me that, in a way, Vietnam did to Crab what the car accident did to Timmy. True, Vietnam wrecked Crab's mind while with Timmy it's his body that'll never be the same. But in other respects, it's almost the same. Both were promising young kids when something traumatic changed their lives forever. The trauma wasn't their fault, wasn't of their making, yet they'll pay the price forever. I just wish I could find some better way to help them.

Staring down at my kitchen table as the shadows lengthen, I drum my fingers a couple times and then pick up an apple from the basket that Anna put there yesterday. Then it hits me. If she were here, she'd add this scene to my list of good things I've done right. Maybe I can, too.

XXVI

When Friday rolls around, Anthony's friends come over for dinner. Timmy's there, and Blake, and Justin, plus Cory, the last member of their gaming circle. Cory is a year younger, just finishing intermediate school, but the boys let him join their game because he's Timmy's friend. Plus, Anthony's convinced that he's good luck. According to Anthony, Cory once saved against a medusa turning him to stone when the odds were bleak, so he's lucky. Hard to top the logic of a fifteen-year-old, I suppose.

But to my shock, it's nearly eight o'clock and the kids haven't rolled a single die yet. Instead, they're all in my living room watching the basketball game, Michigan State against Kansas, cheering wildly whenever the Spartans score. Three empty pizza boxes rest on my coffee table, their salty, cheesy contents long gone. I guess the boys really like having Anna in their game. Enough to stop playing in order to find out how long she'll stay, and if I'll have to join them someday.

As fate would have it, however, I'm safe. The game is an overtime thriller, but Kansas wins in the end, 96-86, for its fifteenth win in a row. The Spartans do well against the Jayhawks' top player, a forward named Danny Manning who fouls out before the game ends, but another Jayhawk named Calvin Thompson rises to the occasion and scores twenty-six points. On the outside, I cheer for the Spartans like everyone else, but on the inside I'm quite content to see Kansas win and have Anna buy my psychology book when school starts in two weeks. A bet's a bet, after all, girlfriend or not.

What encourages me even more than that, however, is that Timmy seems happy and in good spirits, even though I can see that his arm muscles are getting thinner and his shirt is too big for him now. I volunteer to wheel him into the kitchen to begin their game, but it just saddens me once more to see how much one event he couldn't control changed his life. While everyone else plays, I lie on my bed and think about the cosmic injustice. In my sadness for Timmy, though, I finally make up my mind on an idea I've been thinking over.

The game breaks up about ten, and everyone gets ready for their parents to pick them up. Outside of Timmy, Blake is the only one old enough to have his driver's license, but his parents won't let him drive with other kids in the car quite yet, so the rest must wait. As they go outside and keep talking about the horde of zombies that almost took down Blake's character, I decide to share my idea with Anna.

"Anna, I had an inspiration tonight," I say, grasping her arm lightly. She's got on a gray-and-green Spartans sweatshirt with, now that I look closely, a little pizza sauce stain near the collar.

"You're going to join us in our game anyway because hanging out with teenage boys on Friday is so much fun?" she says with her big smile and a wink.

"And how many zombies did Sylvia slay tonight?"

"Not many. Thieves are good for sneaking around. They aren't so tough in big melees, especially when they're only level two like me. I leave that to the paladins like Tony. Anyway, what's your idea?"

"I think I might've found a reason to go to college after all."

Her eyes brighten to go with her smile. "Yes?" Anna says excitedly, now gripping my arm back.

"I was thinking about Timmy a couple times lately, and what lousy luck he had, and wishing I could help him."

"But I thought his injuries are permanent."

"Maybe they are, but I found out there's something called a physical therapist who helps injured people get better."

"I think that takes years and years of school. Are you sure you're up for that?"

"No, but yesterday afternoon after work I called that school counselor you introduced me to. He also told me that being a physical therapist takes at least a bachelor's degree, and that some of them go to school even longer than four years."

"So, why are you so excited, then?"

"I was really downcast when he said that, but then the counselor also said there's such a thing as a physical therapist assistant, and that I can be one of those with an associate degree from the college. That's what I want to be."

"Larry! You finally have your dream of what to be in life!"

"Yeah, I guess I do. Thanks to you, Anna."

XXVII

Several weeks later, it's Wednesday, but I'm not working. I finally quit my job in sanitation and accepted Brad's offer to work for him. However, the construction season hasn't heated up yet, at least not in Port Huron this year, so some days I don't work for Brad, and this is one of them. Instead, I go down to Greg's Motors to check on Crab. I haven't heard from him since that strange day in my kitchen.

He's under the hood of a car, changing someone's oil, when I get there, so I agree to wait until he goes on break. When that time comes, he spends a long time washing his hands before coming over to shake mine.

"Larry, brother, good to see you, dude. I was just gonna check in this afternoon, but you beat me to it."

"Yeah, no construction work goin' on today. You learn anything new?"

"Just yesterday. That's why I was comin' to see you after work today."

Although the garage is nearly empty right now, we step outside to talk. It's a nice day, all in all, just a few clouds. Windy, though, so naturally enough I'm wearing a navy windbreaker and blue jeans.

"So, what've you learned, Crab?"

"Not much, except this. I haven't heard no news of the Barrys for a while from my sources, so I decided to do a little work of my own, except instead of lookin' for the Barrys, I decided to shadow the apartment owner for a bit instead."

"And that turned up something?"

"Yesterday it did, yeah. He was just leavin' his office in the evening when this huge guy meets him at the door."

"When you say huge, you mean fat?"

"Naw, Yogi, just huge. Tall and muscular. Like a pro football player looks."

My stomach tightens. "Was he about thirty or so? Short beard, bushy eyebrows?"

"I wasn't close enough to see his eyebrows, but the rest sounds about right, yeah."

"If it's who I'm thinking it is, Crab, it's Anna's old boyfriend."

"Maybe, Yogi, but wanna know what I heard him say?"

"Probably not. But I asked you to tell me, so go ahead."

"He gets in the owner dude's face, shoulders all puffed out and everything, and growls at him that he heard the owner was having second thoughts on their deal. The small guy denied it, but this big guy wasn't havin' it. Said his friends were gettin' upset and impatient."

"Friends in this case meanin' the Barrys?"

"He didn't use their name, but yeah, that's what I figured because next he said how his friends wanted the deal done quick, and that if the owner ever saw him again, it wasn't going to be pleasant. Then he patted the little guy on the shoulder and walked away."

"See anything else?"

"Not much. The owner goes back inside his office, comes out after a few minutes with a couple folders, and then leaves. That was it."

"Well, Crab, I did my research, too, like I said I would. The Barrys have developed property all over town. Brad's guy in the City Records Department told Brad that they seem to make a lot of deals, but all the deals seem to be on the level. He's never heard anything suspicious. So, either this is a new move on their part, or they're really good at covering their tracks."

"Or the guy in Records is on their payroll, too," Crab offers, eyebrows raised.

"Yeah, there's that, too. I asked Brad about it, but Brad thinks he's honest. Hard to know for sure, though. What do you think we should do, Crab? We can't just walk up to the apartment owner and tell him to come clean to us."

"You want me to drop it? I mean, what's all this intel good for, Yogi?"

"I still don't know, but I just don't like the feeling of all this. Especially now that Rickey's involved. I ever tell you what he did to Anna?"

"Not really. Just what he did to you."

"He threw her across their apartment and almost busted up her shoulder. Bruised her face all to hell. He's got a restraining order against him right now, and he's observed it so far, but if he's got the Barrys in his corner, maybe he'll get bolder. You think I should be worried about that, Crab?"

"I would be if it were me."

"What do you think we should do, then?"

"I'll try to keep an eye on this new guy if I can. He shouldn't be hard to spot."

"Sounds good, Crab. Just be careful yourself. I don't think he tries too hard to cover his tracks, but I don't know him that well. All I know is how dangerous he can be."

XXVIII

"You've kept your pledge, Larry. I still miss seeing you around here, but I know you've done it for the right reasons." Wally reaches across his bar to shake my hand.

"I know, it's weird. I feel tempted sometimes, but Anna helps a lot."

"How 'bout them Tigers? Four wins in a row after yesterday."

"What about 'em? That makes 'em, what, one game better than even? They got a ways to go if they want to get in the pennant chase."

"They got time to turn it up and make a run, though. It's only late June. The season has three months still to go."

"Maybe. We'll see."

"I'm glad you finally let Brad hire you on his construction crew."

"It's takin' some gettin' used to, doin' physical work again, but my back's holdin' up so far, and Brad offers better pay than the City does, especially now that it's June and the work's steadier. But, today's Saturday, so I thought I'd stop by and see you."

"What're you drinking now instead of beer and whiskey?"

"Lots of coffee, mostly. Anna wants me to try tea, too, but I can't get used to the taste."

"My wife tried the same with me, but I'm with you. I just don't like the stuff."

"Oh, and one more thing. Since I've been taking this night class a couple nights a week, Anna gave me something called Jolt cola. It's like Coke or Pepsi, but it's supposed to have even more caffeine to keep your energy up, which I need now that I'm working harder than ever with Brad. Couldn't stand the Jolt, though. Pass on it if you ever have a choice, okay?"

Wally gestures behind him with a broad grin. "I think I've got plenty of drink options here, don't you? How's college goin' though? The quarter over now?"

"Yeah, quarter's over. It went way better than I thought it would. Anna helped me a lot, and I returned the favor when I could, but I did better than I ever expected. I got a B grade in my first class. It's only one class, though. I've gotta pass about fifteen or twenty to get my degree, so you won't see me flashin' my diploma around here for a while yet."

"When you do get your diploma, I'd like a copy to frame, okay?"

"You can't be serious. You gonna put that up in your bar where people can see it? Don't embarrass me like that."

"Nah, not in the bar. In my office. To remind me of the day my friend became the person I always thought he could be." Wally claps me on the shoulder from across the bar.

"Well, like I said, I've got a way to go yet. Don't hold your breath waitin'."

"I tell you, Larry, this woman Anna's been real good for you."

"I think you're right. The only thing I feel bad about now is that I almost turned her down when she said she wanted to date. I still don't know what'll happen in the future, but the present is pretty good."

"I'm not gonna say it," Wally looks down with a grin while he wipes away at his spotless bar.

"You can say it."

"I told you so. That first night when Anna came in here, I told you not to give up on yourself. I had no idea you'd ever actually get together with Anna—I meant it in a more general way—but I told you that you've still got lots to offer. Did Anna ever mention why she had a wedding ring on the first night she came in, by the way?"

"Yeah, I did ask her about that once. She told me she keeps a fake ring in her purse for when she wants to go places by herself and not get hassled by men."

"Good idea on her part."

"I thought it was clever, too."

"I still think it's great the two of you are together, Larry. Although I'm with you that I never expected someone so much younger to be the one to realize how good you are, but maybe it's because she took time to really know you, you think?"

"Maybe. It was an awful lot of coincidences that brought us together, but I'm happy they did. It seems like we complement each other. She doesn't have enough self-esteem, even though she's bright, caring, and very good at school. And then, she doesn't have much help from her family, either. I *think* her parents know we're dating by now, but I wouldn't swear to it."

"And it sounds like she's given you that youthful spark, or optimism, or whatever you want to call it, to shake you loose from the doldrums."

"Hey, easy there," I say sternly, raising a fist, before breaking into a grin of my own and dropping my arm.

"Just don't get mad and punch me in the gut again, okay? Where is Anna today? Working?"

"No, she and Anthony are practicing driving in the high school parking lot."

"The boy finally got the confidence to get behind the wheel, huh? Well, can't blame him after seeing what happened to Timmy. It's good that he's tryin' though. I always—"

Wally's interrupted by the phone ringing in the back of his bar. He reaches it in a couple strides and lifts the receiver. Because it's only early afternoon and not many patrons are present, I can hear his half of the conversation.

"Yeah, he's here."

A pause.

"Sure, I'll let him know."

Wally pauses with his hand over the phone. "Larry, it's Anna. She says something just came up. Might be serious."

"With Anthony and her car?"

"Nah. She says Shawna just called the house wantin' to talk to you. Does Anna know that's the woman you dated a few years back?"

"I don't think I've told her anything about Shawna."

"Just a second, Slugger." Wally lifts his hand and says into the phone, "Is it urgent, Anna? Did Shawna say what she needs to talk with Larry for?"

Finally, Wally gets the idea to wave me around the bar and just hand the phone to me. He stands back while I talk and pretends to go back to wiping the bar.

"Anna, what's going on? You said Shawna called the house?"

"Yeah, she sounded really flustered and nervous and said she wanted to speak with you. I told her you were gone but didn't say where because I didn't know if you wanted to call her back."

"If she sounded like something was wrong, then yeah, I better call her back. Can you relay her number? I don't have it memorized."

"Who is she, Larry?"

I pause for just a split second before deciding to be honest. "An old girlfriend. But don't worry, she's no threat. Just a friend now. She got married about five years back and lives over in Lansing. She didn't mention any of this on the phone?"

"No, she sounded emotional, pretty shook up. Although I think it took her by surprise when I answered instead of you or Tony."

"Do you trust me when I say she's just an old friend, Anna?"

"Yes, I trust you." Unlike me, she didn't pause.

"That's good because she's a big part of the reason we're dating. You've met her once, or at least seen her."

"When?"

"The day you brought flowers to the hospital but then left. Shawna passed you in the hallway. When she came into Anthony's room, she told me you looked distraught with yourself rather than mad at me. If it hadn't of been for that, I probably would've hung up the phone on you when you called me to apologize. So, in a way, she's the reason we're together right now, if you can believe that."

"I'll be darned. I sorta remember a woman being in the hallway that day, but I didn't even look at her."

"Be that as it may, can you give me the number, so I can call her and find out what's wrong?"

After Anna relays the seven digits, I look at the paper. Something doesn't seem right, but I can't put my finger on what. "Okay, thanks, Anna. You sure you're fine with me calling her? I think I owe it to her to at least talk a little bit."

"Yes, I said I trust you. If she's a friend, you should help her out. Just no staying overnight, okay? You only get to do that at my apartment," she teases through the phone.

"Right, no sleepovers at Shawna's house. Got it. If there's anything important happening, I'll tell you about it when I get home, okay?"

"Sure. I love you, Larry."

Although I've heard it many times by now, it still feels amazing whenever Anna says those words. My chest feels like it's expanding, and I tingle a little, too. "I love you, too, Anna," I reply, with no hesitation this time.

Hanging up, I say to Wally, "You hear all of that?"

"Half of it. You need to make another call?"

"Sounds like it. Okay to call from here?"

"Of course. You said Shawna English called for you, right?"

"Yeah, seems weird that she'd call on a Saturday afternoon, but I figure I should see what she needs."

"No problem, Larry. You know how to dial for long distance from here to call Lansing?"

Then the proverbial ton of bricks hits me in the head.

The Long Way Home

"Wait a second, Wally. That's what it is. I knew something didn't feel right about the number Anna relayed to me. This isn't Shawna's home phone number. She gave her home number to me last year when I was in the hospital, and I don't recall all the numbers exactly, but I'm pretty sure this is a different one. Let's get a phone book and see if it's local."

In a few seconds Wally fetches a phone book from under the bar. He looks at the slip of paper with Shawna's new number on it and then scans down the page with his finger.

"Yep, it's local, all right. Lots of people have the same first three digits. Can't tell you where she's calling from though, of course."

"Well, I'll call the number and see."

I dial, at the same time noticing that my heart rate has quickened and my index finger shakes just a bit. Should I be worried? Maybe. The whole situation just has an unnatural feeling to it. The person on the other end picks up on the third ring. It's a man's voice, not Shawna.

"This is the Elmcourt Motel. Can I help you?"

The Elmcourt? That's on my old garbage route. It's here in Port Huron and not one of the nicer places in town. Not the scummy type of place where prostitutes operate but certainly on the cheap end. The knot in my stomach gets a little bigger.

"I was called from this number by a woman named Shawna English. Can you connect me to her room, please?"

"Of course. May I ask who is calling, so I can tell her?"

"Larry Edwards. Mrs. English called my home, and I'm returning her call."

"Just a moment, sir."

I hear a brief silence, and then the phone rings again. Shawna picks up on the second ring.

"Larry, is it you?"

"Yeah, it's me. Why are you calling me from the Elmcourt? When did you get into town?" I strive to sound nonchalant to cover how nervous this is making me. I'm not sure if I pull it off, though.

"Larry, can I see you sometime this evening? Something's happened that's really important I need to tell you about." Shawna's voice is higher pitched than normal, I think, although that could be just the phone. But her words come out very quickly, too, and there's no mistaking that.

"Of course, we can meet. This is pretty short notice, though. Is something wrong?"

"I think it'll work better if I explain in person. Please, will you meet me here? The sooner you can make it, the better. Room 109."

It won't take long. Port Huron isn't that big a place, and the Elmcourt's been there for years. Every local knows where it is. But now I sense the hairs on my arms and neck lifting. Shawna didn't answer me by confirming something was wrong in so many words, but this sure isn't normal. Her parents live in Port Huron, too. Why isn't she staying there?

"Larry?" she says in a shaky voice as I realize I was thinking instead of answering her.

"I'll be there in ten minutes," I say while hanging up. At the same time, I feel the chills begin, and when I try to swallow, my breathing catches momentarily. Again, maybe it was just the phone line, but something in the tone and pace of Shawna's voice sounded very unlike her.

"Isn't good, is it, Slugger?" Wally asks.

"I don't know, but I have a feeling you're right. If Shawna's here in town and says she needs to meet, I think I'd better do it, don't you?"

"You still care about her?"

"Enough that I don't want something bad to happen to her if I can prevent it, yeah."

"Then go. You know how to handle yourself. Maybe it ain't as bad as it sounds, anyway."

———

The Long Way Home

Pulling up to the Elmcourt, I stop in front of 109. Shawna's drawn the curtains and although I see a light inside, I knock cautiously all the same.

After a moment, I hear footsteps on carpet and the latch to the door moves inside. When Shawna opens the door, she stands back from it, almost hiding behind it, while she motions me inside.

"Thanks so much for coming, Larry," she says while sitting down on the bed of her room. I take one of the two foam-padded wooden chairs at the table by the window. Scanning the room, I see two suitcases on the floor and a coffee cup on the dresser by the bed. Whatever the reason Shawna left Lansing to come here, it seems she did it quickly.

Looking at Shawna, her eyes are bloodshot, badly, and her formerly long dark hair is now a much lighter brown and barely shoulder length. Her clothes, a white sweatshirt with a flower print and blue jeans, seem to hang from her body, as if she's lost considerable weight, and her cheeks look drawn.

"Are you in trouble?" I ask, voice quivering just a touch.

"Only trouble of my own making," she replies, looking down at her hands folded in her lap. "I'm not in any danger, if that's what you mean."

"You look like you're on your way somewhere and you're in a hurry."

"I'm going to stay with my parents for a little while. That's what the suitcases are for. I know it looks like I rushed out the door and I'm on the run, but like I said, I'm not running from danger."

"Then why call me from here? Why not just go straight to their house? Or to a friend's house?"

"My parents are out of town and won't be back until tomorrow morning. And I wanted to talk with you first."

"Why me?"

"My marriage is over, Larry."

I just pause and stare for a long time. Shawna's bloodshot eyes look back at me a moment before she wraps her arms around her body and bends over, like she's folding herself in half.

Finally, I find my voice. "Can I ask what happened? What'd Vernon do to you?"

"You're assuming it was his fault."

"It wasn't?"

"Like I said, trouble of my own making," Shawna answers as she draws her legs up onto the bed, pulling them into her chest.

"What happened, then?"

"It's about my son, George."

"Did something happen to him? Where is he?"

"George is fine. He's with Stacy right now. You remember Stacy Thomas, right?"

I nod. She'd been Shawna's best friend when Shawna lived in Port Huron.

"I'm not sure I understand, Shawna. If it's about George, but he's fine, then what went wrong?"

Shawna closes her eyes and puts her head down, squeezing herself further into a ball.

"Shawna?"

"A couple weeks ago I had to admit to Vernon that George isn't his son."

"He's not?"

"No. He's yours."

XXIX

I sit there, mouth open, staring at Shawna as if she needs to say it again for it to be real. Finally, she looks me in the face.

"H-he's my son?" I stammer.

She nods. "Please don't hate me for not telling you before."

"How long've you known? Six years? Since he was born? Or even before that?"

Another nod. "Before. I always knew he was yours."

"I need a minute," I say, standing.

"Larry, don't go," Shawna says, popping up from the bed and taking me by the shoulder. "Please just let me explain before you go," she continues, the sobs beginning.

Feeling a little lightheaded myself, I push her arm away while saying, "You've got a lot to explain."

"Things started unraveling a couple weeks ago," Shawna begins. She's trying hard to keep her composure, speaking quickly while her voice trembles, but still looking me in the eye. "Vernon was playing with George. Vernon's often said how he doesn't think George looks like him at all, and I always tried to tell him George would when he got older. But Vernon was looking at George and finally realized that George has brown eyes while we both have blue eyes. That's when he started asking me hard questions. He knew that George was born about eight months after we started dating, but I'd always been able to convince him George was just premature. He was a little small when he was born, so it worked."

"You met Vernon one month after we parted ways?"

"Just about. I finally told him the truth about George because I thought he'd understand. After all, he's raised George as his son for six years, hasn't he?"

"But he didn't understand."

"No, he didn't. He got so angry with me that for the first time in our relationship I thought he was going to hit me. He didn't, but he was so enraged I thought he would."

"What happened next, Shawna?"

"Remember when I told you how religious Vernon has become in the past few years and how he's always talking about family values? Well, I thought that he'd be understanding and forgiving if I explained everything to him honestly. Instead, he lashed out at me verbally, calling me a deceitful whore, saying I'd dishonored him and polluted our marriage bed, things like that. He shouted that I was nothing but a tramp who's addicted to pills."

"Vernon really flew off the handle."

Shawna just nods, still struggling to stay calm and keep back more tears and then says, "We joined a new church a few months ago. It's even more traditional and conservative than the last one we went to. It's where Vernon's parents go, too."

"Can I guess they encouraged Vernon to divorce you?"

"I never asked them because they've never liked me and thought Vernon made a mistake when he married me, but I'm sure they told him he should. I don't know if he needed any encouragement to do it, but I'd guess they backed his decision."

Shawna pauses for a moment, looking to me for my response. I'm not sure what to tell her, so I rub my forehead and try to think.

"Did I do the wrong thing by telling Vernon the truth, Larry? I really thought I could get him to understand."

"I can't say if you did the right thing or not. I'm not sure I would have understood and just forgiven everything either, if I were him. This is a really big deal, Shawna. Why didn't you just tell him the truth six years ago?"

"Because six years ago I was scared, lonely, frightened, drinking too much, and not thinking clearly all the time," she replies in a cracked voice through the tears. "I didn't want to lose Vernon because I was frightened that I was getting too old and wouldn't be able to meet another man who wanted to raise children. After you and I stopped dating, I was so depressed, and I thought he might be my last chance to become a mother and have a family."

I don't know if it should, but Shawna's last comment causes a squeezing, aching sensation in my chest. It's a feeling I've had so many times myself over the past decade—wishing for a normal family life but knowing my chances of having one were shrinking with each passing day. So, I tell her, "And you were afraid to tell me, too, for the same reasons."

"Yes. And because I know you too well. I knew if I told you, you'd want to take responsibility."

"You're probably right."

"Even after I started getting sober in the months before George was born, I thought about telling you so many times, and I almost did. But you didn't deserve to have me throw that on you when I knew we were done dating, and I knew I'd lose Vernon if I did."

"And yet, you lost him anyway."

"I know it. And it's all my fault. I just didn't know how to tell either of you."

"So, this is what you came up with? Telling me in a motel room six years later?" It sounds more insensitive than I meant it to. The feeling in my chest isn't going away, and it's distracting me.

"Maybe I shouldn't have told you at all. Kept it to myself. Would that have been better? I thought I was doing what you would do. Face up to the truth, no matter how painful."

She has a point. I've always believed that while you can't change what you've done in the past, you can act responsibly in the present. Or, as a baseball coach told me long ago, "You can't change what you did last inning. But you can change what you do this inning." Not all that profound, perhaps, but it made sense when I was sixteen.

"What do you plan to do now?" I ask Shawna.

"Move back here, at least for a while. Get custody of George and raise him the best I can."

"What else?"

"That's it. That's as far as I've gotten right now. I'm not over the shock of everything else yet."

"Does George know everything that's going on?"

Shawna breaks down again. "Yes. He came in from playing outside just as Vernon and I were yelling at each other. He's only just turned six, so he doesn't understand everything, but I tried to explain things while we drove here. Vernon's almost never yelled at me, so he knew things were bad."

I put my hands to my face and rub my eyes for a while.

"I'm so sorry to lay this on you today, Larry. What else could I do, though? Would you rather I hadn't told you?"

"I don't know. That's a tough question to throw at me right now."

"There's another reason I wanted to ask you alone."

"What's that?"

"You're the only one besides Vernon who knows you're George's father. I haven't told anyone else, although my parents probably suspect the truth. Vernon knows because he remembers we were together right before I met him. But I haven't told any of my friends why Vernon and I are splitting up. They all think it's because we decided we weren't in love anymore."

"Is that a smart move, Shawna? Concealing the truth from everyone around you? I'd think the fact that you're here with me right now would show that's a bad tactic."

"I only decided to conceal it until I could tell you. I thought you deserved to be the first person to know."

"Well, I guess hearing it firsthand from you is better than secondhand from someone else."

"And because I want you to know that if you don't want me to, Larry, I'll never tell anyone you're George's father. If you want nothing to do with me after today, I'll walk away, and you'll never hear from me again. I won't use this to try to drag you back into my life or do anything else you don't want to do. I've done enough damage to your life as it is."

The lightheadedness is almost gone now, although I can only imagine what Shawna feels inside. "I'm going to need some time to figure out how I feel."

"I'll be at my parents' house, for the next few days, at least."

"Right."

"I mean it, Larry. I'm not going to ask you to do anything. If you decide to never talk to me after today, I don't blame you."

On the way home, I pull over in a restaurant parking lot, trying to think of what to tell Anna. Of course, I have to tell her something. It's a question of how much. After sitting there for fifteen minutes, though, I realize that there's no playbook for this. There's no good way to give her news this shocking. So, after fifteen minutes, I drive the rest of the way home, intending to tell her everything. After all, hiding the truth is what got Shawna into hot water in the first place. After just being upset with her for covering up the truth, I decide I shouldn't immediately make the same choice.

This ties my stomach into a larger knot, however. I have no guarantee Anna won't walk out the door as soon as the words leave my mouth. Even though a small part of me believes she might be the woman I've been waiting for, I can't say how she'll take this news. Still, I've never lied to her yet, and I won't do it now.

When I park in my driveway, her car is there. No more time to think of what to say or delay the inevitable. I walk, very slowly, to my front door, take a deep breath, and go inside.

Anna's on the couch, psychology book open. She looks up. "Studying already?" I ask her.

"For summer quarter, yeah. I'm finding this stuff really fascinating, and summer school starts a week from Monday, so I'm trying to get a jump on things."

"I'm so happy that you're doing so well in school now." It's true, although when I say it my voice is more monotone than someone who's truly happy.

"It helps that I've got someone encouraging me and cheering for me for once, Larry. How'd it go with Shawna? Is she okay?"

"Not exactly, no."

"Can you help her?"

I pause for a moment. "I don't know."

"Do you want to talk about it with me?"

"It's probably for the best if we do."

"It doesn't involve me, does it?"

"Yes, and no. Are you ready for the whole story? It turns out that there's a lot more going on than I knew when you called me at Wally's."

"I'm not going to like this, am I, Larry?" She closes her book and sits up straight, looking right at me while I sit down in my armchair.

"I can't say, but probably not. You'll have to decide when I finish."

Without hesitating any longer, I repeat everything that Shawna told me at the motel.

By the time I finish speaking, I'm having difficulty swallowing, and the upbeat feeling I always get around Anna has turned to feeling like I'm outside in a storm. When I look at her, she runs her hands through her hair, holding it at the back for several moments before releasing it. I wait to hear what she'll say.

Finally, she stammers, "You didn't know anything about this?"

"Not until about an hour ago. Shawna kept the secret to herself for six years and never told anyone."

"And all of this is true?"

"You mean, did Shawna lie to me? I don't think so. When we dated, she never looked me in the face when she had bad news. This time she did."

"Maybe she's gotten better at lying."

"Maybe, yes. But, if she were out to use me, why not just get me to take a paternity test, so I'll have to pay child support? She said she wouldn't do that."

"Do you believe you're the father of her child, Larry?"

"It's likely. I don't claim to remember everything we did the last month or two when we dated. It was six years ago, and we were both drinking a bit back then. But the timing works."

"Do you love her?" she asks quietly but firmly.

"We stopped dating six years ago, Anna. I broke up with her, not the other way around."

"That isn't what I asked. Do you love her?"

"No, I don't love her. I love you. I've spoken with Shawna three times since we broke up. Three times in six years. Today was the fourth time."

"What are you going to do?"

"I don't know. I've spent the past half hour trying to think of what to say to you. I thought about not telling you until I figured it out myself, but I don't want there to be a lie between us. Not even for a few minutes. You're too important to me for that."

"But you feel like now you must choose between her and me, don't you? Because if you really are George's father, you should help take care of him. Is that right?"

"That about says it. I don't know what to do. It's you I love, Anna, not Shawna. But if I'm the boy's father, how can I turn my back on him?"

Anna stands up, comes over, and gives me a big hug while sitting on the armrest of my chair. "You'll make a good choice, whatever you decide to do." Then she picks up her psychology book and walks to her bedroom.

"Are you upset, Anna?" I call after her.

Turning back, she responds, "I'm not sure what I am right now. I didn't think today would go like this, for sure."

"Me neither."

"Although, aren't you at least a tiny bit happy, Larry?"

"I don't know. Not really. Why should I be?"

"You've told me before that you've always wanted a son and wished you had one. Now you do."

That realization had never hit me yet. Too much else happening all at once. "I know I said that. I just never thought it'd happen like this, and I don't know what to think right now."

XXX

I'm trying to get out of bed Monday morning but haven't. I'm supposed to go to work but don't feel up to it. The shock of Saturday hasn't worn off. Whenever Anna asked what I was thinking yesterday, all I could say was "I don't know." I spent a lot of time with my head down, studying the floor for answers, but there just aren't any good ones.

If I ignore Shawna and George, it's possible I'm committing my son to a life with only one parent and no father. The same life I had growing up. Meaning, in all likelihood, a childhood with limited opportunities, not a lot of money, and a missing authority figure who won't be there to help keep him on the right path and support him. He'll probably end up going to work right after high school for financial reasons. The same life I've lived.

Part of me realizes that I'm doing an awful lot of projecting, envisioning what's going to happen to George and Shawna ten years from now based only on my own childhood, but I can't shake my premonition that that's what'll happen.

Problem is, I don't love Shawna. I wasn't lying when I said that to Anna. It's true, those two times I met her last year she appeared to have grown up a lot from when we dated, but we tried dating once. It didn't work that time, and I can't imagine that it would a second time, either.

Anna, however, I am in love with. At least, I think I am. We've dated more than three months now, I've enjoyed every moment of it, and I feel better than I have in years. People at the construction site comment on it. So does Anthony, even though Anna's stopped playing their game since school ended for him and he doesn't have math to do for a while.

What I need is a way to keep Anna but still be a father to George, but I don't believe those two desires can coincide, and I can't see a way out of this situation that won't hurt at least one of them. If I try to restart a relationship with Shawna for George's sake, it'll drive a wedge between Anna and me. How can she fully trust me if I'm raising another woman's son and that woman lives nearby?

I glance at my alarm clock again. Like it or not, I've got to get moving. Then, I notice it, finally. I've been so lost in my thoughts I never noticed how quiet the house is right now. Getting up and looking into the hallway, Anna and Anthony both have their doors closed. A couple times Anna suggested she move into my bedroom with me, but I guess I've become a little old-fashioned when it comes to sleeping with women. Given what I just learned on Saturday, I should've observed my new rule back when I dated Shawna.

When I get to the kitchen, my stomach instantly curls into a knot, and immediately I feel lightheaded. It's right there, on the table. Anna's handwritten letter.

Sitting at my own kitchen table, eyes tearing up, I don't want to look. But I have to.

XXXI

I try to pick up the paper, but my arm trembles so badly I set it back on the table and read, my heart getting heavier with each line. In an increasingly unsteady hand, it reads:

Dearest Larry,

I am heartbroken for you. Both of the last two nights I wanted to come to your room and comfort you but didn't because I knew you needed to think. I know why you're torn. Anyone would be. For the first time since I've known you, you're indecisive. No one can blame you. That's why I decided to help you with your decision and leave this morning. Your son needs a father. You need to be that for him, and you can't be his father and be with me at the same time.
It may be useless to write anything else at this point, but please know how much I love you. Every time I said that to you, I meant it with all my heart. You rescued me from a dark situation and I'll never forget it. I owe you more than I can ever repay in two lifetimes. So, even though it hurts us both right now, I'm giving you the freedom to be what you've always wanted to be, a father. Do what's right, and don't look back.
Please don't try to change my mind. It'll only break my heart a second time to say goodbye to you in person. I'm crying silently just writing these lines. Know that I love you and I always will.

Anna

Wiping my eyes and sniffling, I read the letter a second time, but the words don't change, and it doesn't take any of the pain away. Then, from behind me, I hear Anthony's door open, and he walks into the kitchen wearing a plain white t-shirt and blue jeans.

"Are you okay, Lawrence? I could'a swore I heard someone crying just a minute ago, but Anna's not here, and I know you never cry."

"You did hear crying. Today, I couldn't help it."

"What happened?" he asks, sitting down slowly, rubbing the sleep from his eyes and then running his hand through his long hair.

"Anna left this morning, Tony."

Anthony's eyes go wide. "Left, as in, she moved away?"

"Yes."

"For good? Like, we'll never see her again?"

"Probably for good. I don't think she'll come back."

"It's all Shawna's fault, isn't it?" I've told Anthony most of what happened on Saturday with Shawna.

"No, it's not her fault, Tony. Not really. It's my fault, like everything else that's gone wrong in my life."

"How's it your fault? If Shawna hadn't shown up and told you that you had a son, you'd still be with Anna, right?"

"Yeah, I think so."

"Then how's it your fault?" Anthony says, his voice deepening and getting louder as he crosses his arms over his chest.

"If George really is my son, I need to be his father, so he doesn't grow up without one like you and me. My mistake was that I had sex with Shawna at the wrong time, didn't use protection, and got her pregnant back when we were dating."

"But she covered it up. You didn't know."

"That's true. I'm not saying she's blameless. What she did wasn't good, either. And her timing couldn't have been worse. But, Tony, when you get to the bottom of things, we're both responsible.

We had sex voluntarily, knowing what could happen. Six years doesn't change that, even if it seems like it should."

He's still got his arms crossed, so I'm not sure he really understands, but all he says is, "Anna's really not coming back? I didn't even get a chance to tell her goodbye."

"I'm sorry I let you down again, Tony."

He continues looking at me intently, as if he's still not sure this can all be real.

"You know what I always say about how hard life can be, right? This is what I meant when I said that. I wish there were magic words that would make the pain go away, Tony, but they don't exist. Not for you, and not for me. Not today."

Anthony just sits for a moment, lacing his fingers and putting his hands behind his head. "I'm not sure what to say, Lawrence. It just doesn't seem right to me."

"Life does that to you sometimes. You can never quite be prepared for it, Tony, no matter what you do."

"Is there something I can do to help?"

"Not right now," I say, patting him on the shoulder as I get up. "Just one more example of how you should learn from my mistakes and not be like me."

Anthony's never volunteered to help with something before. I suppose that's his way of saying he knows it hurts.

After calling Brad to let him know why I won't be at work today, I stop at Wally's Bar in the late afternoon to see him. As I pull up, somewhere off in the distance I hear thunder. Fitting, I guess. After telling Wally the story, he just comes around the bar, sits down on the black bar stool next to me, and puts his meaty arm around my shoulders.

"I don't know what to say, Larry. Your luck was turning, finally. Then this had to happen. I don't believe in curses, but if I did, I'd say this is one."

"Can I have a drink, Wally?"

"Like, a whiskey drink?"

"Yeah, just one, and no more, but today, I think I need one."

"It's on the house. And don't try to argue with me about that."

"I don't have the heart left to argue anything right now. I'm still just sorta numb on the inside."

Wally sets a glass in front of me and then comes back around the bar to sit beside me again, holding a second glass for himself.

"I thought your rule was you never drank your own stuff while the bar was open," I say.

"You know I'm not gonna let you drink alone on this one. I don't know what to say, buddy. It just ain't right."

"But it's a fact. I lost the best woman I've ever met. And it's my fault. Well, at least half my fault."

"Maybe so, but I meant it just ain't fair to you. You were doin' good, goin' to college, and you had this great relationship with Anna. And, just like that, something you did six years ago that you didn't even know you did just comes in and takes it all away."

"I was right about Anna in one way, you know, Wally."

"How's that?"

"Remember last time I was in here and we talked about her?"

"Yeah, you said you felt good about her."

"I did. But somewhere in the back of my mind, I just knew something would happen and she'd leave. I thought it'd be because she'd meet someone younger and handsomer than me. I was wrong about the specifics, but I was right that she'd leave."

"Come on now, Larry, that's bein' pretty rough on yourself."

My eyes start watering, and all I can answer is, "Why does it hurt so much to be right?"

Wally just gives me a hug from the side. "I'd say cheer up, or tell one of my weak jokes right now, but we both know how fake that'd be. I just don't know what to tell you, Larry. You know I've always got your back, but that don't do much good right now."

"I guess it's clear what I gotta do. If Anna's gone, there's only one thing left."

"You told the news to Shawna yet, Larry?"

"No. I'm goin' over there next. Might as well meet George if I can and start findin' out about who he is."

"What about you and Shawna?"

"I have no idea how that's gonna go, Wally. We're gonna have to have some kind of relationship. It's a question of what kind, I suppose."

"You did say she's grown up a lot."

"My evidence being two conversations in hospital rooms and once on the phone, for what that's worth, but, yeah, she was a different woman those few times."

"Will that be enough for a good relationship?"

"Don't know, Wally. Time will tell, I guess, but without Anna I think I have to try to restart my relationship with Shawna, don't I? You think I should go see her today, or wait a day?"

"Can't say. If your mind is clear, you might as well go and see what happens, don't you think? Putting it off only means another day of worryin' and wonderin'."

"Good point. I guess I should."

"You okay to drive?"

"Yeah, I think so. It was only one drink."

"Good luck, my friend. Just don't let the mistakes of the past be the mistakes of the present too, right?"

I nod as I get down from the bar stool and head for my repaired Cheyenne in the parking lot.

I still remember how to get to Shawna's parents' house. It's only a few blocks from mine. It's one of those model two-story houses built in the 1950s with the large living room window downstairs and a pair of bedroom windows looking out from above the garage on the second floor. White paint with dark-blue trim. Shawna was an only child, but I guess her parents intended to have more children at some point. I never asked Shawna why they didn't.

Bobby and Linda Hawkins open the door just a few moments after I ring the doorbell.

"Hi, Bobby, hi, Linda," I say while stepping inside. They both offer hugs.

Unlike Anna, Shawna's always kept a good relationship with both her parents, even during her wilder days. Shawna being an only child, I guess they figured they didn't want to drive away the only kid they had. Or maybe it's that both are unquenchable optimists who always expect that something good is right around the corner. Although both are in their sixties, I'd swear they were younger. Maybe they just look that way today because both are elementary school teachers and now it's summer vacation. I'm almost sure that's how they met, although it's been a while since I heard them telling stories of their youth at the dinner table.

After a bit of an awkward pause, Linda says, "She's in her old bedroom, straightening things up. You remember which door it is, I'm sure."

"We know Shawna put you in a tough situation, Larry," Bobby adds. The ice broken, his old smile comes out. "Just know that whatever you do, neither Linda nor I will judge you badly. We love Shawna and always will, but we always liked you, too, and whatever you say to her today won't change that."

"I appreciate that, I really do," I reply. "But I think I just need to speak with her alone for a while."

They both nod their assent and step aside. I stride through the downstairs living room and up the stairs to where Shawna is. The bannister looks a little worn and the wooden steps have seen their share of traffic, but I guess that's no surprise for a house nearing thirty years old. I always thought the hardwood floors were a nice look in their house, even after a bit of wear.

When I get to Shawna's door, I knock softly and enter a moment later. It now looks more like a guest bedroom than Shawna's old room—fluffy comforter on the bed, flowers on the bed stand, broad mirror over the stained wood dresser, but none of the little trinkets, photos, or knickknacks that mark a room as someone's personal space.

Then, for the first time, I see George, my son, and the resemblance to me is obvious. Not the slightest doubt.

"Hi, Shawna. And hello, George."

"Hello," he replies in the high-pitched voice of a six-year-old.

"Georgie, can you go and play with Grandma and Grandpa for a few minutes? This is Larry, and momma needs to talk with him for a little while."

"Okay. But who is Larry?"

"He a friend of mine from a long time ago. I haven't seen him very often since you were born and we moved to Lansing, but we need to talk alone for a bit, okay? Go on now, find Grandma and Grandpa and ask for an ice cream bar. I told them you could have one today."

The pudgy little kid scuttles off with the stomping run of an excited youngster who's just been promised ice cream. "Be careful on the stairs," Shawna calls after him.

"You might think about renaming him Larry Junior," I say with a smile after George departs and I shut the bedroom door. "He's a dead ringer for me."

"Always has been."

"Handsome for a little guy, too."

"He takes after his father, I guess."

I sit down on the bed beside Shawna. There's nowhere else to sit, but I almost feel like I'm an awkward sixteen-year-old again, trying to decide what to say to her next.

"Have you decided what you're going to do, Larry? That's why you're here, isn't it?"

"Let's just say my decision was made for me."

"How so?"

"I told Anna everything after I left the hotel. This morning when I woke up, she was gone. She left a goodbye note telling me I should go take care of George."

"Is that what you want?"

"Doesn't matter now, does it?"

"Of course, it does, Larry. I told you that if you want me to leave you alone, I will. I meant that. If you tell me never to see you again, so you can go back to Anna, I'll leave town."

I shake my head. "I want Anna and a son. But I can't have both. If I walk away from you and George right now, I'll probably end up with neither. It'd be another failure to compound my previous failures."

"You wouldn't consider an arrangement where we live separately, but you see George part of the time, would you? Like what divorced people do?"

"I thought about that once or twice, but it don't seem right to me. I can't see how that'd be good for George, especially since he doesn't even know who I am right now."

"You're saying you really don't know what you want, aren't you?"

"I guess so. But like I said, Anna's gone. She left by her own choice. I think I need to respect that."

"I tried, Larry. I tried hiding the truth from Vernon for as long as I could, partly because I didn't want to hurt you. But now it's worse than I ever dreamed. My lying has cost me my marriage, and now it's cost you your true love. I can't say how sorry I am."

"It's in the past. You can't change it now."

"You should forget about me. I'll call Anna and tell her to come back to you if you think that'll help. I just wanted you to be happy all these years, but I've stolen that from you, just when you finally found it."

Shawna's on the verge of breaking down again, which wouldn't be good if George can hear, so I try comforting her by gently taking her arm.

"Anna didn't leave any phone number, and I don't know where she's gone. I can't call her."

"Do you even want to be with me, Larry? Or will you resent me for ruining your life a second time?"

"Honestly, right now there's resentment, yes. I can't say if it'll last forever. I've barely talked with you in six years, you know."

Drawing away, Shawna covers her eyes with her hands. "I should never have told you."

"Your parents know, don't they?"

"Yes, because George looks just like you, and I had to tell them something last night. They haven't told anyone else, though, and they won't if I ask them not to. Is that what you want me to do?"

"I still don't know. I came over today to let you know that Anna was gone and to see George with my own eyes. But we're going to have to have some kind of relationship. George deserves a father. He needs a father. I'm proof of what can go wrong with people who don't have one growing up."

"I'm so sorry, Larry."

"You don't need to apologize anymore. It's done. You can't take it back now. We'll figure something out together."

"You think that you can forgive me after all the harm I've done to you?"

"I'm working on it. You know it doesn't come easily to me, but I'm trying."

Shawna draws back, almost shrinking into herself. "I don't deserve it, though."

I try to pat her shoulder. "You want me to come back tomorrow when you're feeling a little better? Maybe by then I'll have a clearer mind myself, and we can talk again. Sound good?"

"Yeah, I guess so. Tomorrow evening maybe we can have dinner together?"

"Okay, Shawna, that sounds good to me. You want me to call before I come over?"

"No, it's okay. Just check with my parents what time on your way out."

"You want them to hear everything?"

"No. I want them to know what time we need to be alone to talk together."

"Oh, yeah, right. Makes sense. See you tomorrow, then, Shawna."

"Goodbye, Larry," she replies, embracing me in a tight hug as I stand to go.

XXXII

"You sure about that, Brad?"

"Absolutely, Larry. Everyone here understands. You've been a model employee since you came on board, and they've got no problem covering for you another day."

"You're sure you're sure?"

"Larry, stop worryin' about it and go take care of things at home. We can manage here without you one more day."

"I'll be back tomorrow, no matter what. I promise."

"You don't need to promise. Everyone understands your word is good. Now, get going, buddy."

Driving away from the construction site, I've about decided that I need to try building another relationship with Shawna. If not a romantic one, at least a responsible one. It's true that she's a different, and, I think, better person than the woman I dated years ago. It feels like a long shot, but I think at my age almost anything is a long shot.

Around 5:30 my telephone rings. It's Shawna's parents telling me that they're taking George out for hamburgers and that they'll try to leave us alone for the next two hours. After hanging up, I grab my keys from the kitchen counter and drive to their house.

Pulling up in the driveway everything looks just right. It's a nice evening after warm sunshine all day, and a light breeze blows through the dogwood trees surrounding the house. Shawna's car is there, a dark blue Volvo sedan of some kind. It always confused me that Volvo models had numbers rather than names, and I don't remember what kind hers is. Not important tonight, I decide as I walk past and ring the doorbell.

It chimes through the house, but I don't hear any footsteps coming to the door to answer. Strange. After the obligatory thirty seconds, I try again. Still no sound. Maybe Shawna's in the bathroom and can't get the door? Doesn't seem likely, though. I'd think she'd at least call out if that were true, especially since she knows I'm on my way. Stepping back from the front door, I look up at the bedroom windows for lights. Shawna's window is open, but no lights. Nothing.

Well, she's expecting me, so maybe she wants me to let myself in? I try the door. Locked. Why lock the door when she knows I'm only a few minutes away?

I bite my lip as I look around, frowning. This doesn't feel right.

Then, I hear it. A loud thump, like something big and heavy hitting the floor. Definitely coming from upstairs. Almost like the sound I remember from when Anthony rolled off the couch while napping one afternoon.

Standing there trying to decide what to do, I hear a faint moan coming through the open window upstairs. I can't tell for sure, but it sounds like the word "help."

I step back a few paces and look at the upstairs windows again. "Shawna?" I call out while looking toward her bedroom. My heartrate has sped up, and I realize I'm starting to sweat. It's a warm evening, but not that warm, and I wasn't sweating when I got here.

While I wait for an answer, in a few seconds I hear the same moan. Again, I can't swear it's a call for help, but I'm almost sure.

Sure enough that I decide to act. Instantly, I remove my polo shirt, use it to cover my right hand and arm, and elbow a hole in the small window above the knob of the front door. Reaching through, arm still covered to protect against shards of broken glass, I turn the knob from the inside and let myself in.

There's the moan again from upstairs. I leap up the stairway, taking three steps at a time, and burst into Shawna's room. Good thing her parents never put locks on the bedroom doors, I think while opening it.

When I see Shawna, I clamp a hand over my mouth and back up two steps. It's several seconds before I take a breath.

She's lying on the floor, the comforter from her bed haphazardly entwined with her body. The white underside of the comforter shows deep crimson stains. Looking at the bed, the white linen sheets do, too. I look to Shawna again and see what she's done. She's cut deep slices on both her wrists, and they're bleeding freely.

Recovering my senses, I scan the room. Good, there's a phone. I grab it and punch in the numbers nine-one-one. My fingers are so shaky, I almost miss the numbers in my haste. In the process, I watch as Shawna extends one shaking arm toward me, mumbling something as more blood drips to the gold carpet. I try to read Shawna's lips—I think she's mouthing my name.

In moments, I get the emergency responder.

"I need help, quickly! My friend's cut her wrists, and she's bleeding to death!" I shout into the receiver.

The person on the line responds in a calming voice. "We'll send an ambulance right away. What's your address, sir?"

It takes me a moment to remember because I'm terrified and it's not my house. "It's my friend's house, it's um, it's—" finally I remember and spit the address into the receiver.

"Okay, sir, help is on the way. In the meantime, here's what you need to do."

"Yes, hurry!"

"First, elevate the injured arm above the heart."

"They're both injured! I can't do that and talk to you at the same time."

"Then listen carefully. Don't hang up. I'll stay on the line until help arrives. First, elevate the arms and apply pressure to the wounded area. When you think the bleeding is staunched, tie a bandage in place. Keep the arms elevated and wait for help to arrive. Can you do that?"

"Okay, I'm trying," I say while setting down the receiver on Shawna's dresser. The cord recoils a bit when I set the phone down, but not enough to drag it over the edge of the dresser. Shawna's eyes have nearly closed, and both her arms now slump at her side. Her head lolls to the left, resting against her bedframe, and when she moves her lips this time, I can't hear any sound.

I kneel next to her while tearing off my belt. Taking my polo shirt, I wrap it around her right wrist to try to stop the flow of blood. Wait, I need to elevate her arms first. "Shawna, this is gonna hurt, but stay with me," I say while hoisting her up from the floor. I position Shawna so that she's on her knees facing her bed, armpits over the edge of the bed, her arms extended across the bloodstained sheets. Again, I wrap her right arm in my shirt before realizing I need something to wrap her left wrist, too.

Immediately, I kick off my tennis shoes and rip off my socks. I maneuver until I'm sitting on her bed with my right hand around her left wrist and my left hand around her right, squeezing as hard as I dare while holding each arm in the air.

I look down at Shawna, but her eyes have closed. "Stay with me, Shawna, stay with me!" I shout at her, sweat drenching me now, stinging my eyes because I can't let go to wipe it away. All I can see is her face, eyelids fluttering slightly when I call her name. The rest of the room is a blur.

Some of the blood seeps through my clothes, staining my fingers. I think the flow is easing up, but I'm so frantic I'm not sure. Where are the medics?

"Shawna," I say to her, loudly but as calmly as I can manage, "Shawna, look at me. Do you hear me?"

Again, her eyelids flutter. At least she can hear me. Her head doesn't move, however.

"Shawna, the medics are coming. Hang in there. Don't let go. You hear?"

Because she slit her wrists, I have my fingers on the arteries in her arms, the ones you use to measure your pulse. I can feel a pulse, but it's weak, and I'm pretty sure it's slowing down while I speak.

"Shawna," I say again, my voice cracking momentarily, "Shawna, your boy needs you. George needs you. You've got to hold on."

I realize her arms are falling lower because my arms are getting tired of holding them up. I raise them again even as my shoulder muscles scream in protest.

Shawna's mouth moves, but I can make out anything.

Finally, I hear sirens coming down the street.

"Help is here, Shawna. You've just got to make it a little longer. Don't give up."

This time, no response. Shawna's pulse is barely there. "No, Shawna. Don't go. Don't go on me. They're almost here. You're gonna live."

As soon as I hear voices at the front door, I shout out, "Up here! Bedroom up the stairs!"

The ambulance team rushes in with all its gear, stretcher included.

"It's okay, sir, we've got her now."

"Her pulse is weak," I say while standing back, trying to stay out of their way. "She's lost so much blood. I think she's unconscious."

The medics shout instructions to each other, but I barely hear what they say. I just sit down in the corner of the bedroom, head in my hands, hoping I was fast enough.

XXXIII

I spend all that evening at the hospital with Shawna, her parents, and George. Before long, George is asleep on a little rolling bed the nurses bring for him, but the rest of us just stare at Shawna sleeping. I left Bobby and Linda a note on their kitchen table before following the ambulance, so they'd know what'd happened and why I busted the window of their front door. That's also when I found Shawna's suicide note, which I'd missed the first time because I just ran upstairs.

She's sleeping soundly, wrists bandaged and restrained, with an IV tube in her left arm. We made it just in time. The doctors told me she had only two to three minutes left—five, tops—when the medics got to her. She'd lost about one-and-a-half liters of blood, and the human body only has four to six.

"We owe everything to you, Larry. If you hadn't have acted quickly, we wouldn't have a daughter anymore," Linda tells me, her voice raw. She and Bobby have spent a lot of time sobbing into each other's shoulders, especially after I showed them Shawna's note.

In her note, Shawna blamed herself for wrecking my life and destroying her own marriage, and claimed she was unfit to raise George. When I sat down in the corner of her room after the medics arrived, I also noticed an empty wine bottle in the back corner of Shawna's bedroom, so I assume that influenced her thoughts, too, when she decided to kill herself.

"I'm just glad I was in time," I respond, my own voice ragged. "I almost wasn't." When I say it, I feel how heavy my eyes are. The adrenaline of the moment wore off long ago, and now I just feel exhausted and sluggish, like I'm seventy-three rather than forty-three. "Even if someone had called me on the phone before I left, or if I had of forgotten something and had to go back, I wouldn't have made it."

"But you did make it, and that's what matters," Bobby replies. "All these things have happened so fast in the past week. Shawna telling us she wasn't married anymore, and finding out about Georgie, and now this. It's just hit so quickly, but I never imagined things were this bad on the inside for Shawna."

"That's right," Linda adds. "When she called us and said she and Vernon were done I told her we'd support her in whatever she needed, but maybe it was our fault for not asking more questions to know how she felt deep down. She sounded sad yesterday evening, but it seemed reasonable for someone who's been through what she has lately."

"I may have had something to do with that," I put in.

Bobby, who has read Shawna's suicide note several times looking for clues about what he might've done wrong, asks, "Why does she think she's destroyed your life? She didn't explain how. Does Anthony not like her?"

"That doesn't refer to Anthony. When Shawna and I talked yesterday, she found out that my girlfriend left me so that I could help her with George." I go on and explain everything else relevant involving Anna and me. "It's not Shawna's fault like she thinks it is, though. Just awful timing and bad luck. For both of us."

"I'll be darned," Linda says. "She never even mentioned that to us. We were hopeful you would help her, but it was because we like you and always thought you were good for Shawna."

Bobby adds, "That's right. I always believed you had a good influence on her when she needed all the good influences she could get." He sighs and shakes his head. "I never even dreamed she would get this down on herself, but I guess that helps explain why a little bit more."

Even though I'm listening closely, I put my head in my hands, rubbing my eyes and cheeks to try to stay awake.

"Why don't you go home and rest for a while," Bobby says to me. "Shawna's safe now, and you've been here all night. We'll call you if anything happens."

"I'll come back in the morning, then," I respond.

Pulling into my driveway, I notice Anthony remembered to turn a light on. That's good. He doesn't always remember.

When I walk up the creaking steps and through the front door, I see Anthony in the living room, watching TV from my armchair. Just as I've almost closed the door, I hear the bushes behind the house rustle and crack. In seconds, Crab comes bursting out, panting and out of breath. After calling "hello" to Anthony, I step back outside to meet him.

"Crab, what're you doing? It's past midnight."

"Yogi, we gotta go. We gotta go now," he says, hands on knees while he bends over to catch his breath. I see droplets of sweat dripping from his chin.

"Crab, I'm beat. Whatever you've got on the Barrys can wait until tomorrow."

"This can't. Grab your keys. I just ran over here from the big dude's house. He's got a woman with him, and not by her choice."

"What'd she look like, Crab?" I ask, grabbing him by his fatigue jacket and shaking it, suddenly reenergized. "Did she have blond hair, straight and tied in the back, about thirty years old?"

"That was her, yeah."

"He's got Anna, then. Let's go," I say, the twisting knot in my chest I get in moments of stress appearing instantly.

I pivot and jump in the Cheyenne, Crab hustling into the passenger's seat. "What else did you find out, Crab?"

"I'll tell you where to go and what I saw. But you gotta get the story straight, Yogi."

"What're you talking about now? Which way to Rickey's house?"

Crab gives directions, then says, "Dude, I'll tell you what I saw, but you gotta pretend you're the one who saw everything."

"Why?"

"The cops know me, man. I've spent so much time in their drunk tank, or bein' high, they'll never listen to me when I tell them what happened. Or, they'll think I was stalkin' someone to steal from them. So, you gotta pretend you saw what I saw, and you know what I told 'em when I called in from the pay phone."

He may have a point. I don't know if he's right about the behavior of the police or not, but I need to hear the story, anyway. Might as well be now. "Go ahead, Crab."

"Okay, you know that big dude you wanted me to keep an eye on?"

"Yeah, his name's Rickey Bradley," I say as I peel onto the street and accelerate. The address Crab gave me is on the outskirts of town. Probably why he's so out of breath after running over here.

"Well, I wanted to help, so I staked out his house today on my day off to see what I could find out about him."

I'm curious how Crab found out where Rickey lives, but I'm even more impatient, so I say, "Get to the point, Crab. Wait, how'd he get a house when he could only afford a one-bedroom apartment before?"

"Perks of the job workin' for the Barrys, I guess. Anyway, I'm watching his house from cover, like I learned to do in the Army. It's gettin' dark, there's no lights on at the house, and I'm about to give up for the day because it don't look like no one's home, when all of a sudden his truck comes skiddin' to a stop in the driveway, kickin' up some gravel. So, I hunker back down to watch, and a woman gets out of the cab with him."

"What happened next?" I say very quickly as I take the turns in the road as fast as I dare.

"It wasn't easy to see everything, but he's got her by the arm, not real rough-like, just firm, and he leads her inside. That's when I decided to make my move and get closer. A couple lights go on, so I creep nearer to those windows. They're sliding windows, and they're open, so I can hear what they say inside."

"What do they say!" I don't mean to shout, but I do. The trees on the side of the road skim by, phantom-like in the darkness, as I try going even faster.

"At first, they were civil. The big guy with the gruff voice tried apologizin', sayin' he's a new man, and all that."

"But Anna didn't buy it."

"No, she said she weren't interested, and he had a restrainin' order, and he needed to take her back to her apartment right away. But this big guy starts gettin' mad, then, tellin' her she's makin' a big mistake. But then, all of a sudden, he gets nice again, and tries tellin' this woman how he's got a good thing goin' and he can take good care of her now, get her nice things, and all that."

"What'd Anna answer?"

"She told him to stop, said she wanted to leave, and she was done with him."

"Then what," I ask, breath panting, heart racing as I peer ahead into the darkness beyond my headlights.

"He says to her that she's his girl, he's gonna show her what she's missin', and she's gonna learn to love him again. Then I saw the blonde woman stand and head for the door, but the big dude grabs her arm and throws her back down on the couch. Just tosses her down like she's a feather or an old shirt. Dude is strong."

As if I need a reminder of that.

Crab goes on. "The lady screamed once, but the guy slapped her, twice, and she got real quiet after that. Then I ran, figurin' she's in trouble."

"And you called the police right after that, Crab?"

"As soon as I could run to a pay phone and dial. You got the story straight, or should we go over it again?"

I repeat back everything Crab just told me perfectly. Fear has a way of bringing my mind into focus. At least, it always did when I played baseball. That's part of why I was good at it.

"Okay, and here's the license plate on the truck," Crab finishes, along with a description of Rickey's truck—a black Dodge Ram pickup.

"We're almost there, aren't we?" I ask, pounding the steering wheel with my left hand while I steer with the right.

"Another block or so on the left, Yogi."

Rickey's house, however he acquired it, is in a secluded spot, but finally, we skid to a stop in the gravel driveway, and I jump down. Crab, meanwhile, stays in the Cheyenne, almost folding himself in half to lie down and stay out of sight. Two police cruisers are in the driveway when I arrive, their blue and red lights casting an ethereal glow on the trees and shrubs nearby.

Striding rapidly, I find the nearest deputy. He looks late fifties, with balding gray hair and a gray mustache. "Excuse me, officer, but the woman you found here's a friend of mine. Where is she? Do you know what's happened?"

"You the guy who called in the tip?" he asks noncommittally. The man's name badge identifies him as Officer Mullins. Like the foliage, his face looks eerie when bathed in the blue and red lights of the police cruiser.

"I am."

"Well, by the time we got here, everyone was gone. But we observed a few signs of a struggle inside, so we're following up."

"You're treating this as a kidnapping?"

"From what you told us on the phone, yeah. After you called nine-one-one, I was the nearest patrol vehicle, so I called for another car for backup, and now we're taking notes on the scene. If you're the guy who called in the report, we're gonna need to take a full statement from you of what you saw. You ready to give one?"

I nod and regurgitate everything Crab told me.

When I finish, Officer Mullins asks, "Anything else?"

"Rickey has a restraining order. He's not supposed to be near Anna."

"Okay, got it. Just one more question, Mr. Edwards. Can I ask how you just happened to be here to see everything?"

"Anna's my girlfriend. She told me where Rickey lives, just in case. I was supposed to meet her today, but when she didn't show and I couldn't get ahold of her on the phone, I just got worried, and this is one of the places I tried looking. But I think Rickey's a very dangerous man, so I decided to call you rather than risk a rescue when I didn't know if he's armed."

I feel horrible about lying to the officer, and I hope it won't get me in trouble later, but I owe Crab, so I decide not to expose him. It's a plausible story, anyway. If this officer ever hears a different story from Anna, well, I guess I'll deal with that when it happens.

"Okay. Well, what we're doing now is I've issued an ATL—that's Attempt To Locate—by radio based on the descriptions you've provided. We'll also visit everywhere it's likely this man might've taken your girlfriend—friends' houses, family, and so forth—in hopes he's at least stopped by one of those places and someone has information. At the same time, we'll find a judge later this morning, so we can subpoena Mr. Bradley's records and use those to help locate him."

I nod as Officer Mullins runs down the procedures.

"Can you tell me the phone number of Miss Nicholson's parents? We need to contact them immediately because any more information about the search needs to go through them first. We'll need their permission to share any further details with people who aren't family. Which includes you, unfortunately."

"I don't know their number by heart. Anna and her parents are a little estranged, I guess you'd say. It's at home. I just haven't memorized it because I never call them."

"Can you call the station as soon as you can retrieve the number? It's vital we call Miss Nicholson's parents, estranged or not."

"Absolutely, I will," I say while kneading my forehead and rubbing my eyes.

"Long day, huh?" Officer Mullins asks.

"You might say that." Briefly, I describe saving Shawna earlier this evening, even though it feels like two days ago by now.

"I'll be damned, man. That beats anything I've heard in a while, Mr. Edwards."

"I wish it didn't. My life isn't this dramatic most days. I didn't want it to be dramatic today, either. I'll be on my way, though, and call in that phone number as soon as I get home."

Officer Mullins hands me his card as I pull my keys from my pants pocket. "This is how you can reach me, but like I said, I can only give you more information if Miss Nicholson's parents agree. That's just procedure."

I put his card into my wallet and retreat to my truck. As I pull away from the scene and the flashing lights recede in the rearview mirror, I say, "All right, Crab, you're safe."

"Thanks, Yogi. Which officer did you talk to?"

"Mullins."

"Good thing I stayed here, then. I think he'd a recognized me. And not for good things."

With the urgency of the situation gone now, my shoulders slump, and I bang my head against the steering wheel softly as I drive home.

"How does all this happen at once, Crab?"

"There it is, man. There it is."

"What's that mean, there it is?"

"It's somethin' we said in 'Nam. You're in a firefight, the guys on your left and right both get hit, and you're standin' there without a scratch. You can't explain it. There it is."

"There it is," I repeat.

After driving in silence for a few minutes, I say, "Wait, I need to drop you off at your place, don't I?"

"Yeah, for once, I don't need to bum a place on your couch, brother."

I drop Crab off at his present home, that home being the loft above the garage at a friend's place, then cruise to my house, the streets dead and empty the whole way. Except somewhere, Anna's out there.

By the time I roll into my own driveway, the time's approaching 3:30 in the morning. To my amazement, Anthony's still up when I go inside.

"How come you aren't in bed, Tony?"

"I got worried when you came home, said hi, but then left again before coming inside. I thought it must be somethin' serious. What's wrong with Shawna, Lawrence? You never said on the phone when you called from the hospital. Is she okay?" After getting all this out, Anthony gives a big yawn. I can tell he's struggling to stay awake.

"Yes and no. Shawna's going to be okay, but it was a close call. I don't think I should say anything more than that right now."

"Did you save her from something?" Anthony asks, raising his eyebrows and tilting his head slightly.

"Herself, I guess you'd say. I'll tell you more later, Tony, when the time's right, but I'm just exhausted right now. I think it's your bedtime. Past your bedtime," I joke with the best smile I can manage. Anthony doesn't have a hard-and-fast bedtime. He's sixteen now, after all, but I just say that out of habit when it's late.

"I guess so," he jokes back. "Nothin' on TV this late, anyway, so I decided to try writing my own D & D adventure. I haven't gotten too far, though. It's harder than it looks."

I pat the boy on his shoulder and try to smile again. "You've got all summer to work on it, though. You'll get it right."

"Lawrence, if you graduate college and get a better job, can we get a VCR someday? A bunch of people at school have 'em and say they're awesome for watching movies at night."

"We'll see, Tony, we'll see. There's something else I need to tell you, though, and it isn't good. The reason I had to leave before checking on you a while ago isn't because of Shawna."

"Does it have to do with Anna?"

I nod gravely.

"Did she say she doesn't want to see you anymore?"

"No, it's not that. Her old boyfriend, the one who beat her up, kidnapped her tonight."

"She's gone?"

"We don't know where they've gone, Tony."

"But Anna's okay, right?" his voice quickens.

"We just don't know. We just don't know. I need to call the police and give them the phone number of Anna's parents right now. But I don't have anything else to tell you. That's all I know."

"I thought he had a restraining order, or whatever those things are called."

"He does, but they don't always work."

"What are we gonna do?" he asks, staring at me as if that will force the answer out of me somehow.

"As hard as it is to say, there's nothing to do right now. You've gotta try to sleep for a while, okay, Tony?"

"But Lawrence, we gotta do something to help!" he says, jumping up from the couch like he's ready to march out the door.

"All we can do is let the police do their work. Sometimes, that's all a person can do, Tony. Maybe we can talk more later this morning, okay? Just try to get some sleep, buddy."

After looking me over again and realizing there really aren't any answers, Anthony just nods slowly and shuffles down the hallway to his bedroom, and I follow as soon as I call Officer Mullins.

Then, however, on my way to my room, I detour to Anthony's bedroom, just to make sure he's okay.

Walking in, I sit down at the foot of Anthony's bed and just shake my head while covering my eyes with my palms. "I don't know what to do, Tony. I don't know what'll happen to Anna." And for the second time in Anthony's presence, I break down and cry, the tears running down my arms. "I'm so frightened, Tony. I love Anna so much, and I just want her back safe," I say while keeping my face buried in my hands.

I'm so distracted with this, it takes me by surprise when Anthony drapes his quilt around me, puts his arm around my shoulder, and says, "Me, too, Larry. I miss her already. I just want to see her again."

I hug Anthony back, and it strikes me this might be the first time since he came to live with me that we've really hugged each other. Then, Anthony says, "If you want, I'll take your spot at work tomorrow, so you can try to help Anna and Shawna. Tell Brad he can count on me to work all day if I have to."

For the first time in hours, I smile a full smile. "I'll do that, Tony. I'll call him in a few hours and let him know. You're acting like what a real man would do. I'm proud of you."

I hug the boy one more time and then trudge to my own bedroom, but on the way, I pass Anna's room. I open the door and look in. There's the bed, made perfectly, just like she left it, and the vase with the fading flowers, daffodils and crocuses, by the window. Silently, I shut her door, go in my bedroom, and collapse on my bed. I don't even remember closing my eyes, but I wake up to my alarm clock a few hours later, my clothes still on.

XXXIV

It turns out Brad's happy to have an extra pair of hands in my place, so Anthony gets his first job after I fill Brad in on everything that's happened since yesterday morning. I've had Anthony mowing the lawn, washing my truck, and doing occasional other chores ever since he came to stay with me, but he's excited when I pack him a big lunch and drop him off at the construction site. He keeps yawning because he didn't sleep any more than I did last night, but I hope doing something new and active will keep him going all day. I also think it'll be a good distraction for him, so he spends less time worrying. Then, after calling the police station and learning they haven't found out anything they can share with me yet, I drive back to the hospital to check on Shawna.

This time when I get there, she's awake. And alone. I guess her parents finally decided to go home and get some sleep themselves. Shawna gives me a feeble smile as I sit down next to her.

"I was here with Linda and Bobby most of the night," I begin.

"I know. When I woke up about three, they told me you'd been there with them."

"Is that when they left?"

"Yeah, they said they'd come back as soon as they'd slept a bit."

I say nothing for a while because I'm not sure what to say next. Small talk doesn't seem quite right considering what happened yesterday, but how do you know what to say to a friend who just tried to end her life? This is another one of those things that doesn't come with a blueprint. Maybe Shawna's even upset with me for saving her?

She doesn't seem sure what to say, either, so finally I stammer, "You scared me so badly, Shawna. I almost didn't get there in time."

"I was so stupid," she replies, eyes starting to tear up when she looks me in the face.

"Don't cry now, Shawna. Don't get upset again. Yesterday is over. It's okay now."

"Why did I do that? I don't even know why I did it now except that at that moment I just felt so bad about everything. I thought I'd ruined your life and mine, both. And maybe because I hadn't taken my medicine in several days."

"Your medicine?"

"You probably forgot, but my therapist recommended some medication to help me with my anxiety and depression. But when Vernon got upset with me that day, he told me I was worthless and that I was nothing without my drugs. So, I stopped using them just to prove I wasn't worthless and could cope without them. Maybe he was right about that, though."

"I don't know, Shawna, maybe you just needed to ease off them instead of stopping all at once?"

She doesn't answer directly. Instead, Shawna closes her eyes to try to stop the tears and just says again, "Why was I so stupid, Larry?"

Since the doctors restrained Shawna's wrists, she can't wipe tears away, so I do it for her. After brushing away a stray lock of hair that's fallen into her eyes, I tell her, "Don't think about that right now. Just worry about feeling better. There'll be time to talk about that later if you want to."

She smiles a thank you and lies quietly for a while, staring up at the ceiling. I don't know if she has any drugs in her system right now, but I just give her time. After a few minutes she turns her head back to me and says, "How's Anna doing? Have you seen her lately?"

I debate if I should lie to her and say things are fine. Shawna certainly doesn't need more stress or anything that might make her feel even worse than she does already. But I hate lying. So, I decide to tell her most of the truth. "I haven't seen her since she left. Haven't talked to her, either. I don't know how she's doing right now."

"I'm so sorry about that, too. I—"

I put a hand on her arm to stop her. "You don't need to apologize again. Don't worry about it now. Are you still tired, Shawna?"

"Yeah. The nurse told me I needed some blood transfusions when I got here. I think I'm still getting used to having someone else's blood in me," she says with a weak smile.

"Do you want me to stop talking, so you can sleep for a while? You'll probably want to be rested when your parents come back. I'm sure they'll want to talk with you a lot."

"That's probably a good idea, yeah." Shawna closes her eyes and relaxes back into the pillows.

I stay by her side, watching her rest. After a little while, Shawna opens her eyes halfway and says, "Thank you, Larry, for saving me from myself."

Before I can answer, she closes her eyes again, so I let her be.

When Bobby and Linda return to be with Shawna, I take a break and go home for a nap. We talked at length last night, so I don't have much new to say to Shawna's parents. On the way home, I check with Brad at the construction site and fill him in on everything I know. He replies to take whatever time I need and says that Anthony's doing fine in my place.

When I find Anthony, I ask, "How's it goin', buddy? You gettin' the hang of things?"

"Not exactly, no. The other guys won't even let me use the tools."

I laugh. "Have you ever used these tools before?"

"No."

"Well, that's why."

"How can I ever learn if they won't let me try?"

"You're supposed to learn on your own. If you make mistakes at the construction site, it costs time and money to fix them."

"Good point, I guess, Lawrence. Mostly all I do is move stuff around and clean up after people."

"Those jobs need to get done, too, so don't feel bad. Keep workin' hard, and you'll get a chance when the time is right."

"Do you know anything new about Anna yet, Lawrence?"

My smile disappears. "No. Hopefully, we will by tonight when you're done with work."

Now I'm at home again, so I decide to check and see if there's any news about Anna. I get Officer Mullins on the line.

"Is there any news, Officer Mullins, that you can tell me about?"

"For one thing, I've spoken with Miss Nicholson's parents. They tell me they're thankful for what you've done and to tell you everything I tell them."

I didn't expect that. Especially given that I've never spoken to either of Anna's parents in person. Instead of bringing up that fact, however, I just ask, "What can you tell me, then?"

"We have some news, Mr. Edwards, but some is good, and some isn't."

"What's happened?" I say, my pulse immediately racing in anticipation he'll say *We've found Anna, but* . . .

"We put out an Attempt To Locate on the license plate you gave us, and we've located the truck. Turns out, it didn't even belong to Mr. Bradley."

"It didn't?"

"The truck is registered to Paul and Chet Barry, local real estate developers. When we called their company, Chet Barry informed us Mr. Bradley is an employee of his but had taken company property without leave. So, he and his brother are almost as interested in locating Mr. Bradley as you are."

I doubt that's quite true, but instead I reply, speaking quickly before my mind can imagine new horrific scenarios, "And what about Anna? You found the truck. What about her?"

"That's the bad news. When we found the missing truck, she and Mr. Bradley were nowhere nearby. We suspect he hotwired or otherwise obtained another vehicle, and they are still on the run."

"In other words, you aren't any closer to finding out where she is."

"Not quite. These kinds of cases come up from time to time, sadly, but that does mean we have some procedures in place to better solve them. We've notified Mr. Bradley's credit card company to inform us when and where he makes any purchases. That will help us to track his route, unless he steals someone else's credit card also. We've also notified his parents and other close relatives to contact us should they hear from him. When searching his house for evidence this morning, we also located an address book and we're in the process of contacting the names in that book with the same request."

"I see."

"You are anxious to know of Miss Nicholson's whereabouts, for sure, but it's rare that kidnappings happen without the perpetrator informing at least one other person of his or her plans. It's been less than twenty-four hours, and these searches do take a bit of time."

"May I ask, Officer Mullins, if the house where Rickey lived was really his?"

"It is also the property of the Barrys, which they were renting to Mr. Bradley. They said his apartment building burned down some months ago, so they allowed him to rent the property from them. They've given us full permission to search the premises and have been very cooperative."

"Thank you for your time, Officer Mullins."

"It's okay, Mr. Edwards. We know you're worried. I promise to contact you if we have a break in the case."

I sit down on my couch and just breathe for several minutes. When I drove home, I meant to take a nap, but now I decide it's probably a good idea to go back to the hospital and see Shawna again. I just need a quick break. Closing my eyes, I sigh, intending to open them again immediately. Without meaning to, I drift off.

XXXV

The crunch of tires in my gravel driveway jolts me awake. Glancing at my watch, I find I was out for nearly forty minutes. Shaking out the cobwebs, I try to think of who'd be coming to the house. Brad? He should be at work. Unless Anthony screwed something up.

Rising slowly, I start for the door to see who it is. Before I get there, however, the front door opens, and Anna walks in. Tears stain her face, her eyes are red, and so baggy I'd swear she hasn't slept in two days. I can also see the bruise on her cheek from where Rickey slapped her last night. She's got on the same Spartans sweatshirt she wore two months ago when we watched basketball together.

Rickey stands in the doorway right behind her. In his hand is a six-shot revolver.

"Stand over there, Larry. You too, Anna," he says to us, waving Anna and me to different corners of the living room with his weapon. I expect a snarl or a growl from him, but his voice is normal. Normal, but he's speaking very fast. The words come out so quickly I barely catch them. I also notice that his left arm twitches a couple times. Sadly, that's the one without the gun. "Stand apart now. We're going to play a little game."

"Rickey, don't!" Anna cries, speaking for the first time. She's sweating heavily and almost hyperventilating. "You've been using coke. Please don't. You aren't yourself."

"Oh, I'm fine, trust me. In fact, I've never felt better or more alert. Cocaine does wonderful things for you, if you use it right. But you wouldn't know about that, Anna. I always figured you were too timid to try it with me. Guess I was right about that, too."

He's still talking fast. I don't know what using cocaine does to a person, but I decide to try helping Anna talk to Rickey reasonably. "Rickey, calm down. Things don't have to go this way. Please, just relax, and let's talk things out, okay?"

"And you," he says, jerking the gun in my direction, "you're a lying bastard. You just shut up. You've been scheming to take Anna from me, haven't you? Ever since that day with the car battery, you've wanted her, right?"

"Rickey, that isn't how it is," Anna pleads with him before I can respond. "It isn't like that. You have to believe me."

"Save your lies, tramp. I know the truth. All of it. Even the parts you wouldn't admit last night when I had you." While he says it, a grin slowly expands across his face. "That's right, she's still mine, Larry."

My concentration's fixed on Rickey, so I don't see Anna's reaction, but her whimper of fear suggests at least some of what he says is true.

"Now, here's our game. You like games, right, Anna? Come on, you like them, right?"

"Yes," she whispers.

"And you, Larry, well, I don't know, but today, you're going to play along. You like this gun, Larry?"

"I don't know anything about guns," I reply, hoping to throw him off guard and buy time until I can think of something. The muscles in Rickey's left arm keep twitching, but I don't know for sure what that means.

"It's a beauty. A Colt Detective Special. Caliber is .38 Special. I know it don't have much of a barrel, but believe me, the bullets'll kill a man all the same. Or a woman."

"Wait, what are you talking about?" I shout.

The Long Way Home

"Oh, now we're in the game!" he taunts back. "You see, Larry, the gun holds six bullets. There's two in it right now. I ain't gonna show you, but Anna can verify it's true. Right, Anna?"

"Yes," she whispers again, so quiet I strain to hear her through all the tension.

"See? She's a good sport. Don't think about makin' a move, though, Larry. One of the two bullets is ready to fire. But, in a minute, I'm gonna spin the cylinder of the gun, so no one'll know what'll happen when I pull the trigger. See, that's the game. I'm gonna aim at you first, then Anna, and then me. I'm gonna keep pulling the trigger until both bullets fire. So, maybe you'll live, maybe you won't. Ready to play?"

"Why, Rickey?" Anna pleads again. "Why must it end like this? Just put down the gun and let us help you."

"No more lies, Anna. You aren't very good at it. Never were. I still don't know why it took me so long to figure out you were fucking this loser behind my back, but I finally did. But I'm tired of talking. Let's start the game."

Before either Anna or I can say another word, Rickey spins the cylinder and faces me, all in one motion. He pulls the trigger.

Click. Nothing.

"Your lucky day, Larry!" Rickey shouts. "You'll get to play round two! Anna's turn!"

As he shifts to face Anna, some instinct kicks in and I launch myself at Rickey. I won't let him kill Anna.

Maybe he was expecting this, but Rickey swings the gun back in my direction and pulls the trigger again.

Bang!

This time, it fires, and the bullet hits me just below my right shoulder. In shock, I stumble backward against the wall of the living room, even as the pain screams at me and I see the blood stain spreading under my arm.

I stumble to the floor, and my head smacks the wall, hard. I'm sitting there blinking in shock when I hear Rickey say, "You broke the rules, Larry. No one likes a cheater. You know what the penalty is for cheating? You get the next bullet, too."

Even though I'm trying to look up at him, already my vision is getting hazy. I blink a few more times, but my eyelids are heavy. I hang in just long enough to see Rickey level his pistol at me when Anna jumps on his back, arms around his neck, screaming words I can't quite make out because my ears ring so loudly. Rickey just shrugs her off and throws her across the living room with his left arm, like a football player stiff-arming a tackler. Anna crashes over my coffee table and sprawls out on the floor, screaming as she collides with the table and then the floor.

The last thing I see is Rickey turn back toward me, gun pointing at my body from four feet away. He pulls the trigger for the third time as I prepare for the end. Click.

He shrugs and takes aim again. Just as I see the barrel of the gun perfectly in line with my face, the stars in my eyes intensify and the blackness takes me.

XXXVI

When I come to, I'm still in my living room, although I see emergency medics gathered around me. Anna's there, too, holding my hand in hers. Judging by how wet they feel, she's been crying again. I can see new bruises on her arms, presumably from where Rickey threw her across my living room, but she's smiling down at me.

"You're gonna be okay," she says tenderly.

"He's awake," I hear one of the medics say. He's a man of about my age with a brown mustache and short brown hair. Crouching down next to me, he asks, "Can you hear me, sir?"

"Yeah. What happened?" I wonder as my blurry vision slowly focuses. I rub my eyes with my left arm.

"Just take it easy there, Mr. Edwards. You're going to be fine, trust me. Go slow, though. Take your time."

I suddenly notice Rickey is nowhere in sight. "How did Rickey get away? Why didn't he kill me?"

"He didn't get away," Anna says softly. "He's in police custody now."

"But how? He was gonna shoot me, and I blacked out."

"Your guardian angel saved you."

"What?"

"Just rest. I'll explain once you've recovered a little more, Larry."

The medic speaks again. "Your wound isn't that bad, Mr. Edwards. I know it's going to hurt like crazy, but the bullet didn't strike any bones. You've lost some blood, but you'll be okay in time."

"But the human body only has four to six liters of blood," I protest, remembering what happened to Shawna. "How much've I lost?"

"Nowhere near that much," the man says with a smile. "It looks like you passed out from the shock of being shot, or maybe from your head striking the wall, rather than from the amount of blood you've lost."

I sit there, looking back and forth from the medic to Anna as if that was the most ridiculous thing anyone could say.

The medic smiles again. "Don't feel bad, Mr. Edwards. It happens more often than you'd think. Some people go into shock at the sight of their own blood. It appears you might be one of them. It's nothing to be ashamed of. It's not like it's something you want to practice experiencing, either."

Finally looking at where Rickey shot me, it appears the medic is being truthful. He's wrapped a large ace bandage around my arm and shoulder, but no blood soaks through.

Sitting up slowly, I turn to Anna and ask again, "What happened?"

She opens her mouth to answer, but then Officer Mullins strides into the living room, Anna's parents right behind him. "Anna!" they both shout while rushing to embrace her. Another woman about Anna's age is there, too. Her older sister, presumably.

"Hi, Mom. Hi, Dad," she says, virtually disappearing into the chest of her father Benjamin who, now that I see him in person, I note is a very tall man. Almost as tall as Rickey. Six-four, maybe? Georgia, Anna's mother, hugs her next, followed by her sister.

Anna spends a few moments answering the panicked questions of her family and trying to fill them in on what's happened. They explain how they drove from Chicago to Port Huron as soon as

Officer Mullins called them early this morning. Then, Officer Mullins clears his throat loudly. Everyone stops and looks at him.

"Miss Nicholson, we're going to need your full statement on everything that's happened to you. I see several other people here who also want to know what's happened in the past twenty-four hours. Perhaps we can satisfy everyone if you'll sit down and explain things carefully?"

Nodding, Anna takes a seat on my couch. Officer Mullins sits in the reclining chair, puts his notebook on my coffee table, and takes out his pen. Anna's family crowds around her behind the couch, her mother's hand resting on her shoulder as she begins. I stay where I'm at on the floor, leaning back against the wall.

"Where do I begin?"

"At the beginning. How did Mr. Bradley find you?"

"I'd been saving up money to get a new apartment or house to rent. Rickey and I were living together before our first problems when I had to get the restraining order against him. I was going to keep living there, but then the fire happened. Larry was kind enough to offer me a place to stay, but I knew I couldn't stay here forever. So, I decided to move to a new place of my own and ended up renting a house. I was going to get a roommate, but events moved a little too fast for that."

"And what was the address, Miss Nicholson?"

After providing it, Anna continues. "It turned out that a friend of mine, David Bolden, is the property manager for the company that owns the place I rented. At least, I thought he was my friend, but he must've told Rickey that he'd seen me. You probably want to talk to him, officer."

Mullins nods, "David Bolden. Got it. And what is the name of the company that you rent from?"

"Barry Enterprises."

That explains a lot. Anna had no way to know that the Barrys had hired Rickey as their muscle, so she couldn't have known she was putting herself in danger by renting from them. I didn't know they rented properties as well as developing them, but, apparently, they do.

Anna goes on. "Yesterday evening, between nine and ten, Rickey pulls up in front of my house in his black truck. Except, I was popping popcorn at the time, so I didn't hear him until he'd barged into the house. He took me by surprise and told me I was coming with him."

"And was Mr. Bradley armed at that time?" Officer Mullins asks.

"I think so, although I never saw the gun until later. There's only one way out of my kitchen, though, so I had no chance to escape from him. He wasn't angry or rough with me then, but he insisted I go with him, even though I kept reminding him about the restraining order and how he was getting himself in trouble. But he wouldn't listen and just insisted I go. Since I couldn't get away, I did."

"Is that when you drove to Mr. Bradley's place?"

"Yes. It was about ten at night when we got there, I think. He made me go inside and tried to talk me into getting back together. He talked to me for a long time. Sometimes he was nice, sometimes he got mad and shouted. When I finally told him no for about the tenth time, he got angrier than ever and slapped me twice." Anna points to the bruises on her face as evidence.

Anna's father and mother have shown remarkable restraint as she tells her story. I guess it's the military discipline, but her father just stands there, statue-like and expressionless, while she speaks. Anna's mother pats her on the shoulder every now and then.

"Had Mr. Bradley consumed any alcohol or drugs at that time, to your knowledge?" Mullins asks Anna.

"I never smelled any alcohol on him. After we left his house, he drove north for quite a while. I knew he meant to take me to the Upper Peninsula. His family owns a cabin up there."

"Do you know what changed his mind?"

"After a while he started cursing and muttering something to himself like, 'No, they'll think of that. That won't work.' So, next he turned around but needed to stop for gas. I thought about trying to run away when we stopped, but I was too frightened because he warned me not to. That's when he first showed me the gun." I see Georgia's grip on Anna's shoulder tighten, the knuckles of her fingers whitening.

"I was so tired by then, but Rickey just kept going like nothing could bother him. Once at his house, and then again at the gas station, he took out the cocaine and snorted some, a little at a time."

"How do you know what cocaine looks like?" Georgia Nicholson finally breaks her silence. "Those drugs are awful."

"He told me that's what it was."

"Officer Mullins, what are the effects of cocaine use?" Benjamin asks. "I am familiar with the name but do not know the consequences." Although he's stood still the entire time, I can see sweat beading on his balding head and hear the slightest quiver in his voice.

"It's a drug that's coming into more widespread use the past few years, sadly," Mullins responds. "But some of its effects are to make the user more alert, more talkative, and give them confidence—a sense of invulnerability, so to speak. They don't tire easily, which would explain why Mr. Bradley could keep up his energy for such a long period. The negative effects, however, include illogical and unusual behavior, sometimes including violence. Some users also get more irritable and suspicious of the people around them. Paranoid, in fact, even toward friends. It can even kill the user instantly."

"Like Len Bias, if you saw that story," I put in.

"I don't know that name," Benjamin says.

"Yes, that's right," Mullins replies. "Len Bias was the University of Maryland basketball player who was the number two overall pick in this year's NBA draft. But he used cocaine, and it killed him about ten days ago."

Benjamin nods as if satisfied, resuming his stoic demeanor. After the explanation from Officer Mullins, I realize his description of the side effects of cocaine fit Rickey's actions perfectly. That probably explains why he came back here and made us play Russian Roulette. He felt invulnerable because of the cocaine in his system.

Anna starts speaking again. "All along, as we kept driving, I kept trying to tell Rickey that he'd made a mistake and it'd be better if he let me go, but he wouldn't do it. I pleaded with him. I begged. Nothing would change his mind."

"Where did you stop last night to sleep, or did you stop at all?" Mullins inquires.

Anna looks at the floor, and her voice gets quiet. "At a motel some distance north of here. That's where Rickey forced me to have sex with him. After that, he sat by the door, gun in his hand, and snorted more cocaine to stay awake."

Anna's mother gives her a hug around her neck while her sister rushes to do the same.

"The bastard," Benjamin intones.

After a few moments and thank yous to her family, Anna brushes away the hugs, so she can continue.

"Finally, he told me to shut up and that he wanted to end this for good. That's when he drove here, to Larry's house."

"Did he already know where I lived?" I ask, momentarily forgetting I'm not supposed to interrupt.

"I don't think so. He snorted another line of cocaine and then made me tell him where to go. When we got here, he forced me into the house at gunpoint and said it was time for a little game."

Anna then recounts the details of the past hour, pausing when she gets to the part about Rickey shooting me and throwing her across the room.

"How did you manage to subdue Mr. Bradley, then, if you were on the floor and Mr. Edwards had passed out?" Mullins asks, eyebrows raised.

Anan pauses again. "We had help."

"From whom?"

"I don't know who the man was. But he just appeared from out of the kitchen and clobbered Rickey on the head with a wooden baseball bat. The man was medium height, had a trimmed beard, and he had on one of those green jackets that people in the military wear. He sneaked up behind Rickey, then wound up and delivered one blow to the head. Rickey went down unconscious, and, after kicking Rickey a couple times to be sure he wouldn't wake up, the man took the phone and called for help. Then, he took the phone off the wall, unhooked the cord, and used it to tie Rickey's hands behind his back. He stayed here a few more minutes to help me to the couch and check Larry's wound, but when he heard the ambulance coming, the man left. He never told me his name."

Crab! He must've left for the same reason he didn't want Officer Mullins to see him last night.

"Where is this baseball bat?" Mullins asks.

"Back in the kitchen, between the fridge and the cabinet just to its left, where the man put it before he went out the door. He put the bat there, called nine-one-one, and then left after making sure I was awake and the ambulance was nearly here."

Must've been Crab. He's the only one other than Anthony who knows I keep a baseball bat there, just in case.

That's when I figure I should just tell Mullins about Crab. Not only was he the hero, but I think Mullins deserves to know about the new leaf Crab's turned over.

"I can tell you who it was, Officer Mullins."

"You can? A friend of yours, Mr. Edwards?"

"It was Crab Parker who saved us. Although you maybe know him by Alan Parker, too."

Mullins gives a huge grin and shakes his head. "You don't say."

"It's true. His family and I have been friends going back to high school. Longer than that, even."

"You mean the same Alan Parker I've taken off the streets dozens of times for public intoxication over the years? The one who came back cracked after Vietnam?"

"The same one. You might not believe it, but he's been clean for a couple months now. I don't know why he came over today, but he got here just in time to save both of us."

"Why not stay to get the credit, then?"

"He's scared of you, Officer Mullins. I think that now that he's finally straight and sober, he doesn't want attention because people only remember the old Crab and won't believe that he's trying to change."

"Can you take us to see him?" Benjamin asks me. "If this man saved my daughter, he deserves my thanks. In fact, if he's the one who thwarted Anna's kidnapping, I'd like to repay him if I can."

Everyone's looking at me. I don't know what Crab would want me to do, but I hope he's okay with getting the credit he deserves. I tell them his address.

XXXVII

When the fourth of July arrives, Anna, Shawna, and I are sitting in the back yard at Bobby and Linda's house, all of us sipping different drinks from lawn chairs. Although Anna and I are back together, the three of us have agreed that outside of that, there's no hurry to make any decisions about our future relationships with each other. I suppose we could have saved everyone a lot of drama if one of us had thought of that back in June, but no one writes advice books for people in our situation.

I'm surprised, but pleasantly so, that Anna agreed to come over to Shawna's house and meet her. I feared she'd be insecure about seeing me with Shawna after everything that happened in June, but she was willing to do it. Hopefully, it's a sign Anna's grown more comfortable with herself and believes me when I tell her the depth of the feelings I have for her.

George watches a black snake firework grow on the patio cement, Linda and Anthony watching to make sure he doesn't touch it. Meanwhile, Bobby works the barbeque. Putting down her iced tea for a moment, Shawna says to me, "Well, you and Crab really started something with your little 'investigation,' didn't you?"

I nod over the lip of my can of Pepsi. "After Rickey got all the drugs out of his system, he fessed up to being the muscle for the Barrys, threatening the owner of the apartment complex that burned down, and opened up the bribery scheme in exchange for a lighter prison sentence."

"And my former friend David corroborated his story. I think he regretted telling Rickey about me, and that was his way of making up for it," Anna adds.

"Anyway," I continue, "Rickey, David, and the apartment owner had plenty of evidence on the Barrys. Especially since the apartment owner was smart enough to record some of his phone calls with them. They're gonna have a hard time explaining that away in court."

"You think the Barrys will sell out the fire chief, too, Larry?" Shawna wonders.

"I'm betting on it."

"I'm still wondering one thing," Anna puts in. "How did Crab happen to be at Rickey's house when Rickey brought me there? You've never told me that part of things."

"Where is Crab, anyway?" Shawna asks. "You were supposed to invite him, Larry."

"I did invite Crab. He told me to say thank you, and that any other day he'd be here, but fireworks scare him. Something to do with what happened to him in Vietnam, I think. He told me he bought earplugs and was gonna try to find a place outside of town where the noise wouldn't be too bad."

"I remember his brother Todd. He was a handsome guy, and I had a crush on him for a little while in high school. I was hurt when I learned Todd died over there," Shawna confesses with a relaxed smile.

"As for how Crab knows things, Anna, I never ask him about that. He's spent a lot of time on the streets of Port Huron, you know, and our town isn't that big. Crab knows just about everyone on the streets, including some folks a little on the shady side."

"Maybe this can be the start of something new for him. I hope he enjoys being the hero. You and I wouldn't be here if not for him," Anna tells me.

"And I wouldn't be here, either, if you hadn't have saved me, Larry," Shawna adds.

"Me, neither," Anna says while swirling her drink with a straw.

"How do you figure that?" I ask Anna.

"Well, Larry, don't forget that you threw yourself at Rickey when he was going to fire at me. The bullet that hit you in the armpit would have hit *me* if you hadn't done that. That means I'm probably not alive, either, if you hadn't risked yourself for me."

"Maybe," I say. "But I owe each of you something, too. Part of me always wanted to have a son, and now I do because of you, Shawna. And Anna, in your own way you helped me get my life back. Or, at least, my purpose in life. Now, I finally want to be something, and knowing how much you helped me get there, I guess I owe you, too."

"So, tell me, Larry, how long until Sir Lawrence the Greathearted joins our adventuring party?" Anna wonders with a teasing laugh. "Tony said I had to ask you that today," she adds with a giggle.

I just smile. "I don't know that I'm brave enough for that. But I'm happy that Tony has his math tutor back. I saw his old math teacher, Mrs. Wilkinson, at the grocery store the other day, and for once I could walk by her without ducking my head and hoping she didn't have anything to say to me."

We all have a good laugh with that one.

Shawna speaks again. "Anna, Larry tells me you've started speaking with your parents again."

"Yes, I guess my kidnapping finally broke through all the walls we'd built up between ourselves over the years. I know it's partly my fault it took that long, and partly theirs for being so stubborn, but it looks like our relationship might finally get better. I think it's time that it did. Larry's shown me how much it helps to have a responsible figure in my life."

"And it's wonderful what else your father did, Anna. He volunteered to pay for you and Larry to go to college. Now you can both be what you want to be in life. You can open your day care for children someday, and Larry can be an assistant physical therapist and help injured people get better."

"Starting with myself," I joke. "That gunshot might not've been too dangerous where it hit me, but it still hurts."

Anna kisses my cheek as she stands up. "I'm gonna go and play with George. He's almost as cute as his father."

I'm left looking at Shawna. "The two of you are wonderful together," she says. "If I wasn't so thankful to just be alive right now, I'd feel even worse for nearly breaking up your relationship. I guess fate really did want the two of you to get together."

"Next time, though, I'm gonna ask fate to plan things out a little more directly. There were so many times along the way I thought I'd never see Anna again. She probably feels the same."

"I really am happy for you, Larry. You deserve this. More than anyone. Even against the odds."

"There it is," I tell Shawna.

She pinches her eyebrows together. "There what is?"

I laugh. "It's what Crab told me the other day. When something happens that you can't explain, you just say, 'there it is.'"

"And Anna plans to move back in with you?"

"Yeah, for now."

"For now?"

"For now. Until we both have college degrees and can afford a bigger house," I answer with a wry smile.

After Shawna's laughter dies down, she says, "Tony finally cut his hair."

Another chuckle. "The guys at the construction site teased him a little for looking like a girl. He doesn't want to quit and give me my spot back because he likes making some money, but he doesn't like them riding him, either, so he had me cut it the other day."

"It looks like your good habits finally rubbed off on him. He's following in your footsteps, at last."

"Now I just got to make sure he follows in the good footsteps and stays away from the bad ones. I have plenty of experience at both kinds, you know."

"I think he'll be okay, Larry."

"Anna deserves credit for that, too. She's a great influence on the kid."

"Like I said, the two of you are wonderful together."

"You know what though, Shawna?"

Shrugging, she waits for me to continue.

"You aren't so bad, either. I'm glad you're in my life, too. Like you told me in the hospital last year, regaining an old friend is just as good as making a new one."

"Since when did you get all wise and thoughtful like that?" she asks, grinning.

"Must be all that college learning. You think?"

"Whatever it is, I like this new Larry even more than the old one. If I ask nicely, will the new Larry stick around for a while?"

"I think he's here to stay."

I'd like to thank everyone who purchases *The Long Way Home* for reading my book. If you enjoyed reading it, I would be grateful if you'd leave a short review of the book on whatever website you purchased it from. Favorable reader reviews are very important to authors like me. They help tremendously in attracting new readers and spreading the word about existing books that you think others will enjoy.

Thank you!

If you want updates on future books, please join my Reader's Club mailing list at robbauerbooks.com.

About the Author

I'm Rob Bauer, author of historical fiction and nonfiction books and owner of Rob Bauer Books. I hold a PhD in American History and was a Distinguished Doctoral Fellow at the University of Arkansas.

My fiction has two purposes—entertaining readers and explaining historical injustice. Although I enjoy adventure and humorous books as much as the next reader, I'd like my books to stand for something a little bigger. All my studies in history put me in a position to do that. Whether I'm writing about how racism damages the individual psyche, the deportation of the Métis people of Montana, the South's prison labor system, or the utter terror of the Belgian Congo, with my books you'll find yourself in powerful historical stories.

I also write nonfiction about baseball history because I've always loved the game, its history, and its lore. I sometimes joke that baseball may be the one thing in life I truly understand. Although I love the statistical side of the game, if you don't, never fear because my histories go light on the statistics and heavy on what baseball was like in the past. They're stories about baseball, but stories with a point.

The history blog on my website offers posts on a variety of interesting historical figures and events. I'd love to have you follow along.

When I'm not working on my next story or writing project, I enjoy spending time at the beach. And, oh yeah, I still read a history book or two. When I'm not watching baseball.

Acknowledgments

I also want to thank the people who helped make this book possible, especially Jim Soular for his help with editing. Ali Holst gets the credit for the cover art and design. Thank you to Jennifer Lodine-Chaffey and E. M. Bosso for reading and making suggestions.

In addition, there are several people who helped me with specific parts of the book. Thank you to Angie Giancarlo for sharing information about her hometown of Port Huron. Jake Michelson provided valuable insight on the finer points of automobile makes and engines from the 1980s. Officer Cory Clarke of the Kalispell Police Department was nice enough to explain how a 1980s police department would handle a missing person case. Jeannie Ringo helped with some questions regarding the chain of advancement typical of supermarkets. Finally, my editor Jim Soular, who is also a Vietnam War veteran, helped educate me on the long-term effects of Post-Traumatic Stress Disorder on veterans.

Made in the USA
Coppell, TX
20 April 2021

FLATHEAD VALLEY COMMUNITY COLLEGE
LIBRARY